THE SALSA CONNECTION

AN INTERNATIONAL ROMANTIC THRILLER
And
WINNER OF THE ROYAL PALM LITERARY AWARD

written
by
JOHNNY RAY

The story moves from the salsa clubs of St. Petersburg, Russia to New York to Louisiana and, finally, to Italy. The red-hot thread of the dance runs through a novel that explores the Russian mob, slavery and prostitution rings, and the art world, as well as love, loss, revenge and the strength of family ties.

When Nickolay Panov left St Petersburg, Russia to go to New York City for an international ballet competition 25 years ago, he was considered one of the best ballet dancers in Russia. The Americans say he was murdered. The Russians say he defected. In any case, he never returned. Just before Nickolay disappeared, several priceless paintings and icons from a major museum were stolen. While he was accused of the theft, no solid proof has ever been offered to tie him to it. However, evidence shows that the stolen goods were shipped to America. The CIA and the Russian Government are still pursuing all leads connected to the heist, and so is the Russian mafia.

Sveta was three years old when her father disappeared, so it's a shock when, in the mail, she receives an invitation to a salsa dance competition in New York. At the bottom of the invitation is a note: "Please come to the competition and enter, my little lady." No one but her father has ever called her that. Why has her father surfaced after all these years? Sveta wants answers, even if it means entering the late-night, sultry world of salsa dancing in St Petersburg and New York City and coming into uncomfortably close contact with the Russian mob.

ALL RIGHTS ARE HEREBY RESERVED BY JOHNNY RAY

JOHNNY RAY is an award winning novelist who won the Royal Palm literary award for best thriller and is quickly making a name for himself as the master of the romantic thriller. He loves social interaction with his readers and can be found on
Twitter
www.twitter.com/sirjohn_writer

Facebook
www.facebook.com/authorjohnnyray

He can also be reached by e-mailing at
sirjohn@wwisp.com

or you can just follow him on his blog at
www.sirjohn.us for updates and future releases.

Johnny Ray's other novels include:

DRONES
Published by Sir John Publishing in 2013

A WAR HERO RETURNS
Published by Sir John Publishing in 2013

JOHN RAIN – THE HAWAIIAN AFFAIR
Published by AMAZON DIGITAL in 2013

MODELS AND LOVERS
Published by Sir John Publishing in 2012

HER HONOR'S BODYGUARD
Published by Sir John Publishing in 2012

FOR LOVE AND VENGEANCE
Published by Sir John Publishing in 2012

SCANDAL – THE DEATH OF A LEGACY
Published by Sir John Publishing in 2012

THE JOURNEY TO WHITESTONE
Published by Sir John Publishing in 2012

STALKING LOVE
Published by Sir John Publishing in 2012

CHAPTER 1

Present day, St. Petersburg, Russia

"Oh my God, he's alive," Sveta gasped, as she failed to contain the words rushing past her trembling lips. Oh papa, is this really from you? In the solitude of her tiny kitchen she quickly felt vulnerable, knowing the torture she'd be subjected to if discovered. She couldn't believe the invitation she was grasping in her trembling hands. She had prayed for this sign of her Papa being alive ever since he had disappeared twenty-five years ago. Papa, my papa!

With the rush of joy swelling in her chest and presenting her with such newfound hope, she had to stay focused to fight the deep shock attempting to overtake her. As her body quivered, and her eyes filled with the tears of joy, a gripping fear suddenly flooded her thoughts. Had anyone else read the coded message?

Sveta studied the signs of wear and tear on the tattered envelope from America. The stamps made absolutely no sense at all, but looked official. If the invitation had been tampered with, any intrusion would be hard to prove, but yet she knew how interceptions of mail were so common in Russia. She analyzed every part of the envelope to determine if any clues existed at all. While she imagined many possibilities, she saw nothing conclusive.

The invitation inside the envelope was in much better condition, but still showed the weary signs of battered and wrinkled edges from the long trip. The invitation described how several salsa clubs in New York were sponsoring an international competition to determine the best salsa dancers in the world. She studied the rounds of eliminations extending over several weeks to determine the finalists. Since the long list of rules written in English didn't make complete sense to her, she would have to translate them better later. Although she had learned English in school since the fourth grade, she still needed help with some documents such as this one.

It was, however, the note scribbled at the bottom of the invitation that made her think her heart would stop beating. The note written in English read, "Come to the competition and enter, my little lady." Only her papa had ever called her my little lady, and he had disappeared while attending an international ballet competition in New York City years ago.

She remembered how the Americans had contended that he had been murdered, and also how the Russian government had always insisted that he had defected. In any case, he had never returned. Memories of how a large number of priceless paintings stolen a few weeks before her papa had vanished returned to haunt her. While he had always been accused of being involved, no one had ever presented any solid proof tying him to the crime. As the shock paralyzed Sveta, she waited on her mom, Mariya Panova, to arrive soon. Perhaps she could make more sense of this invitation.

After the door rattled with the sound of keys turning the locks, her mom quickly opened the massive door to their flat. Sveta, however, didn't move when her mom entered the room. She could only imagine the many long hours ahead of them trying to understand the meaning of this note. While it would take some time for each of them to recover from the initial shock, she had no doubt in her mind—her papa was alive.

Mariya had been a great mom and her best friend ever since her papa's disappearance. With tears still falling from her eyes, Sveta watched her mom rush to her to ask, "Sveta, what is it?"

"Mom, I received this invitation in today's mail. I think it's from Papa."

Mariya reached for the letter. "An invitation to what?" She quickly scanned the letter, but looked confused at the English.

"It's an invitation from America to enter a Latin dance competition, but here, look at the bottom of the invitation. Please, tell me . . . oh god . . . please tell me what you think."

Much as Sveta had earlier, she watched her mom slide into one of the chairs at the table. Tears quickly flooded her mom's eyes and ran down her face, as she appeared to recognize the handwriting. "Sveta, either he's alive, or someone is playing the worst trick on us we can ever, ever imagine."

Sveta fought back a smile. Could this be true? Is he alive?

"Have you shown this letter to anyone?" Her mom leaned forward as her body trembled. While Sveta watched her mom attempting to stay poised and in control, she realized even the most elegant and proper women of the world would have problems coping with the news she had just received.

"No, I just received the invitation a few hours ago. Here . . . look at the envelope. Do you think anyone has tampered with it?"

Mariya started turning the envelope over, examining it. "For some reason, I don't think it's been inspected. If someone had examined the invitation, I don't think we would have received it, but who knows for sure."

"Mom, we need to hide it. You know how dangerous it would be if they find this invitation."

"Don't worry. I know the perfect place to hide the invitation—in the garden." She continued to study the invitation by turning it over and over. Sveta knew her mom knew very little English.

An additional wave of excitement swept into Sveta's voice. "What do you think this means?"

"I think it's obvious he wants to make contact with you, but why . . . after all these years…I don't know. I've hoped for a long time that he would contact me, just to let me know that he was all right. He was . . . …and still is . . . the love of my life. I'll never forget him." She leaned over the table, dabbing at her tears.

The idea of going to New York City felt totally impossible to Sveta. Such a trip represented a fairytale that was too great to imagine, and in reality, she had to admit the trip would never happen. Her job as a sales clerk in an art gallery would never pay enough to make such a trip to America. After all, it required everything her mom and she could earn to make ends meet. "There's no way we can afford an expensive trip like this! Papa has to know we have no money."

Mariya raised her head. "I know, but I think more information must be coming later. I just don't know what to think."

"I understand we've discussed his disappearance many times before, but Mom, I need to know if you remember anything else I should be aware of concerning Papa. Can you think of anything at all you haven't told me? I'm a big girl now."

"Don't remind me you're twenty-eight years old. I still can't believe you haven't married, like most of your friends your age. All the good men are already married, and the other men may think you have something wrong with you."

"Mom—"

"I'm just concerned." With a tiny smile, Mariya indicated she wasn't going to argue with her daughter tonight. "You know the stories concerning the Lisin crime organization involvement. Being one of the largest crime families in Russia, they're the kind of people you don't mess around with. They've been around forever, trying to find out what happened to your papa, and they also don't believe your papa died. The family is still run by the older brother, Ivan Lisin, but it's his younger brothers who are so damn ruthless."

"I've heard these stories all my life, and I know to do nothing to make them upset." Sveta nervously glanced around.

"Yes, and because of them we'll need to proceed very carefully since they would love to know about this invitation."

Sveta's thoughts returned to her mom's concerns about her not marrying. "I know I've committed some mistakes concerning men, and how I should have done differently on many occasions, but life is as it is. I've learned to live with my bad decisions in the past."

While time passing slowly, leaving Sveta time to ponder her past, it also allowed her mom several moments of silence to digest the news. Finally, Mariya stood and spoke. "Well . . . tonight I think we need to celebrate a little bit, even if we do so in the privacy of our home. We need to remember the good times when we were a family. I own a bottle of Georgian wine that I've saved for a time like this. What do you think?" New twinkles quickly emerged from Mariya's watery eyes.

Sveta smiled at the idea of a slight celebration. "Sure, we need to observe our past."

"Good. I'll open the bottle, while you find your father's folder we've saved for all of these years."

Sveta crossed the room to a large cabinet, where they stored many of their clothes. The one-room flat they lived in didn't offer many places to accommodate the few belongings they owned, and efficient use of space was required. "I could also use some chocolate," Sveta sighed. "It would also be fantastic if we had some of the strawberries from the garden, but I guess I can live without them for now."

Mariya managed to open the bottle after struggling with the cork for a while. She returned to her place at the table. The two wine glasses in front of them were from Czechoslovakia, and while they were old, they were also elegant in design. Sveta remembered using them to celebrate many times before.

"I love this wine. It would be so great to visit the winery one day." Mariya squinted and read the label.

"Mom, you've told me this dream for years."

"Perhaps . . . but I would also like to go other places to see wineries. Another place I would like to go visit someday is where wine is produced in Italy." She smiled briefly. "It's something I know your papa talked about wanting to do one day."

"Yes, they do produce some great wines, but this trip to Italy will remain a fairytale, and exactly like this one of me going to America to dance in a competition." Sveta sighed, rubbing her eyes with her hands. "So tell me, what do you think of it being a salsa competition? I don't even know how to do salsa dancing!"

"It's popular at many clubs around St. Petersburg, and I know you've seen salsa dancing many times."

"Yes, but watching salsa dancing and dancing it are two different things."

"You know you possess the ability to dance, much like your papa. Yes, your papa and I loved to dance, but he danced incredibly, and I danced . . . well okay. His talent is why he received the invitation to go to America back in 1987 to represent Russia in an international ballet competition, and I had to remain here with you."

"Do you think Papa is into salsa dancing in America now? That's a big change from ballet."

"I don't know what to think, or what to make of this invitation, but I'm sure we'll obtain some more information soon. That is, if the next letter isn't intercepted first."

Since it remained a strong possibility, new tears trickled down Sveta's face, as she whispered, "I was only three when he disappeared, and I can only so vaguely remember him. But . . . I've dreamed of him being alive, and of him coming and taking us away from all of this."

"Yes, his disappearance will always be etched in my memory. The questions the police asked, and the hell I went through over the next several years was so intense."

"I understand how hard this is on you, but I want to go over what you remember again."

"You mean, right now?"

"Yes, please! I want to go over what you remember once more, so please think if there's anything at all you haven't told me before that I need to be aware of now."

"Okay, what they told me was that the Americans had asserted that he had been abducted from the hotel where he was staying the night before he was to perform by someone who had attempted to rob him. They said he was murdered later during the night, and a witness had seen him being pushed off a bridge, but the Russian government had insisted that the Americans had lied and that he had defected and gone into hiding. The one fact I've not told you before is that the witness to your papa's death was a member of the Lisin Family."

"What do you think really happened?"

"I'm not sure, and I always assumed I would never know. That is . . . until now." Mariya pointed to the invitation.

"Why would he defect? I remember hearing the stories about some priceless paintings stolen at the time of his disappearance, and the allegations that he was involved. But . . . all of these allegations were never proven, were they?"

"Correct, they never proved them, but the paintings and other items were never recovered either. I remember, however, that some proof had surfaced about the paintings being smuggled to America, but nobody was ever tied to the crime officially." Sveta knew her mom's thoughts of her husband being a master thief had haunted her for years, but she would never allow herself to fully believe it. "When your Papa left," she sighed, "I have no doubt he had full intentions of coming back. We also had plans to conceive another child when he returned. He wanted a son he could teach to dance like him."

A sense of embarrassment tingled Sveta's spine. "I understand you wanted me to dance ballet, like you and Papa, but it wasn't the life I wanted. I'm sorry if I let you down. The money from the ballet school where you teach barely keeps us alive, and the hours you work are too much for a woman your age."

Her mother shrugged. "Well, it's something I love. In a few years I can retire, and we'll see what happens to us then." Mariya poured them another drink before she raised her glass to make a toast. "To your papa, wherever he is, and to whatever he's up to."

Retrieving her glass, Sveta tapped one side against her mom's glass. "Yes, to my papa, Nickolay Panov, and to whatever plans he has for us." She swallowed a sip, as she enjoyed the complexities of the wine. "Mom . . . is it hard to obtain a visa to go to America?"

After taking another sip of the red wine, Mariya tilted her head backwards as if in deep thought before smiling. "It's not easy, and can take some time. You'll need to find a sponsor to invite you, and to be responsible for you, but the other requirements can be obtained at the embassy here in St. Petersburg. Are you thinking you might actually go to America?"

"I don't know what to think. I want to understand what the requirements are and learn how much the trip costs. Also, unlike ballet dancing, if I dance in a salsa competition, I'll need a partner. The chances of accomplishing all of this in time will be next to impossible."

"Yes, it's a huge task. Perhaps this is why he sent you this short note now, you know, so you'll start doing research for the trip."

Sveta felt a frown growing across her face as she contemplated what she had to do. "I have access to a computer at work that I can use to search the internet. It's too bad we don't have an internet connection at home."

"A computer and internet connection is too expensive for us, and if you do research at work you'll need to proceed carefully and not give away our secret."

"It's not a problem." Whatever it required, Sveta needed to find some answers.

CHAPTER 2

Sveta didn't sleep much during the night as thoughts of her papa, and many other unanswered questions, haunted her dreams. She was lucky though as on Saturdays, her day off, she loved to sleep late. The gallery where she worked had professional clients who came in during the week but never on the weekends, unless the shop had a special showing or exhibit.

As she watched her mom dress in her usual garden work clothes, she realized that her mom had apparently been awake for some time. They maintained a small garden they loved to care for, which was located at the edge of the city. Her mom wanted to hide the letter somewhere in the garden for safekeeping.

"I see you're finally awake," Mariya said as she smiled. The tiny flat didn't provide any privacy, but remained cozy in a way only those who lived there would know.

"I didn't sleep at all last night." Sveta stretched and yawned. "Olya wants me to go with her to shop for some clothes she's wanting. I hope the shopping will not take too long."

Her mom looked sternly at Sveta, as if to warn her. "I don't need to tell you how important it is for you not to discuss the invitation with anyone, even if you're tempted to do so."

"Trust me, Mom. I don't want to get in trouble either. Last night I decided to learn everything I can about salsa dancing, and since Olya loves to dance at some of the clubs, I thought that if I approached the subject correctly, she could be a big help."

"I don't want you to disappear like your Papa. You can trust no one. Is that understood?"

"Yes, it's fully understood." Sveta hated being lectured to as if she was a child, but realized her mom would never change.

With the morning vanishing, her mom wrapped her head and moved toward the door. "Try to come to the garden and help me as soon as you can. We've a lot of work to do right now."

Sveta locked the door after her mom left, knowing it would take a while to style her hair and put on her make-up. She ran her fingers through her thick shoulder-length hair as she contemplated her problems in keeping her hair up and looking elegant. While sometimes she preferred to pull her hair tight over the top of her head and use a clasp to hold it in place, she wanted to look good for her friend today.

While the water her mom had boiled for tea earlier still remained hot enough, Sveta poured some of the tea from the tea pot to a teacup, and then added some of the hot water. The aroma smelled especially good this morning, as she forced her mind to concentrate.

Sveta's cell phone rang before she finished the last of her makeup. "Hi, are you ready?" she heard Olya ask.

"Hello." Sveta glanced around. "I'm almost ready. Where are you?"

"I'll be at your place in five minutes."

"Great, I'll meet you downstairs." Sveta glanced at her clothes. "How's the weather outside?"

"It's going to be fantastic today! The weather man promised no rain."

"Okay. I'll see you in a few."

The weather in late June could be warm, as Sveta

thought of how it would be fun to go to the countryside and enjoy a picnic. However, other more important matters needed attending to, she thought, as she raced down the steps. Reaching the bottom floor, she breathed deeply when she felt the warmth of the morning and saw her friend approaching. "I thought I would save you the stairs this morning."

"I appreciate that." Olya offered Sveta a hug. They had been close friends for a long time. Olya had been married at one time, but divorced her husband because of his heavy drinking. This had been against the advice of many of her friends, but Sveta, however, had stayed dedicated to Olya all along the way, and had allowed Olya to find her own way. Despite what she had gone through, Olya was a cheerful and loving person with short red hair that was now glowing in the full sunlight. Her slightly plump figure only added to her jolly nature.

After leaving Sveta's building, they headed across the park and toward the metro line which would take them to Nevsky Prospekt that ran next to the Neva River. Sveta enjoyed the late June season, and especially the White Nights festivals currently in full swing. She noticed how many of the partygoers, visitors, and vendors must have finally retired for the night and probably to rest for another night of fun.

"How did you sleep last night?" Sveta asked, as they hurried to the metro.

"The lights last night kept me awake for most of it. Since we're going out tonight, I knew that I needed to obtain some sleep last night, but I just couldn't."

"I had the same problem." Yes, of course, not the real problem, but the light did have some effect on her, and now it was a convenient way to blame her lack of sleep on the never ending days, and get away with it. While Sveta wanted to tell her friend of the letter, she knew better.

"We're still going out tonight, aren't we?" Olya's face beamed with excitement.

"Sure, but I don't have a lot of money to spend." Sveta's voice reflected a little embarrassment.

Olya patted her shoulder in sympathy. "Don't worry about it—we won't spend much, and I have some if we need it." Sveta thought of Olya's work as a painter. When she sold some of her paintings, she had money. If none sold, she crumbled into an extremely bad situation, since she had no husband to help support her anymore. "I sold one of my paintings yesterday!" Olya squealed. "I'm rich . . . well at least tonight I am."

"Which one?"

"I sold the abstract nude I've been working on. You know, it's amazing which kind of work sells these days, but at least I feel rich now." The recent sale explained how Olya managed to go shopping. Nevsky Prospekt remained hectic, as they strolled along the avenue.

It would be a long hike today from the Alexander Nevsky Monastery to the Admiralty, but the time together would be great. Sveta enjoyed glancing into the different shops. "Which store are we going to?" The answer didn't really matter to Sveta since she wanted to study the whole avenue today. Since salsa bars and palaces were not the kind of places she normally visited, she needed to locate what she had never paid attention to before. In the five kilometers of shopping, dining, and entertainment along the avenue, she kind of remembered seeing many salsa bars in the past.

"I'll show you when we arrive at the shop. It's going to be fun to finally buy something new!"

As they entered one store after another, Sveta noticed how styles had changed in some respects, but remained the same in many aspects. Kind of like the city, she thought, which offered everything from baroque to modern architecture. While strolling down the streets, she noticed the gypsies lurking along the gutters and entrances to alleyways as well as the Nouveau Riche who shunned them, but were walking along the main boulevard like they were. Scattered along the extremes of both wandered the tourists. Their clothing and mannerisms made them so obvious.

A sign caught Sveta's attention. The name of the place ahead of them read, "The Salsa Palace." While she had never noticed the sign before, this time she paid attention to it. Trying to be subtle, Sveta pointed to the sign. "Have you ever tried salsa dancing before?"

Olya glanced at Sveta with a slight look of astonishment in her eyes. "Yes, and I love it. I've never visited this club, but I've heard it's a great place to dance." Olya's eyes sparkled as she reached over to tickle Sveta. "What do you think? Maybe we can meet some hot guys dancing tonight?"

"I've never danced that kind of dance before. Is salsa hard to learn?"

"For you, salsa should be easy. It's different from ballet, and you do need a partner. I'm not too good, but I can help you get started." Olya could be a fun-loving girl when she wanted to be, and it would definitely be good to have her along and not have to go to the bar alone.

Forcing an inquisitive smile, Sveta decided to ask another question in a soft voice. "We'll see. What kind of clothes do we need to wear?"

"This is a Latin place, so we need to look the part. Don't worry; I have a dress you can wear tonight."

"I don't know how I let you talk me into these kinds of adventures." Sveta whispered a thankful prayer for making the outing seem like Olya's idea, and it would definitely keep her from asking too many questions.

Not far from the salsa place, Olya stopped and smiled. "Okay, this is the shop. I hope you like what I found." She giggled with excitement.

"I'm sure I will. I can't wait to find out what you've been dragging me along to see." They entered the dress shop, and walked to the far back corner.

Olya soon stopped in front of a rack. "Here it is. What do you think?"

The black dress looked elegant and sheer, and clearly made of high-grade expensive material. It was a type of gown that could only be worn to a fancy party of some kind. "Where do you plan on wearing this, Olya?"

"I don't have a specific plan for it, but I love it." Olya held the dress close to her body.

"I understand," Sveta laughed. "Well, let me see what the dress looks like on you."

As Olya went to the changing room to try the dress on, Sveta stepped around the shop and looked at the prices on the stylish dresses. While she couldn't afford clothes like these, she hoped she could one day.

Sveta watched Olya emerge wearing the dress. "You look fantastic." Olya's light-brown eyes twinkled in her excitement, as her freckles faded with the rush of redness filling her cheeks. Normally a fashionable belt would hold the dress snug to the waistline, but in her case the loose hanging material hid her stomach perfectly.

Olya smiled deeply. "I hoped you'd like it. I know I'll buy the dress now." She hurried back to the changing room to change again.

Carrying the purchase out of the door, they both laughed while continuing to enjoy the sites along Nevsky Prospekt. "Look." Olya pointed to the sign of another salsa palace off to their side. "At ten tonight, they're offering salsa lessons here for free. What do you think?"

"I like the idea of free lessons, of course, but you need to promise not to laugh at me." Sveta turned to stare at the entrance to the club.

"Laugh at you; I think you'll be the one laughing at me tonight. You know, if we stay out this late, we may need to wait 'til the morning to return home. The bridges will be raised most of the night to let the ships pass."

"I know, and I was thinking about that. I'll let my mom know we'll be out late tonight so she won't worry about me, but please do me one favor—don't tell my mom, or anyone we know that we're going dancing here tonight."

"I understand. Is your mom still giving you a hard time about not wanting to dance ballet?"

"I think she's finally gotten over my not going to the St. Petersburg Vaganova School of Choreography many years ago. I know she always hoped I'd follow my father as a great dancer, but after the disgrace and shame my mom and I went through after papa's disappearance, ballet became something I simply couldn't do."

"Don't worry. No one will ever hear about us dancing at the club tonight from me." Olya patted Sveta on the shoulder to confirm that her secret remained safe.

"Thanks." Sveta thought how easy her plan had worked out to make sure word of her going to a salsa bar would remain quiet. She would need to tell her mom to act as if she heard nothing, but, of course, she would tell her mom everything she learned.

"What time do you need to go help your mom?"

"I'm afraid I need to leave right now, since she's counting on me to help her. We have a lot of work needing attention in the garden right now. When I come to your place later, I'll bring you some of the strawberries ripening now. I would love to eat some before we go out tonight."

"Great! I'll see you a little later. I have a few more shops I want to visit before I go back."

"Okay, I'll see you later also." Sveta headed for the bus stop. It would take about an hour to travel to the garden in the nearby countryside.

Sveta relaxed, knowing she had someone to go with her to the salsa club. She had some scary thoughts about going out at night alone to some of the clubs, and facing men drinking too much vodka, but thanks to her friend going with her she would feel much more comfortable. She admitted to herself that learning a new dance could be exciting tonight. With the questions raised by the invitation continuing to eat at her, she had a real interest in learning now. She had so many questions—questions which she now demanded answers for. She had waited long enough.

***

Sveta looked forward to the thirty-minute trip from the bus stop to the garden house. Even as beautiful as the city was, with all its magnificence, it felt great to travel to the countryside for a change in pace. There she could clear her head and think, which was exactly what she needed to do right now.

After the bus stopped close to the garden that Sveta and her mom had cultivated for many years, a car soon trailed behind her as she navigated the trail to the garden. The large, expensive looking car, something you didn't find too much outside the city, gave her a feeling of being stalked. Was someone in the car watching her walk on the trail? She turned around to stare at the car. The car stopped, and slowly turned around on the side of the road to head back in the other direction. Was she being paranoid? Had someone followed her? Damn, she wished she knew for sure.

After arriving at the garden, she searched for her mom. "Hello, where are you?"

"In here," Sveta heard her mom yell from inside the garden house.

Sveta loved the garden house and the times she had spent the night there. She remembered those fun times, and especially growing up in the garden in the summer time. "What are you doing?" Sveta smiled at her mom, as she entered.

"Close the door," Mariya ordered, as she waved for her daughter to hurry. "I've located some papers I want to show you."

She quickly sat beside Mariya. "What are you looking for?"

"These are some of the newspaper articles and other papers written about your papa when he disappeared. They had accused him of being part of a large robbery of Russian art stolen from a museum, but the exact pieces were never fully disclosed. Even the role he may have played has never been proven. The KGB at the time hid most of the details in total secret. Many members of the Lisin organization have ties with the government, as you know. All people in Russia loved these paintings, and considered them part of their Russian heritage, and as such attached extremely high patriotic value to them."

"But Papa was simply a dancer. How could he have had anything to do with this?"

"Yuri Zotov was head of the Department of Culture when these items were stolen. He had personally arranged for the Russian team to participate in the competition in America. Needless to say, but they did find, supposedly, one of the stolen paintings in your father's room. It was an inexpensive painting, but enough to make the theft look like he had been involved. The rest of the stolen objects were never discovered."

"Yes, I know who Yuri Zotov is. While I've never met him, he's one of my biggest clients. He likes to buy items at low prices and then sell them later for large profits. I understand he has an impressive art collection in his house. He has also purchased many paintings and pieces of art from my gallery, including my best painter from Italy."

"Yuri has always asserted that your Papa didn't defect with the objects or sell them to someone in the United States. He thought America was covering up something, and lying about him being murdered in the room where the object was found, as well as him being later thrown off of a bridge. It's others in the government, and members of the Lisin family, who have accused him relentlessly over the years."

Sveta wiped the tears from her eyes before her mom continued. "We've lived with this unknown piece of history all our lives. It's unreal to think his body was never discovered, or that he's never surfaced. But this letter . . . . Why does he finally show up now?"

"I wish I knew, but I think we'll obtain more information on this salsa connection soon."

"Speaking of salsa, I have some exciting news. I'm going with Olya tonight to a salsa club to learn to dance. She thinks she's pulling me to this club, and it's her idea."

"Sveta, don't you think you're rushing things? You only received the letter yesterday. What if someone saw it? You could be followed, and if caught trying to contact your Papa, you could in up being in big trouble."

"Yes, but what choice do I have? I've wanted to know the answers to my Papa's disappearance for years. Since I think I might have received a chance to do exactly that, I'm taking it."

"You know that I'll help all I can. I just don't know what I can do to help."

Sveta knew she would. "Time will tell, but right now we have some work to do. I'll find the water bucket and start watering the plants."

"Okay, Sveta, I'll join you soon. I'll need to hide these papers again since it wouldn't be good to have someone discover them now."

Sveta glanced at the many vegetables growing in the garden that needed tending. She loved her miniature garden consisting of only about fifteen meters by twenty meters and the little house with the one room. However, the garden house did contain a loft above it on the rear. She understood how important a garden was for many Russians to have in order to have a place to grow fresh vegetables and fruits, like apples.

Emerging from the house, Mariya asked Sveta, "Would you like some tea?"

"I would love some, but let me work a little more first. We've some vegetables needing to be picked, and the strawberries look good as well as the new potatoes. Who are we going to give some of the harvest to?"

"Don't worry. Many people in our building want some. Also, we need to pick some of the flowers and enjoy them at home."

The work went quickly, and while Sveta felt tired from the hard work, she still looked forward to dancing at the salsa club later. "I need to hurry. Olya will be waiting for me."

"I need to put in a few more plants, but I'm leaving in a minute also so that we can go together." A smile crossed her mom's face. "I've been secretly mad at your father, thinking perhaps he had abandoned us, but I never wanted you to know. However, I now think he's alive and that he'll make a good life for us soon. I don't know why I think this, but I've this feeling in the air around me. It's as if he's sending his love to us right this very minute."

"It's strange—yes. In fact, I started to say I was receiving the same feeling, but I have so many questions I want answers to."

"We'll have them soon. I know it."

CHAPTER 3

Sveta glanced toward Olya's flat. Since she couldn't see her on the balcony, she decided to make her way up the flight of stairs to the fourth floor. Her building contained many flats with large ceilings, making it the perfect place for her to use for her studio.

The weather looked great, and the prospect of an exciting night with her best friend felt exciting. Being her best friend, Sveta again wished she could tell Olya about the letter, but knew to keep the invitation quiet, at least for now. Sveta breathed deeply, and knocked on the door.

Obviously impatient, Olya quickly opened the door. "I've been waiting for you—what took you so long to get ready?"

"I wanted to look good tonight, and you know me and my hair. I also stopped and purchased some chocolate for us. It's a new one that I've never tried before, but I heard it was fantastic."

"You know I love chocolate. Let me see what you purchased."

Sveta handed her the chocolate bar, and dropped onto the sofa, where she noticed a dress Olya had placed on one side for her. While the dress looked a little big for her, it was better than anything she owned. "I don't know how the dress will look on me. We're not the same size." Sveta pouted and pushed her breasts together to try to make them look a little bigger.

"Don't worry about it. We'll make the dress work." Olya's large but firm breasts came from her being a little overweight. While she had worked on her weight problem some, she had more interest in working hard at painting than going to a gym to exercise, and as a result she possessed more of a common girl look. Sveta knew that any elegant looks she had were obviously inherited from her mom.

Quickly obeying her friend, Sveta removed the dress she wore, and glanced at her body. Like most ballet dancers, her legs looked slim, but well toned; in fact, they looked slightly muscular. She could do nothing about her petite breasts but laugh.

After pulling on the black dress, Olya tried to adjust it as best she could by locating some pins, and pulling part of the material tighter. Sveta felt amazed to see how much better the dress looked a few minutes later. The dress would do until she could afford to buy something else. "Thank you. I'll be careful with your dress tonight."

"You're welcome. I've almost completed a salad for us, but we need to hurry. I want to arrive at the bar in time for the lessons."

"Okay. I'm also hungry from all the work today."

After eating, they left the flat and crossed several streets before entering the metro, heading toward the festival. With the crowds already starting to swell when they arrived at the Neva River, they hoped to cross the bridge before the operator raised it for the night. Luckily, they rushed across only minutes before they would need to find another route.

A large man hurried to cross with them. Sveta thought she had seen him on the metro behind them, but wasn't absolutely sure. She turned around to study him again as the man quickly buried his face into a paper, and acted like he was reading. Perhaps it was a feeling or a hunch, but she wondered if he was following them. She decided to keep an eye on him to see if he stayed with them.

The white night festivities had attracted many locals and visitors who were enjoying the entertainment scattered along the way. With so much to see and do, not to mention the large crowds, the trip to the salsa club became painstakingly slow.

"We need to hurry. It's about to start, and I want to receive the free lessons." Olya laughed loud.

"Me too. I definitely can't afford lessons, but I want to learn something about this kind of dancing."

Finally, they arrived at the salsa club and studied the entrance. Sveta had very little money, and needed to be careful about how she spent her limited funds. A man stood at the door. "How much does it cost to go inside?" Sveta asked, as she approached him.

"Tonight's ladies' night, and you can enter for free."

"Wow! That's great." The two stepped around him and into the club. As Sveta entered, she glanced over her shoulder to see if the stranger was still following them, but she was relieved when she didn't see him anywhere.

While the time was approaching nine thirty, and the light outside still remained bright from the northern lights, inside the dark club, with its dim lighting, they needed to let their eyes adjust to view their surroundings. They slowly passed by a foyer where patrons normally left their jackets during the winter months.

Sveta studied the next room, full of small tables and chairs for either two or four people. While most of the tables were positioned to the right side of a long room that seemed to go on forever, the left side of the room had a bar stretching for maybe thirty meters or more. As her eyes adjusted to the dim lighting, she studied the many lights advertising brand-name drinks. Even the back wall had decorative lights shining on the various bottles, showing off the brands particular style, or color.

"What do you think?" Olya asked, as they headed toward the back of the room.

"It's fascinating, but still dark. Can you see okay?"

"Yes, my eyes are adapting well, but I don't see many people in here yet. I think we arrived a little early, and before the dancing starts. That's good since we need some time to become acquainted with this place."

The five, or six bartenders behind the bar stayed busy setting up their workplaces. They were obviously expecting many people later. Two of the bartenders watched them as they passed. Like many places, the more ladies the bar attracted, the more the men came, and they were the ones who had the money to spend on drinks.

In the chairs around the tables sat maybe forty to fifty people. Many of them had food in front of them that they were enjoying before the dancing started. Finally, in the back of this long room, Sveta noticed an open space—a dance floor.

Sveta studied the thirty-by-thirty meter dance floor. The hardwood floors had many lights hanging above it, which added to the atmosphere. In addition to these lights, an additional array of white sparkling lights and mood lighting of various pastel colors decorated the dance floor.

While the bar ended where the dance floor started, one spot at the end allowed patrons to order drinks directly from the bartender without waiting for a waitress. After looking beyond the dance floor, Sveta examined the band stand. Several members of a live band had arranged some equipment, and a few of them were still actively checking out their instruments. "I see the band stage—I think they own a lot of equipment," Sveta said as she glanced over toward Olya.

"I see it. Where do you want to sit?"

"I don't care, but somewhere close to the floor. I want to watch as much as we can. It's going to be so much fun to enjoy this kind of dancing."

As Olya sauntered over to the far right wall and started to sit, two guys approached them. "I'm sorry, but you can't sit in this section. We're removing those tables to make more room for dancing. You can sit over by the bar . . . if you want." One of them pointed to some tables a few rows back.

With a big smile, Sveta answered, "That will be fine. We didn't know."

"I understand. This must be your first time here. Are you here for the dance lessons?"

"Yes, we think salsa would be great to learn. Do they still offer them tonight? We saw a sign out front."

"Yes, we offer thirty minutes of dance lessons every night before we start. You'll enjoy it. The instructors who offer the lessons own a dance studio close to here, and they pick up many clients by giving away these free lessons."

"I've never danced salsa before—is it hard?" Sveta asked, as she studied the closest guy's face and his body language.

"I think it's easy, but I've been dancing salsa all my life. I hope you enjoy it." He smiled as he left, and joined the other guy to take some more chairs to a room at the back of the stage area. After realizing that they had much to do, Sveta didn't want to keep them any longer, but it would be fun to talk with them more when they had time.

After reaching their table, Olya and Sveta adjusted the chairs to observe the dance floor easier. The walls, which were painted black, helped the club look much larger and spacious, and allowed the decorations and lights to capture their thoughts and imagination to a higher degree.

A waitress strolled over to their table. "Good evening. What can I offer you from the bar?" She smiled, and waited for a response.

"We aren't too thirsty, but I think I would like a beer. What would you like to drink, Sveta?"

"I'm not sure. . . ."

Obviously observing the look on her close friend's face, Olya leaned over closer to her. "Don't worry about it, tonight is on me. I made a good sale yesterday, and I have money for tonight." Olya turned toward the waitress. "I think we'll take two Baltika number threes."

"Sure thing. I'll be right back with them." She headed across the room toward the bar to retrieve the order.

The guys kept coming and going to remove more and more tables and chairs, as the dance floor grew much larger by the minute. She assumed that during the dinner hour they used the space for serving meals, but now they converted the space into the entertainment part of the night. The guy she had spoken with glanced over at them each time he returned to retrieve more chairs.

Noticing the attention, Olya reached over to tickle her friend and to tease her. "I think you have someone interested in you already." Olya laughed. She always had a certain way of teasing Sveta.

Sveta studied him again when he retrieved the last load of chairs. He looked to be in his early thirties, and with a modest amount of a Latin look in him while still retaining many Russian features also. With no noticeable accent, she assumed him to be a local. His eyes looked dark and piercing, but his face reflected a smooth, almost boyish smile. With extremely good posture, he could pass for a Russian ballet dancer.

The waitress returned to the table with the two beers. "That will be seventy rubles."

Olya produced the money and handed it to her. Both girls lifted their beers, and looked at each other, trying to think of a good cheer.

Finally, Sveta spoke first. "To a night of salsa."

Olya nodded her head. "To a night of great dancing."

Another couple arrived, and sat across from them. With them dressed in Latin-style clothing, you could tell that they came to the bar to dance.

The beer tasted fantastic and was exactly what Sveta needed. Not wanting to be a burden on her friend, she decided to drink the beer slowly, knowing the night would be long. The place soon came into better view as her eyes adjusted better to the low light.

Several more men arrived on the stage. As the band grew larger, she saw several large congas situated in the middle of the stage, and next to a large bass. With many microphones set up, she assumed many of the members might be singing also.

Soon, many more couples entered the room, and ventured to the edge of the floor. It wouldn't be much longer now. "Olya, have you been here before?"

"No, this is the first time here. I've visited a few places before, but never this one. Remember, you promised not to laugh at me."

"I think we exchanged a mutual promise. I can't believe you talked me into coming here."

"Relax! We're going to have some fun tonight."

About seven girls came in and quickly pulled two tables together. They must have danced at the club before, perhaps regulars. Two of them stood, and shifted their hips in a definitely Latin circular type motion. Olya pointed to the dance briefly to obtain Sveta's attention, but not so obvious as to attract the attention of the girls dancing. "That's what you'll need to learn. Latin dancing has a certain movement to it.”

“I think it’s going to be fun.” A tingle of excitement began to grow along Sveta’s spine as the fascinating movement dominated her attention. She almost missed watching the dance instructor coming into the room. He stood tall, almost six feet, and slender, with a well toned body of an expert. His dark hair, which he combed directly to the back of his head, and his high cheekbones made him almost pass for a professional model. As his looks mesmerized Sveta, she suddenly noticed the lady stalking behind him. She was a perfect match for him. They had to be the dance instructors.

As they reached the center of the room, they split, and started to greet the people around them. He approached their table first. “Are you here for the dance lessons?” He offered a big smile full of white teeth.

“Yes, we are.” They both answered at once.

“Hello, my name is Dima. I’ll be the dance instructor tonight, along with my wife Natasha. Since I see that the band is almost ready to begin, we’ll be starting in a few minutes. Have you ever danced salsa before?”

“This is my first time, but Olya has danced some before.”

Olya extended her hand in a slight protest. “I’ve danced a few times, but still know almost nothing. Sveta’s an excellent dancer. I’m sure she can learn quickly.”

“I understand. What kind of dancing do you do?” His attention centered on Sveta, as he waited for an answer.

Olya, however, answered for Sveta. “She’s a ballet dancer, and her mother’s an instructor at a ballet school.”

“What’s your mother’s name?” Dima leaned toward Sveta, apparently wanting her to speak.

“My mother is Mariya Panova. Why?”

He studied her face. “Wow! You must be Kolya

Panov's daughter."

Sveta felt a wave of shock. Her head became dizzy. Her father's legal name was Nickolay, but only his closest friends called him Kolya. "You've heard of my father?"

"Yes, I've heard a little about him from my parents. They said he danced extremely well. It was terrible that he vanished when he had so much going for him. Since I've always had an interest in his story, I'd love to talk to you more about this later. Here's my card. Please call me sometime." He quickly handed Sveta his card before turning to meet others who had entered the salsa bar.

Turning to Olya, Sveta asked, "Can you believe this—he's heard of my father?"

"Your father was a fantastic dancer, and you should be proud of him." Olya paused for a minute. "I wonder who his parents are."

"I'm not sure, but I have his card, and I'd love to find out what he knows." Her heart fluttered. She wanted to tell her friend what she received in the mail, but no—it wouldn't be a good idea. Since the time that her papa disappeared had caused her mom so many hardships, it would be best not to bring up future problems until she learned more about what was going on.

Sveta was soon lost in her thoughts until Olya tapped on her shoulder to let her know that the female instructor had moved over to their table. "Are you ready to learn some salsa tonight?"

"Yes, we're looking forward to it. Are you one of the instructors?" Sveta smiled.

"Yes, I'll be teaching with my husband. You talked to him a few minutes ago. It's really easy, and you can make many friends while you're dancing."

"We hope so." Olya glanced around the bar, and where many men were now waiting at the sides.

Natasha noticed the smile and added, "We usually have many men here looking for someone to dance with. You'll have a lot of fun, and they'll help you learn more tonight after we finish with the lesson." As the band hurried into final preparation, she spoke quickly before rushing to be with her husband. "We'll see you on the floor in a minute."

On a count of three, the band erupted into a Latino rhythm which invigorated and electrified Sveta's mind, body and soul. They played extremely good, especially the conga players, who produced a beat that she could definitely feel.

"Welcome to the club tonight," the bandleader announced as he moved to the front of the stage. While speaking Russian, he had a Latin accent of some sort. "We have some great Latin music for you, and I hope to have all of you dancing on the floor shortly. For those who have never danced salsa before, we're fortunate to present two of the best dancers around St. Petersburg to offer free lessons tonight. So . . . let's all welcome them to the dance floor!"

The band stopped for a few seconds, allowing her heart to flutter in anticipation of some big event about to burst onto the floor, and then the music started. The coordination sounded incredible as the mixture of instruments coming together intoxicated the room with a definite Latin rhythm.

Moving to the center of the dance floor, Dima met his wife entering from across the room. They merged into one with the music instantly. The movements were so fluid that they must have been joined together at birth. When he raised her hand, she executed two spins in the blink of an eye before returning into a perfect rhythm with him. She next parted briefly from him, and after fully extending away from his hold, she paused for a second. After finding her hand, he pulled her back, where she wrapped her legs around him. In a sudden freezing of the movement, she glued tightly against him. The moment intensified and became extremely sexy and passionate as she stared deeply into his eyes. They became so much as one with the music that everyone stood awestruck watching them dance.

The intricate steps increased more and more, until he finished with her doing a deep backward dip. As she lay almost entirely backwards, he pulled her in a long, arcing circle. Suddenly, she snapped back into his arms, wrapping her leg around him again as if to say, "Yes, we are one."

The music stopped, and the audience clapped loudly as they had just witnessed an extraordinary dance. While Sveta loved the performance, she whispered to herself, "I don't think I can ever dance that good. What was my father thinking? He wants me to go to an international competition in salsa. This has to be a joke of some kind."

CHAPTER 4

Having watched professional dancers most of her life, Sveta understood talent, and these two had the gift. She knew they must have danced together for a long time to demonstrate that kind of connection. Sveta could also tell they loved each other, and love was the one quality which creates fantastic dancing by couples.

The clapping lasted for a long minute or two as the crowd demonstrated their appreciation for the great performance. The dance instructor soon accepted the microphone as many of the crowd drifted to the floor. Sveta assumed that many had received lessons here before, and knew what to expect.

Nevertheless, he soon announced. "If you want to participate in the free lessons tonight, and we hope you do, please come on over to the dance floor." He attempted to pull everyone arriving late into the salsa bar to come join in the lesson.

Sveta and Olya looked at each other and exchanged a familiar laugh, knowing they needed to step onto the floor. Sveta recognized the awkward moments when people first start, and this time allowed no exception. The people on the dance floor ranged from both young to old. Some were in great physical condition, and others looked to be tourists who were just out for a change of pace.

As Dima moved to the left side of the floor, his wife strolled to the right side. "I need to have all the men in front of me, and all of the women in front of my wife." The crowd obeyed him instantly, indicating that they wanted to learn as much as they could.

"Salsa dancing is a lot like many dances, but still different in its own way. You'll also notice many different styles of salsa dancing. Tonight, we're going to learn the basic steps. I know we have many people here who love to dance and to expand their knowledge of this fantastic, and of course, one very passionate dance."

Sveta watched Natasha, the instructor in front of her, and admired how graceful she floated across the floor. She must have received at least some training in ballet, she thought. "Here goes nothing." Sveta leaned forward and whispered to her friend before flashing a quick smile.

Dima smiled before he started giving instructions. "I know you girls might hate it, but on the dance floor . . . the man is always in charge. While it's up to him to decide which moves you make, it's your job to be totally connected to him so you'll understand exactly what he wants you to do. So let me hear all the ladies say they agree to follow their partner's lead, and no matter how ridiculous the movement looks."

A lot of laughter filled the floor, as they all finally gave in, and reluctantly replied. "We agree."

Next, he turned to the men and said, "Men, you can all thank me later. However, we have one requirement for you also. It's your job to make the ladies look good. If you want them to follow you, you need to give good signals. You not only need to know your steps, but their steps."

He walked to the center of the floor before he continued. "Since this dance originates in Cuba, we'll start with the basic Cuban, or Cantina salsa. This dance has a lot of hip action, which gives the movements the signature Latin rhythm. First, push your hip forward, and to the far right. Next, push your hips to the far left. Please follow this by pushing them backward and to the far left, before finally pushing to the far right rear corner. In other words, you're making a circle. But on each corner, you're hitting that spot on a beat. It's kind of like this…" He motioned to the band to give him a rhythm beat.

He produced a perfect circle, hitting each spot perfectly, and creating a sexy movement of his hips, which generated nothing less than a pure Latino movement. Turning to his wife, he said, "She'll now teach you ladies how to make your movement to coincide with your partners."

"Yes." She smiled, picking up on her cue. "To make our bodies melt together, we'll need to make a circle to complement his. To do this, we first need to push our hips to the rear and far left, then to the rear and far right, followed by moving forward to the far right. We follow this with a movement to the far left, but still forward."

Both instructors turned to look straight at their students, and with a finger reaching over their heads they counted one, two, three, and began moving to the beat of the salsa music. The guys attempted to follow him, while the girls followed her lead. Some danced well, and some looked funny. One overweight guy in particular had a hard time learning the movement. Sveta and Olya locked eyes with each other while both attempted to keep from laughing, but the lesson continued, as everyone worked to produce the correct movement.

After turning around to his partner, Dima raised his hand. "Let's see what the steps look like together." With the two instructors facing each other, they proceeded through the movements again. As they danced in perfect harmony and complemented each other so well, it became easy to understand why they moved in such a direction.

"Now, let's learn the basic step. I want the guys to step forward with their left foot and transfer their weight onto it. Next, step back to where you started and transfer your weight to the right foot. Proceeding, step backward with the right foot and transfer your weight to it. Finally, you bring the right foot back home and transfer your weight to the left foot. It's the transfer of weight which gives you the hip motion."

Next, Natasha started to teach the ladies their steps. "Please remember, girls, you are always right, so keep in mind this one thing—always start on your right foot, but by stepping backwards. If you stay connected to your partner, he'll lead you in where you're supposed to be." She completed the steps several times before joining her husband, and saying, "Let's watch how the steps look when we put them together." The two went through the basic step, where the dance looked perfect as expected.

For the next twenty minutes, they went through the basic step again and again and eventually added the hip movement. Finally, Dima raised his hands before he spoke. "Okay, we need to try this with a partner. If you brought someone with you, that's good. If not, you need to find one." He started matching several couples.

Two guys with big smiles rushed over to Sveta and Olya from across the room. They both looked like typical Russian men wanting to have a good time. For the next few minutes, they all attempted the new basic steps, which felt easy enough. As the lesson ended, the men introduced themselves and said they would love to dance with them in a minute, to which both girls replied at once, "That will be great—we want to learn."

After the girls returned to their table, the full band on the stage started to play their music. The girls raised their glasses in a quick toast before several men approached them, asking to dance. After a quick wink at each other, they headed back to the floor. These two guys knew salsa dancing well, and also realized that the girls were relatively new at it. They helped them learn the basics all over again, while slowly moving them into more and more difficult steps.

The music played louder as the night progressed. As each new guy asked Sveta to dance, she could barely hear the name of the guys or really know exactly what they were saying to her, but she knew they wanted to dance. The dancing increased her thirst, and the beer soon vanished.

As they approached their table, Sveta lifted her empty glass, looking for anything left at all. The last guy she had danced with, and who had followed her back to her table quickly acknowledged the situation. "What are you drinking?"

"We're drinking Baltika number three," Sveta responded with a smile. "But you don't need to buy us one, we're fine." Instead, he winked at Olya before heading for the bar to place an order.

While he worked his way through the crowds, another guy came to ask her to dance. "Thank you." She smiled. "But if you don't mind, I need to rest a few minutes, and one guy is bringing me a beer. I'll be glad to dance with you in a little while."

"Okay." He glanced at her out of the corner of his eyes before crossing to another table on the other side of the room.

"You're getting good." Olya leaned over toward Sveta. "I watched the turns you made with the last guy. He isn't bad looking either. What do you think?"

"He seems to be a good dancer, and he's at the bar buying us some drinks." Sveta pointed to him at the bar where he was waiting on them.

"Wow, a man after my heart," Olya offered in a joking

but teasing voice.

"I'll tell you what, Olya . . . you can have first shot at him. I need to go to the restroom for a minute, but tell him I'll be right back."

"I'll be glad to," Olya answered, as she still teased Sveta.

As Sveta crossed the floor to the restroom, she noticed one big guy sitting at the bar and drinking by himself. She wondered if he could be the same man she thought she noticed following her earlier. As the invitation invaded her mind again, she felt paranoid, knowing that she still didn't know if the letter had been tampered with, or not.

A few minutes later she returned from the restroom, but definitely looking for this man. She didn't see him anywhere—good. While Sveta breathed easier for a minute, her thoughts lingered on the invitation. If intercepted, she knew the mafia could be following her, wanting to know the truth.

"Here you are." Olya smiled, as Sveta returned. The guy who had ordered the drinks sat at the table with Olya, and another guy she hadn't seen before had joined them. In the few minutes she had disappeared to the toilet, Olya and the guy buying the drinks had become deep into a conversation as they leaned closer to each other.

The newest guy at the table stood to pull Sveta's chair out for her, as she smiled briefly at him before accepting her seat. While she thought he might be a friend of the guy buying the drinks, she wasn't sure. "My name is Denis," he said in a deep Russian voice, as he slid into a seat next to her. "Is this your first time here?"

"Yes. Does my dancing reflect badly of me on the dance floor?"

"No. You're not bad at all, but I haven't seen you here before. I watched you dancing, but so many guys were after you that I haven't had a chance to ask you yet. When you get your energy back, I'd love to dance with you." His shiny, light-blond hair, with his slightly Swedish looks glowed in the low light of the club, as his eyes radiated a deep but bright-blue color she could see even in the dim light.

"Do you dance much?" She asked, as her curiosity about him continued to increase.

"Yes, I love to dance whenever I receive a chance. This place only offers strictly salsa dancing on Saturday nights, like this. This club does offer some salsa dancing on Wednesday night here, but it's also a mixture of other dances."

Sveta lifted her glass and drank some of the refreshing beer. While the dance floor stayed crowded, she decided to rejoin the other dancers after feeling the beat of the next song. "Okay, show me what you know. I'm a quick learner."

He flashed a large smile at Sveta, and pushed his chair back before standing. He extended his hand to her, helping her to stand. "It will be my pleasure."

As Sveta stood, she tapped Olya on the shoulder. "Why are you not on the dance floor?"

Olya shrugged her shoulders to indicate she didn't know.

The man in front of her, the one who had purchased the beer, quickly extended his hand toward Olya, indicating that he was eager to dance.

Sveta entered the floor, but couldn't find much room to dance. As she turned around, and raised her arms in a perfect frame for ballroom dancing, Denis looked at her, but quickly lowered her arms to her side. After taking both hands, he started to move in a Latin motion. She remembered this basic step from the lessons earlier, but he made the steps feel so much smoother and comfortable. "Relax and feel the music." he said, as his face leaned in closer to her.

While the music played so loud that she could hardly hear him, she still knew what he was attempting to tell her. As the crowd of dancers pressed in closer to her, she was left with much less space to dance. With the other dancers constantly bumping into her, he pulled her closer into him, and changed direction in a turn which moved her to a spot on the floor where fewer people danced. His stare remained intense but considerate, and she loved his full attention on her.

He placed her left hand on his shoulder, and entered into a relaxed frame. She could understand how high elbows would never work on such a tight floor. The movement from many of the dancers became provocative and sexy. This presented her with a different style of dance, and one she had never tried before. Salsa felt so new, and exciting.

Eventually, Olya came over, pulled her from the floor, and back over to the table. Sveta knew she looked tired and thought Olya had acted to save her from being stuck on the floor, but Sveta loved the attention and the dance instructions.

After arriving back at the table, Sveta introduced Denis to Olya, and Olya introduced her new friend. When the four of them had sat together to rest for a minute, Denis offered to buy some more beer by pointing to the empty beer glasses. Everyone thanked him before he left to go to the bar.

"I think you like this guy," Olya teased, leaning closer to be heard.

"He's a good dancer, but many of the guys in here seem to dance a lot."

Overhearing their conversation, the other guy at the table spoke first. "It's still early, and the best dancers arrive in a few hours."

"Wow, why so late?" asked Olya.

"I think they like to give the bar time to thin out a little. They're energetic and lively, and they need more space to dance. Most of those on the floor readily give them that space, and it's like the floor belongs to them for a while. You'll see."

Suddenly, the dance instructor approached them, and extended his hand to Sveta. "Please, come show me what kind of dancer you are. If you're anything like your father, I know you'll be brilliant."

She accepted his hand. "This is the first time I've ever tried salsa, and I don't think my papa ever tried salsa either." She could hardly resist the invitation, as a free lesson from a dance instructor was something too hard to pass up. She followed him toward the dance floor, as she yelled over her shoulder to Olya. "Tell Denis I'll be back in a minute."

"I will, and good luck!"

Arriving with her on the floor, he immediately went to work on the hip movements to get her in the rhythm of the music. He added the basic step, and soon had her in tune with the music. He next led her through several turns and twists, making her flow across the room. He ushered her through more turns, as he demonstrated his professional teaching techniques. Sveta felt a real pleasure in dancing with him, but a few minutes later he reached over and led her back to the table. She knew he had mastered a certain ability to dance with many ladies during the night and not become entangled with anyone for long periods of time.

"You have a lot of potential," he said with a smile. "I would love to know how you're doing in a few months.

We do offer dance lessons at my studio, and I think you should come by and take some."

"I'd love to, but I don't think I can afford to take any right now."

"You have one of my cards. Please call me, or come see me." He paused for a second. "The first lesson is free." Noticing Olya looking intensely at him, he handed her a card also. He looked over at the man sitting at the table and asked him, "Do you mind if I have one dance with her?"

"Not at all," This guy only smiled briefly before responding, "Just remember to return her to the same table."

With a quick smile, they headed for the dance floor, leaving the two at the table. Reaching over the table, Sveta extended her hand and said, "I couldn't hear your name a few minutes ago."

"It's Slava, and I think you said your name was Sveta?"

"Yes, that's correct. Thank you for the beer also."

"You're welcome."

Noticing the new beer on the table, she remembered Denis going to order it. "Where is Denis?"

"He glanced at you on the dance floor and left. He said he'll return in a little while."

"He didn't get mad at me for dancing and not waiting for him, did he?" She felt slightly bad in leaving.

"I don't think so. He had some things he needed to attend to for a minute. Don't worry, he'll be back soon."

Sveta danced with several more men during the night, and learned many new steps or movements with each new dancer. They all had something to teach her, but many of the dancers became drunk as the night progressed. Sveta also realized that she drank maybe too many beers, but someone always purchased her a new one as quickly as she finished one. With many of the dancers settling in with one specific dancer for the night, their movements became much more sensual and provocative.

This last guy she was dancing with offered no exception to the others as he pulled her into many close movements, keeping her snuggled next to him while his hands became too exploratory. She had to constantly remove his hands, which were moving low on her back and several times to her rear. Perhaps many of the dancers were accustomed to dancing like that on the floor, but such contact made her feel very uncomfortable.

Finding a short break in the music, she decided to thank this last guy and head for her table, as she watched Olya doing the same. While new beers, of course, waited on the table for them, they had no idea who ordered them. Olya lifted her glass, and indicated for Sveta to raise her glass in a toast. "To the good life."

"To the good life." They both tapped their glasses together, and sipped the free beer.

When the music paused for a second, Sveta noticed many people moving from the floor. A single horn suddenly played for a second as the conga player stopped playing. The shift in music quickly attracted everyone's attention in the bar. After standing to glimpse pass the crowd, the two girls studied Denis edging toward the center of the floor. A woman on the other side of the room wearing a black dress with elaborate flowing lace walked out to meet him in the center of the floor. While the cut on one side extended to her hip, revealing a shapely leg, her dark and full hair hung long and added to her gorgeous looks. She instantly dominated the crowd's attention.

Reaching the center, he grabbed her hand and pulled her toward him and into a double spin before reaching him. Her arm slid over his shoulder, as she wrapped her arm completely around his neck in a firm but solid connection. She pulled from him, only to be pulled back to him again. This time, however, he stopped her in front of him and held her, steadying her as she bent backward in a full dip. He guided her far off to the left before slowly swirling her around to the right, and upon reaching the far side she snapped upward and back into his arms again.

The dramatic movements and perfect timing with the music dominated everyone's thoughts while they intensely watched the performance. The dancing went on for another five to ten minutes, and became more passionate with each new introduction of movement. The dance quickly excited Sveta, but scared her also. How could she be expected to master such a dance?

Soon, several other dancers entered the floor, and proved to be as talented as Denis and his partner. After looking over at Olya, her eyes sent a message both of them understood. With dancers like these on the floor, they would sit and watch. This they did for another hour before deciding to leave.

Denis, however, quickly approached their table as they stood. "I see you're still here."

"Yes, but I think we're leaving. These dancers are too good for us, but it was so exciting to watch them. You're extremely talented. Watching you and your girlfriend dance is almost like viewing a fairytale."

Denis smiled. "She isn't my girlfriend. She's a good dancer, and we dance together often, but that's it."

"I understand. By the way, thanks for the beers. We really enjoyed them."

"You're welcome, and I enjoyed meeting both of you. If you want to learn more, I would love to teach you."

"That's nice of you, and perhaps we can run into each other again soon."

"This is a huge city. If you give me your home number, I can call you. There're many places to dance, but you need to know where and when."

Knowing he was right, she looked at Olya, as if to ask what she thought. Olya quickly nodded her approval as Sveta retrieved a napkin from the table and reached for a pen in her purse. "This is my number at work where you can give me a call later. I work at the Sergeevich Gallery."

After glancing at the number, he placed the napkin in his pocket. "Good, I'll call you later."

Sveta waved at him, and headed for the door. With Olya behind her, she thought about how good the dancing had been all night. Upon reaching the front door, she noticed the two instructors standing there, talking to an older man who looked like he might be the owner.

"Hello." The instructors smiled as the girls approached. "We're going to eat something at a pastry shop around the corner. Would you two like to join us?"

A glance between the girls indicated at first a definite "no", but Olya checked her watch before answering. "Well, I think we need to kill a little time, since the bridges won't be lowered for a while."

Realizing this, Sveta agreed as she turned toward them. "We'll be glad to, but only until we can cross the river."

"Good, it's only a few minutes from here. This will give me some time to ask you about your father. The stories are fascinating, and I haven't heard anything about him in a long time."

"I don't know if I can tell you any more than what you probably know. If anything, it sounds like you may have answers to questions I have about his disappearance."

After walking outside, they studied the sky still casting a silvery glow, and many people still wandered about on the street. She knew most people had a hard time sleeping when the sky never turned fully dark.

While a large crowd packed into the small shop, they managed to obtain a table in the front near a window that provided an excellent view of the street and the constant traffic along the sidewalk. They all agreed a good strong tea would be excellent for clearing their heads. "How do you know of my parents," Sveta finally asked.

He looked like he knew this question would be asked, and had prepared for it. "I danced at the same school where your father danced when I was younger, and my father also danced there before me. Your father's name has arisen on many occasions. I think everyone knows of the missing icons and paintings, and how many of the true facts have never been disclosed. Since no one knows whatever happened to them, I think your father became the perfect person to blame this on."

"I've heard this before, but I still don't believe he had anything to do with the theft. From what I've learned he loved his country, and more than anything he loved to dance."

"I didn't mean to upset you. This had to be hard on you growing up."

"Yes, it's been hard on me and my mom. It's not easy living without a father in Russia, and especially when people think your father was a thief."

"I'm sorry, and I'm sure it was. In the twenty-five years since he disappeared, have you ever learned any more about what really happened to him?"

"As I said, you probably know more than I do. Yes, I'll agree that on many nights I've cried and hated him for leaving us. If he really defected, and started a new life in America without ever contacting us, the news would be hard to take now."

"I'm sorry for making you sad." With a brief smile, he

changed the subject. "I enjoyed watching you dance tonight. For some reason, I think your father would love to know how his daughter has turned out."

Trying to change the subject again, Sveta asked, "Did you say the first lesson was free?"

"Yes. It's an introductory lesson, but one that I think you'll like."

Olya spoke next. "We don't have a lot of money for lessons, but we would love to if we could."

"The lessons aren't too expensive. I'll offer you a special package when you come by." He handed both of them a brochure from his studio. "The times are on the back, and I really think you'll enjoy it. Also, if you have any friends who enjoy dancing, tell them also."

"Thank you. We'll think about coming soon." Sveta stood to leave. "We need to go home. I live with my mom, and I'm sure she's still waiting for me."

"I understand. We hope to meet you again later," the dance instructor's wife said, as she offered a farewell smile.

CHAPTER 5

At almost ten thirty the next morning, Sveta woke to smell the aroma of fresh tea floating across her flat. She rubbed her eyes as she studied her mom quietly working at the kitchen table, knitting away on a new scarf she had planned to present to one of the girls in her class later. She spoke without removing her concentration from her work. "I see you decided to wake up this morning."

"Yes, we stayed out much later than I planned."

"How's your head?"

"Trust me, you don't want to know. Many guys purchased beer for us last night. I hope Olya's doing better than me."

Finally, her mom shifted her attention to Sveta. "Well . . . tell me, how do you like salsa dancing and what did you find out?"

"The music is very different, and we enjoyed watching a lot of dancers who were fascinating. It's nothing like ballet, since salsa has no hard-set rules. I'm going to the art gallery in a little while to work on the computer since I'm interested in getting online to find out what I can about salsa." She looked at her mom, who looked tired and like she hadn't slept all night. "You don't look so good this morning—are you okay?"

"I didn't sleep much since the letter we received yesterday troubled me all night. If he's alive and hasn't contacted us all these years, he'd better have a good reason for doing so. I've lost so much sleep, and I've been through so much because of him."

As Maria leaned over and quietly whimpered, Sveta rushed over to her. "Mom, I understand. I have such a vague memory of him, but I've wanted to know him all of my life. Can you really believe there's a chance he might be alive in America somewhere?"

"I don't know, but I do know that some powerful people looked for him for a long time."

Smiling at her mom, Sveta reached toward the heating unit for the water, and lit the heater. "I need to take a shower because of last night. Since no one works at the art gallery on Saturday, I'll have a good chance to search the internet without raising questions."

"Please be careful. I don't trust anyone, and I won't be surprised if they don't monitor where you go on the internet."

"I understand, but I need a way of searching, which is hard to trace. A friend of mine showed me how to do it on the system." Sveta removed her gown and went into the bathroom, which served as their laundry room also. She knew washing her long, thick hair required some time, but it was necessary for her to look good. Drying her hair would take more time, but she needed to talk to her mom a little longer to make sure she'd be fine while she went to her shop.

"Do you mind helping me comb through this mess?" Sveta asked as she strolled back into the room with a towel wrapped around her.

"Not at all. You did always have such thick hair. Your hair reminds me of your papa's hair." With a pleasant change of mood, she laughed faintly. "I wonder how thick his hair is today. I'd love to know."

The middle of the day felt warm as Sveta left the flat where the bright sun forced her to reach for her sunglasses. Since the gallery wasn't too far away, Sveta decided to walk and save the little money she owned. With the thoughts of money reentering her thoughts this morning, she knew that a trip to America must be expensive, but the cost of the trip would be the first item she would research when she arrived at the gallery.

In addition to money, she knew she needed to obtain a visa. Since she had no knowledge of how to do this, she hoped she could figure this out on the internet, and wondered how she would to do this without raising questions about why she wanted to go to America to compete in a salsa competition, a dance she knew almost nothing about. This had to be one of the stupider things she'd ever contemplated doing, she thought while she continued to walk.

As she rounded the corner to the gallery where she worked for the last seven years, she studied the gallery's deserted look. Solitude was good, since she didn't need to have someone else working in the gallery while she surfed the internet. She quickly unlocked the door, and glanced around quickly. While she didn't notice anyone following her, she scanned the area specifically for the man she thought had followed her the day before.

Once she entered the building, she locked the door, walked to her private office, and quickly shut the office door behind her as well. Inside her office, she felt comfortable and secure. After resting for a minute, she reflected on her career, and how she had learned so much about art. The owner had taken her under his wing, so to speak, when she decided not to follow a career in dancing.

She powered up the computer and waited for the internet connection on her personal computer, which operated slowly but surely. Sveta quickly visited the American embassy site to learn about obtaining a B-2 visa. It didn't look too hard to obtain, but how was she to really know?

Next, she started pricing the cost of a trip. The round-trip air fare was expensive, but she had already suspected that it would be. It was the cost of staying in New York City that shocked her. "They have to be kidding. The rooms cost more per night than I make in a week." Her heart sank, since this would be impossible. However, she continued to add up the cost out of curiosity. The trip would cost more than she could save from two to three years of hard work.

Since she didn't have the invitation with her, she had forgotten the exact name of the competition. After a long search, she finally located the site on the internet. The large list of salsa bars in New York City fascinated her as she counted over one hundred of them. Finally she located what she looked for: the New York International Salsa Dance Challenge. Many of the clubs were joining together to promote their clubs and salsa dancing, and the competition itself would be held at several clubs. To qualify, you needed to win at one locally sponsoring club. From this one win the couple would advance to the finals.

While the more she read about the contest the more excited she became, she knew she couldn't accomplish all of this. Thoughts of such had to be a joke. Still intrigued, she studied the many sites on salsa dancing around the world. She quickly learned how this dance had grown worldwide and was still gaining strength.

She located many special forums where many people entered to chat about salsa. While she found a few in Russian, most were in English or Spanish. She remembered the English she had learned in school, which was far from perfect. Perhaps the sites presented a good method to practice her English, she thought. With the prospect enticing her more and more, she started to bookmark the pages, but stopped abruptly. What am I thinking? The one thing she didn't need to do was leave any kind of trail that someone could follow. After unmarking the site, she decided to make mental notes of the locations so that she could return later.

The dance instructor had said there were many kinds of salsa styles. As she did more research, she discovered that he was absolutely correct. While the dance had moved from Cuba in the fifties to New York and Washington, salsa also had spread to Moscow and St. Petersburg. With many Cubans living in Miami, salsa also grew dramatically in the typical Cuban style. The dance had constantly evolved with the new hip-hop style salsa danced in Los Angeles, California, for an example. Some of the words didn't make sense, like on-one and on-two, but she knew she had much to learn.

Suddenly, she heard someone outside her door. She rushed to close the window to the site, and opened her mailbox moments before the door opened behind her. "What are you doing here today, Sveta?" She heard her boss, Mr. Sergeevich ask her.

Acting shocked, she swirled around in her seat to face him. "I didn't know anyone was here. When did you come in?"

"I just arrived and noticed that your light was on."

"Yes, I was walking close to here, and I thought of something that I needed to check on. I received an e-mail from Antonio in Italy a few days ago, and I was concerned about when his painting was going to arrive. Since we need to let Mr. Zotov know on Monday, I was going to type him a new e-mail to confirm shipment. This way, I'll have something concrete to tell him when he calls."

"That's a good idea, since he usually calls early in the mornings. I still don't understand what he finds so fascinating about Antonio's work. He doesn't do a lot of painting, but I'll agree the few that he does paint are extremely fascinating."

"I've thought about his work also. I think one day his paintings may become valuable, and if the price does, Yuri Zotov should be able to sell reprints to all the work he hoarded. He's a smart buyer. Have you ever viewed his collection? It's said to be worth a fortune."

"I'm sure the collection is, since he's worked as head of the Department of Culture for a long time. Be careful when you deal with him, or talk about him, he has some important friends and ties to organize crime."

"I understand. I'm just so thankful that he sends me a special finder's fee for getting the painting to him. It's also very nice that the painter gives me a large bonus on his sales. It's too bad how this painter, Antonio, is a recluse, and no one knows really who he is. I think when his true identity in determined, his art work will be very valuable."

"You might be right—only time will tell."

"I love his work, and I wish we could keep something where we could enjoy it here. However, I know Zotov wants all of his work as soon as it's delivered."

"I'm not going to stay. Be sure to be careful and lock the door when you leave."

"Okay, I will, and thank you for checking on me."

That felt close. As the loud sound of the lock told her he had left, she knew that she would have to be more careful in the future. Holding her breath, she opened the internet site again. With Zotov suddenly dominating her interest, she went to a search engine to do some research on him. After all, he had been the one who held ultimate responsibility for the lost paintings, the ones for which her father had been blamed with stealing. While he had never accused Nickolay directly of the crime, other men under him had pursued the theft aggressively for years and years. She knew these men had direct ties with the Russian mafia.

From what she could tell, he acted like most politicians in that it remained hard to determine exactly where their loyalties really were, but he did have a great heart for the arts and Russian icons. Many Russians never believed Nickolay died since his body had never been turned over to the authorities. The evidence presented of someone tossing him from a bridge, and his body never surfacing didn't satisfy the Russian police, or the mafia.

She had always believed that much more existed to her father's story than what she had been told. She would love to be able to talk to this man directly and candidly, to add some closure to what had haunted her all her life, but she knew that would never happen.

As the idea of going to New York City became more exciting by the minute, she knew she would need to come in many more times to do some research. New York—can you imagine me–yes me in New York City! She hurried to perform one last search on salsa dancing in New York. After seeing the large number of sites, she thought that just perhaps many more people there danced salsa than people did in St. Petersburg. She had to leave and do some thinking. A walk by the Neva would do her good.

CHAPTER 6

The next morning, Sveta's mom shook her gently to get her awake and ready for an early morning. Sveta knew she needed to get to the office before her boss and do some more research. Her mom had been interested in what she had learned, and had proposed many more questions for Sveta to think about. "It's time," Mariya whispered.

"I'm crazy for waking this early. What was I thinking?" Sveta felt still half asleep, but she knew that she had to move fast.

"Sveta, when I get to the school, I'll go to the library and search for whatever I can find out about salsa also. There may be nothing in the library, but you never know."

"Thanks. The main question I want answers to is why my papa has never contacted us, that is until now."

"Perhaps in time we'll know. Believe me; I have a few questions for him as well."

Minutes later, Sveta rushed out of the door. She wanted to have access to the computer before she had her boss over her shoulder, and asking questions.

She soon entered the gallery and turned on the lights before locking the door behind her, since the gallery wouldn't be officially open for several hours. The unique shop offered many impressive high-quality objects for sale, and the polished marble floors and rich wood walls presenting an elegant look where many extraordinary painters from around the world hung their work. Since her office looked exactly the way she had left it, she quickly went to work on connecting to the internet.

Immediately, she navigated to the New York salsa sites where she located perhaps over a hundred salsa bar sites with thousands of links. After she flipped and flipped through the sites, she learned much about dancing in New York. In the flipping, she clicked on a site for salsa dancers, and soon connected to a chat room. The list at the side showed over a hundred people on the forum. With the screen advancing fast as many people chatted, primarily in English, the pace and slang used by everyone was too much for her, exciting to be sure, but just too much information for her to process.

Continuing, she noticed many large forums with tremendous amounts of information in them. It would take some time, but she would work on translating them later. On one forum she located a list of intriguing blogs, but before she knew it all her time had disappeared. The internet ran slow, but it was better than nothing. With the time approaching ten, she needed to open the shop. The two other girls who worked in the gallery would be in soon, as well as the delivery guys. She shut down the internet connection and headed for the door.

After she unlocked the door, and placed the open sign in the window, she glanced around, to see her boss entering the door with a strong determined gait and a very serious frown. "Sveta, have you read the paper this morning?"

"No, I just arrived a few minutes ago, and I decided to open the gallery. Why, what is it?"

He handed her the paper, and pointed to the front page which had an article, and a photo of a man shot the night before.

"That's terrible." Sveta felt nauseous.

"Do you recognize who he is?"

Slowly, her eyes located the name under the photo of

Pavel Pavlovich Lisin. "Ohmigod," Sveta gasped and threw her hand to her neck in disbelief. He was the first deputy commander under the Minister of Internal affairs. She knew his face well, for he was the man who had made life for her mom and her horrible for years. Not only had he accused her father of the theft so many years ago, he still pushed for more investigations into it on occasions.

Finding a seat, she collapsed to read the full article. He had been executed with a bullet to the back of his head, obviously the work of the mafia. It had been a well-known fact for years his family continued to be the main force running the Russian mafia. "I would say I'm sorry, but—"

"I understand your thoughts exactly." He raised his hand as if to apologize for interrupting her. He had treated her like a father for a long time and insisted she come to work with him at the gallery.

"Why do you think he was killed?" Sveta glanced at him.

"Who knows? He had friends in and outside the mafia, and he had a long life with the government. I'm sure both sides will blame the other, and like many times before, the truth will be swept under the rug. Honestly, I'm surprised the facts were reported in the paper like this. Maybe his death was a warning to others, but you never know for sure."

"I understand he had become wealthy over the years. That's an incredible feat for someone in his position."

"He earned his money buying and selling art like Zotov. When I hired you, he threatened me with many things, but he knew to avoid pushing it because of clients I service, like Zotov."

"I'm sorry." Sveta hated to have caused him problems.

He waved his hand dismissively. "Don't worry about it. I think he finally received what was coming to him."

Stopping at the main showroom, he turned to Sveta. "He has many connections, and I'm not sure how all this will play out. It will be good for you to be careful for a while."

"I know he has three other brothers who were also reportedly to be in the mafia, but they keep a much lower profile, however."

"Yes, but it's the half-brother, Michael, who controls things. He has a reputation of being very violent, and no one wants to mess with him. He's a rough-looking man with a ruddy face. While he dresses extremely well in designer suits and wears the typical gold Rolex watch and expensive rings, there isn't too much he can do about his face, which without a doubt, reflects a lot of fights."

"I've heard about him, as I think all of Russia has."

"The other brother, Boris, is the lawyer for the family. While he's quiet and stays out of the limelight as much as he can, he's still greedy and shifty."

She snorted in amusement. "Well, despite all of their tricks, they've all made the news many times."

"Yes, they have, but it's the older brother Ivan, who talks to the news the most. He has tried to gain respectability for years, and to eliminate the bad mafia image. He's been chased by the government and the media for years, but because of that they may have forced him to go legitimate in many ways."

Sveta needed to place this out of her mind. "Anyway, we have a shop to run, and perhaps we'll have some good clients today. The tourist traffic should start coming in soon." She paused. "Our largest client also needs some special attention today. I haven't received a confirmation on the painting from Italy."

"I'm sure Antonio will contact you soon since he does all communications by e-mail. It's going to be so fascinating to examine his work." He gestured at the walls.

"I would love to put his work on display, but I know that might never be possible."

"How has Zotov been able to purchase all his paintings?"

"When he discovered the first piece Antonio sent to us, he fell in love with the work. He made an offer to Antonio where he would purchase all his work of such quality, but only if he could receive a significant discount. Zotov is fully convinced one day all this work will be worth a fortune, and he's hoarded the paintings ever since. That was seven years ago."

"I know; I started selling his paintings soon after I started working here."

"Yes, for some reason Antonio likes dealing with you. His true identity has never been discovered. Since all the paintings come from Italy, I have always assumed that he lives in the mountains in the north."

"I think he must be a great guy. One thing for sure, I love the commissions he gives me on his sales."

"I would love to visit his studio one day. It has to be enormous! Most of his paintings are about the same size, two meters by three meters. This is too large for most families, but perfect for large estates. Let me know if you don't receive any confirmation on the shipment later today. I know Zotov will be calling soon."

"Yes, I'll send another e-mail right now."

Over the next several hours, a few tourists entered the shop, but most of them came in the shop simply to browse. While it had remained hard to concentrate on work with all that had happened in the last few days, she tried her best. When it was soon time for lunch, she yelled over to one of the other girls, "I'll be back soon."

She had only walked about ten meters out of the gallery when she noticed Denis standing next to a side of a building. "What are you doing here?" She felt almost breathless at the shock of seeing him standing still, and apparently patiently waiting on her. He had looked good the other night at the club, but he looked much better in the full light. With his bright-blond hair radiating in the midday sun, she studied the natural glow of his boyish face. When he smiled, he seemed to light the world.

He stepped closer to her. "I was close to here, and I was hoping to catch you on the way to lunch."

"Why didn't you come into the gallery?"

"I came to the door, but I saw that you were busy with a customer. To tell the truth, I wasn't sure if you would remember me or not."

"Don't be silly, I had a great time dancing the other night. It was the first time I've ever tried salsa dancing. The salsa bar was a remarkable place."

"It's a good local place to dance, but there are many salsa palaces in the city which are much better."

"I watched you on the floor, and you're very good. How did you learn to dance like that?" Sveta leaned closer toward him.

"It's a long story, and perhaps I can tell you over lunch."

"I'd love to, but I only have a few minutes for lunch today. The other girls in the gallery have to go to lunch soon." Sveta allowed a remorseful smile to cover her face, hoping to let him know she felt truly sorry,

"I understand. Perhaps I'll find you on the dance floor again." He turned to leave.

"Wait! Can you tell me where you'll be dancing next?"

With a small, childish smile, he turned around, and said, "On Wednesday several bars cater to salsa dancers. If you want, I can come by and pick you up around seven. That is, if you want to go."

"I don't know. Is it okay if I bring my friend with me, the one you met the other night?"

He seemed to be thinking about the request for a minute before he answered. "Sure, I'll bring a friend of mine who's a good dancer as well."

"Thank you, I'm looking forward to it."

Denis quickly smiled and left, as Sveta thought about how great it would be to have someone to teach her. It felt great, knowing how the events were working out for her perfectly.

###

As she forced her mind to focus on the customers in the gallery, the afternoon passed quickly. Her mom would want to know the news about the assassination the night before, that is, if she hadn't heard already. If she hurried, the evening news might contain more details on what happened. Before heading home, however, Sveta had to stop by and visit Olya. She hadn't seen her since Saturday night, and she wanted to make sure she was okay. She quickly ascended the four flights of stairs to her flat and knocked on the door.

"Here you are." Olya smiled as she opened the door.

"I'm fine, thanks, but how are you?" Sveta asked, as she entered the flat. Olya's place reflected a sort of controlled madness, as her flat also doubled as her painting studio. She had various art supplies everywhere. "I'm so sorry I didn't come by yesterday or call you. It was late when I woke, and I had to do something."

"That's fine. I had a bad headache from all the beers the night before, and I lounged around all day." With a slight squeal in her voice and a hint of mischief, she added, "That was a lot of fun the other night, was it not?"

"Yes, I'll admit it was a fun night, and . . . we met some guys."

"Yes, we did! Tell me what you think of the guy I danced with, the one who bought us beer all night?"

"He seemed like a nice guy, but I didn't have much time to talk to him."

"I remember the guy you danced with—he really looked cute. What was his name?"

"His name is Denis. Guess what? He has already visited me today at the gallery."

"He came to see you today! Wow, that didn't take long."

"Exactly, and he wants to go dancing again on Wednesday." Sveta fluttered her hands with the excitement.

"I think you're starting to like this salsa dancing. I told you salsa was contagious."

"Oh, yes, I asked him if you could come along with us—he said yes." Sveta hoped she would be excited about the invitation.

"I don't know…" Olya batted her eyes in a flirty manner.

"He's going to bring a friend of his who also knows how to dance."

Olya offered her a sideways glance. "What does his friend look like?"

"I have no idea. Who knows, but this may be the guy you were dancing with. Anyway, we can learn more about salsa. Please . . . I told him you would come."

"Okay, but I can't drink so much beer again." Olya produced a big grin.

"Great. I can't stay long since Mom is expecting me home soon to help her with some cooking. Would you like to come by and eat with us?"

"Sure, I can come over later if you want me to. Since I did so well on the last abstract, I'm going to start a new one. It will take a little while to rough out the basic form." Olya pointed to the canvas.

"I'm sure this painting will be as good as the last one. Good luck on it." With a quick hug, Sveta walked out of the door and headed home. The never-ending daylight always gave people, including her, the impression that the time remained early, even when it became late at night.

When Sveta entered her flat, her mom glanced over at her for a second before continuing her preparation of a salad and a homemade strawberry jam that came from the berries in their garden. "I hoped you would be home soon since this is getting to be more time consuming than I had planned tonight. We can drink some tea with pelmini— would you like that?"

"Yes, I would. Listen, I'm sorry I'm late, but I had to stop by and check on Olya about tonight. We have some guys wanting to take us out dancing again on Wednesday night."

"Really?" Her mom turned to stare at her. "I assume this is salsa dancing again."

"Yes. The guy I danced with on Saturday night I told you about came by the gallery today. He's really cute."

"It's good to watch you going out and having fun."

"I have some more news tonight also… did you read the paper this morning?"

"No, what was in it?" Her mom asked, as she kept working on the salad.

"Pavel Lisin was killed last night by someone shooting him in the back of the head. I saw this when my boss handed me his paper at work. I didn't see too much about the murder in the paper, but I hope we can obtain more on television tonight."

Her mom stopped and froze where she stood. While a definite show of fear flowed over her, a sign of relief emerged at the same time. It was hard to know if she felt happy to have him gone, or scared of the people responsible for his death. "Do they know who did it, or do they have any suspects?"

"I don't think so, but Gleb Sergevich did tell me a little bit more about him today. As we know, Pavel worked for both the government and the mafia. It would be hard to say who he made mad this time."

"Come in here and help me with the TV, the news should be starting soon. I really want to hear what they have to say, if anything."

The news soon started on time, and they covered many events, but this major story of the day never appeared. The government must have decided to bury the information.

CHAPTER 7

After another sleepless night, Sveta had a hard time getting out of bed when her mom called her since the endless possibilities of what had happened to her papa constantly ate at her. She glanced at the clock on her bedside table and realized she had to hurry, since she needed to search the internet undisturbed for a while. While she would love to have a computer connection at home, a computer and internet connection simply cost too much for them.

"Good morning." Sveta told her mom, as she stretched on the sofa she used for a bed at night.

"Good morning to you." Her mom replied with a smile. She always has been an early riser, and had never seemed to require the sleep Sveta needed.

"Wow, it's getting late. I need to hurry. I have many things I want to use the computer for this morning. Can you water the plants on the balcony for me?"

"I'll take care of them, don't worry. If you purchase a paper on the way to work, please bring it home. I want to read it if you see anything about Pavel Lisin at all."

"Yes, I plan on buying a paper first thing, and to check on the internet as well. It's hard to believe that the news told nothing last night about his death."

Sveta went to work on her hair. The long, thick blonde hair looked beautiful, but required so much work in the mornings. She had considered cutting it so many times, but she had always changed her mind before she did.

"I'll see you after work," Sveta yelled at her mom as

she headed for the gallery.

The stroll across the tiny park in the early morning air refreshed her. From above her she heard the sound of several nightingales. Since she loved to hear them, and knew they wouldn't be singing for much longer this year, she stopped and paused to listen to them. It was so amazing how something so simple could relieve her mind, at least for a minute. She felt so thankful for them and the peace they brought her, but while she could have stayed in the park all morning she knew that she had to hurry.

Before arriving at the gallery, she stopped at a vendor's shop to purchase a paper. "Good morning," Sveta said cheerfully as she handed him money for the paper.

"Good morning," he replied smiling. "It's going to be warm today."

"Yes, I hope it will be. Thanks." Sveta returned the smile before she started walking and reading at the same time. After glancing over the front page, she discovered nothing regarding the murder. She decided to wait until she arrived at the gallery to check the rest of the paper.

With no one at the gallery when she arrived, she opened the door and went inside. To make sure she would not be disturbed, she quickly locked the door behind her. After walking inside a small kitchen, she placed some water on to boil. A cup of tea would be fantastic this morning, she thought, as she rushed to her office and attempted to connect to the internet which remained slow, as usual. While waiting for the connection to start up, she realized she hadn't received a confirmation on the painting from Italy. She would have to check on it again, since she needed the commission from the sale of his painting.

As soon as she obtained a connection, she went to a search engine to check on Pavel Lisin. Since he had been around for a long time, she found many articles about him.

While he had worked for the government for most of his life, it was well speculated that he had also maintained his crime family connections. In Russia, she knew how many people thought the mafia ran the government, while others thought it was the government who ran the mafia. In either case, she knew most people simply tried to live with a situation they couldn't control.

Finding out nothing more than what she already knew, she decided to go to the New York salsa sites she found so interesting the day before. She located many lists of places to go, and places to take salsa lessons. While almost all the places had a web site trying to attract patrons to their salsa bar, she finally clicked on the place where she had seen the large chat room and forum earlier. To enter the site, she had to register. What was the user name and password she had used earlier? "Oh yes." She blinked her eyes as she remembered. Her user name was Danceprincess, and the password she had selected was therussiangirl. She had to fill out a short profile, and supply a small amount of data, which she faked.

After she logged on to the site, she saw a note on the screen: "You have two messages." That's intriguing, she thought. Looking around to make sure no one had come into the gallery, she clicked on the button. The first message materialized, "Welcome to The Salsa Connection. We hope you like this site as much as we do. Feel free to explore all the information and links provided. If you would like to advertise here, please click on this link."

She clicked on the next message button. It came from someone in the forum who must have read her profile. His user name was Salsaking. Interesting. She decided to click on the full message. The note in English read, "Hello, and welcome to The Salsa Connection. I found where you had entered the forum last night, and I see where you live in Russia. That's cool. I love to salsa dance, and I'm always interested in learning how people in other countries dance the salsa. If you're interested, I would love to chat with you sometime. I know that this site is large and can be frustrating. I have a private chat room attached to my blog, and I hope you can come to it so that we can chat. It will be nice to hear from you." He signed off as "The Salsa King."

Wow, she thought. Sveta wondered how well she knew English. While she didn't feel totally comfortable with the language, this would be a good chance to practice. Out of curiosity, she clicked on his profile, just to satisfy her curiosity. His real name was Danny Martinez. He lived in New York and was 26 years old. She quickly noted his blog address, and his e-mail posted on the site.

After her curiosity became too much for her to ignore, she decided to go to his blog which detailed a daily account of things going on in his life. While the blog had been in operation for about a month, his comments continued to attract her attention. She noticed very few replies to his posts. As an actor, he had been to auditions for parts in many plays, but was not having much luck. Meanwhile, he was working as a waiter to make ends meet until he received his break.

Yes, he could be someone to chat with while working on her English. She wrote his web address on a piece of paper and hid it in her desk. She next went back to the newspaper and read it slowly, but found no other information on Pavel Lisin and his murder.

Thinking about the shipment from Italy, she quickly used the phone to call the shipper. She was in luck: the painting had been received, and would be delivered to her today, but it would be late in the afternoon. Fantastic—she needed the money.

###

Lunchtime finally came, and while she did feel hungry, she had somewhere she needed to go. With the card of the dance instructor clutched in her hand, she wanted to visit his dance studio and ask some questions. At almost a half-run, she headed for the metro stop.

As she entered the metro with perfect timing, she knew that to become good enough to dance in a competition, she would need to learn salsa fast. Considering how many people had been dancing the salsa all their lives and had a natural rhythm in their soul, she didn't know how it would be possible, but somehow, deep inside her heart and very soul, she had a hope that maybe, just maybe, this would make sense to her later and it would all work out.

Soon the metro stopped close to the dance studio, and she soon stood in front of the entrance. She saw a sign in the main window advertising dance services, but otherwise it looked unimpressive. Upon entering the studio, she noticed that it consisted mainly of one large dance floor, but with an office and one small changing room in the back. While she did see a dance pole stretching along the edge and a few chairs scattered around, the studio mainly consisted of the large wooden dance floor.

At first she didn't notice Natasha kneeling by a little desk on the other side of the room, but she did as she stood. Natasha's elegant walk gave her away. "Can I help you?" She finally asked, clearly not recognizing her.

"Yes, my name is Sveta. I met you and your husband at the salsa club last Saturday night."

A smile swept across Natasha's face, indicating that she finally recognized her. "Yes, I remember you now.

How did you like the salsa dancing the other night?"

"I loved it. I've heard of salsa all my life, but I've never been to where they actually danced it. My parents were both ballet dancers, and ballet is the only type of lessons I've ever officially received."

"Do you dance ballet now?"

"No, I don't. My mom still teaches, and I might stop by occasionally to stay in shape, but I don't have the heart and soul of a dancer."

"I think I understand. My husband told me your story. Life must have been hard on you, growing up without a father."

"Yes, and it was much harder on my mom. She has never quit loving him."

"Are you thinking about taking salsa lessons?"

"Lessons would be great, but I don't think I have enough money to do so."

"Unfortunately, it does cost money to become good at it, and as you know dancing takes a lot of dedication. However, salsa is a lot different from ballet, where the mechanics are rigid and formal. Dancing salsa, you won't be on a pedestal for the entire world to observe. As you remember from the club, salsa is danced in tight quarters."

"I noticed that. To tell the truth, I wasn't comfortable, and many of the dancers were kind of rude in the way they constantly bumped into you."

"It's a different world. In the sophisticated world of ballet, many people have large spheres of personal space around them they are used to. That isn't the case in Latino dancing, where other dancers give you no space at all."

"I like the dance. The music is different and hard to understand, but the experience is . . . so very intoxicating."

"I think that's a perfect way to describe it. Anyway, the first lesson is free, and afterwards you can decide if you want to go further with it. When would you like to have a lesson?"

Thinking quickly, Sveta said, "I'm free on Thursday night, and my friend would also like to learn. She was the girl with me the other night. Is it okay if I bring her with me?"

"Yes, of course, that will be fine." She glanced at her appointment book. "I can do it at six, if you like. We have a group dance social at seven, which you're welcome to stay for also. Our students are encouraged to come to this group dance social to be able to dance with other students. The more practice you have, the quicker you'll advance. It's always free to those taking lessons."

"That sounds much better. I normally don't leave work until seven, but I'm sure my boss will let me off earlier this one time."

"Good, we're looking forward to seeing you and your friend on Thursday." She handed Sveta a brochure with more information about the studio.

After thanking her again, Sveta headed for the door.
###

The rest of the day remained uneventful, as Sveta had more time to think about her newfound interest in salsa. While she wanted to find out all she could about salsa, she also knew she had to keep a somewhat low profile, as she felt like someone was watching her most of the time. It was something she had learned to live with, but perhaps with Pavel Lisin no longer around the fear would soon vanish.

Her boss came over to her minutes before closing. "I have good news . . . the painting has arrived in the back."

Her heart fluttered with the excitement of the fantastic news. The two rushed to the shipping room at the rear of the building, where the enormous painting remained sealed in its crate.

"We need to check the painting before we send it to Zotov."

Gleb quickly indicated to the deliverymen that he needed help in getting it out of the crate. Within a few minutes they had opened the crate. The massive painting looked incredible, and as they all expressed an understanding of why it required so long for one of these masters to be completed, Sveta continued to examine the elaborate details in the painting. With this painting depicting grapes being harvested in the mountains of Italy, she could practically feel the rich and colorful traditions of the wine makers hard at their work. This kind of painting with so many intricate details had to be studied over and over. It told a story better than a writer could ever hope to do in a book.

Gleb searched for any kind of damage during the shipment, but when he could find nothing wrong he breathed deeply in relief. "Very good." He rubbed his chin, reflecting his satisfaction. "Let's place the painting back into the crate, and I'll decide if we can deliver it to him first thing in the morning. I know he's been waiting for this one for a long time."

Sveta felt a big relief to find the paintings in good shape. Anytime something went through customs, there was a chance the article could be damaged. It helped a lot to have Zotov's name attached to the shipment.

"I'm sure he'll be happy with it. If he brings me the money for the painting tomorrow, I'll be able to pay your commissions to you also. This painter has also always insisted on paying a bonus commission to the salesperson. You should be thankful you sold his first painting since he's made you a lot of money in his sales."

"Yes. I wish he painted more, but I know a painting like this takes a lot of time. I think I'll celebrate a little tonight because of this, and have my friend Olya come by to join my mom and me at home. You're welcome to come also, if you wish."

"Thank you for the invitation, but I also have plans tonight. Please say hello to your mom for me." Sveta knew he'd made good money from this sale, and would be doing his own celebration.

"I will. Have a good night, and I'll see you in the morning." She flashed a big smile as she left the gallery, knowing she would be paid tomorrow, and paid well. She stopped by the store, and purchased a bottle of champagne and some chocolate. It would be a fantastic night to celebrate her good fortune.

She walked to Olya's flat and climbed the stairs to where she found Olya busy with her painting, and mixing paint in an attempt to obtain the color she wanted. The basic form of a human body became evident, but the distortion she worked on still remained somewhat unclear. Since the last one had been so powerful and moving, the next work would be hard to duplicate. Only time would tell as to how she did on this one.

"That looks . . . different," Sveta said as she finally ventured an opinion.

"Thanks," Olya replied as she laughed loudly.

"I received the painting from Antonio a few hours ago, and to celebrate I stopped and purchased some champagne and chocolate. We also still have some strawberries from the garden. I hope you can come to my flat and enjoy them with us."

"That sounds good to me. I need to get away from this painting for a while, and maybe rethink what I want to do with some colors. It will take me a few minutes to clean up."

"Okay, take your time. I also went to the dance studio today where we have free lessons. I hope it's good with you, but the lessons are on Thursday at six."

"I can make the lessons for sure. Are you sure they're free?"

"Yes, I checked on the cost, and I told them that we have no money for lessons. They also have a group practice lesson after our lesson which starts at seven, and it is for the students to dance with each other—we've been invited to it, as well, for free."

Reaching over to tickle Sveta again, Olya said, "I think you're getting into this salsa dancing. The guy you met the other night must have stolen your heart already, humm?"

Sveta's bright green eyes twinkled as she blushed. "Not yet, but he's cute. I'm excited about tomorrow night also. I think he's going to take us to a place where they dance strictly salsa on Wednesday night. Since he dances a lot, I'm sure he knows the best places to go."

"I'm sure he does, and . . . I'm still interested in seeing who I'm getting set up with also." Olya rolled her eyes to dramatize the fun she enjoyed having with Sveta.

CHAPTER 8

The next day all went as planned, and she received her commission with a large bonus from the painter, and just as she had been promised. Zotov also left her an envelope with money for helping him purchase the painting.

As her interest continued to grow, she managed to log online for a minute at lunchtime when the other girls went to lunch and started reading about salsa and the history of the dance. The evolution of the dance became very entertaining as she learned that the salsa hadn't been invented at any one particular time or place, but had been handed down over generations, with Spanish and French influences. It also contained a combination of African and Caribbean music, which all seemed to gel in Cuba back in the 1950s. From that time, salsa had been transported to places like L.A., New York City, Mexico City, Miami, Columbia, Moscow, St. Petersburg, and many other places. As all places added to the music, salsa had evolved with the cultures of the various locations. She could easily understand how over time this sound had been eventually crossbred into what it is was now. So while the music would sound the same, to some extent, salsa had evolved differently around the world.

Much like the music, the dance styles had evolved. While the basic Cuban salsa had been transported abroad, it also advanced on its own in Cuba over time. In L.A. and New York, the on-two style developed. Currently, in L.A. the dance evolved by the local influence into a hip-hop salsa. In competition dancing, the influence of ballroom salsa from Europe existed. In the mix of all of this, you had regular people who wanted to have fun and do a freestyle dance containing a mixture of whatever they knew.

Since there was so much to learn, it would take a long time to master only the basics of this dance. However, the more she read, the more she became interested in learning. As she started to terminate the site, she decided to click on the blog of the American dancer. He had entered a long blog for the day about his life. While he had worked hard today, he still planned to go out salsa dancing later tonight.

She decided to click on the comments and leave him a note. She wrote slowly in English, "I have decided to make acquaintance with you, and find out more about salsa dancing in America. I am from St. Petersburg, Russia, and my English is not so good. If you are interested in communicating with me, I would be happy. I will await your reply—Dance Princess." As soon as she had sent it, she had second thoughts. While she didn't know what could be traced and what could not be traced, she hoped for the best.

The rest of the day passed slowly, but soon it became time for Olya to arrive. She wanted her to be here when the two guys came for them. For her friend's sake, she hoped Denis would bring someone nice.

At seven, the large front door opened, and Olya strolled in. She had washed and dried her hair, and looked clean and fresh, which was far better than just a few hours earlier. While most of the time she looked like a starving artist, tonight, she had a clean, radiant glow about her. "Look at you. You look like you're ready to go dancing and have a good time tonight."

"You never know, but first we need to see what I'm

being set up with tonight." She rolled her eyes to have some fun with Sveta. "Have you heard from them?"

"No, I haven't. The one time I talked to him was here on Monday. Denis knows I stop working at seven, and he said he'll meet us here."

As she walked around the gallery, Olya studied some of the work on sale. "I could paint that," She finally announced as she admired one piece.

"I'm sure you could even do better; however, the painters we have in here are famous and have large followings pushing up the prices of their work. I hope you'll become as prominent as them one day," Sveta said, as the two became so engrossed in the paintings that they didn't notice the two boys entering the gallery.

"Hello," Sveta heard Denis yell in her direction. After quickly turning around, she saw him with another guy. As she joined them with Olya following her, Denis turned to his friend, and said, "This is Andrew. He's a friend of mine and a good dancer."

Sveta looked at him and thought about how Denis had made a good choice for Olya with this guy who looked muscular yet trim. He had jet-black hair, and deep-brown eyes. "I'm glad to meet you, Andrew. This is my friend Olya," Sveta announced as she turned briefly toward her friend. "And by the way, I'm Sveta."

"It's good to meet both of you. Denis said you wanted to learn to dance and the club we're going to should have a good band tonight."

After looking over at Denis, Sveta said, "You look nice tonight." He had dressed in black pants and a tight black shirt with some Latino-looking embroidery in it.

"Thanks. This is an old shirt I have—nothing special." He glanced at his watch. "If you're ready, we can go. It's about a fifteen-minute walk from here, and all of the good seats will be taken soon. I hope you enjoy the dancing tonight." Denis quickly offered his arm to Sveta.

The walk felt good, and it allowed everyone time to talk. Both guys talked about working together in the shipping industry where they loaded and unloaded freight, which explained why they were both in such great shape. It required hard work, but paid well.

The scenery along the way looked beautiful, and had many tourists constantly glancing around to enjoy the sights. However, after living here all of her life, Sveta had witnessed the same sites every day, but The Nevsky Prospekt really did define the heart and soul of the city. The buildings looked so different from other parts of the world. The city offered so many sites to visit, that is, if you had the money to do so.

As they passed the Fontanka, the cool water below looked so inviting, since the weather still remained so humid outside. They soon stopped in front of a large building, adorned with many sculptures of half-naked men. While the large columns stretched all the way to the top of the building, the building looked like it had been recently updated to some extent, but evidently maintained the modern décor.

As Sveta studied the many large doors entering the building, Denis moved over to the far right side of the building, and to a door leading to the basement. She noticed no signs on the door to indicate what was inside, but St. Petersburg had ordered most signs removed several years ago. The city managers considered large signs a distraction to the beautiful architecture for which the city had become famous, and as a result, in this city you had to know your way around. She thought about how hard it was for even locals to find spots like this sometimes.

Denis opened the door and waited for the others to

enter before he again walked ahead and down the steps to the basement. At the bottom, he opened another door for everyone. A man by this door obviously wanted money for them to enter. Denis paid him, but also asked for a table, which cost extra.

After walking Inside, Sveta soon studied the tables at the other side of the casino. With dark, elaborately carved wood covering the walls of this very unique place, it would be nice to know what this casino had been used for before the owners converted the space to a club. A bar located in the center of the room consisted of a central cube, making it easy for customers to order drinks from all sides. While the three bartenders inside actively arranged glasses and prepared for the night, multiple colored lights sparkled on the counter in the center of the cube. They obviously did most of the work preparing the drinks inside this cube where the many different bottles of alcohol were highlighted in the array of lights.

"Let's go around this way." Denis pointed to the right where about fifteen or twenty people frolicked around the bar, enjoying drinks and laughing. Many of them appeared to be locals.

As Sveta followed him, with the others in close pursuit, she saw many chairs along the wall, and occasionally a small sofa or lounge chair. In front of the chairs, petite coffee tables added a perfect touch.

After weaving along the tables, they soon arrived at one table in front of the dance floor where a band was busy preparing on the other side of the dance floor. With most of the band members working on the stage, she assumed they would be starting soon. After glancing above the band, Sveta studied the many multicolored lights, like you would notice on a Christmas tree.

"Thank you." Sveta said, as Denis pulled a chair out for

her.

The four sat quietly, as other people came in to find a table. As she further analyzed the surroundings, she loved the Cuban charm and style of decorating, which became very evident. It was easy to understand the style was one they wanted to create. Many of the waitresses hustling around also looked to be Latin.

"Are you hungry?" Denis finally asked. "They have Cuban food here, if you want to try something different."

Sveta had never had Cuban food, and at first wanted to turn down his offer, but after looking over at Olya, who indicated she would like some, she relented and decided to try it. "I've never had Cuban food before. Is it spicy?"

"Sometimes it can be, but I'll ask if we can order you a Cuban sandwich with only a little spice."

"If that's what everyone wants, I think I'll try one also." Sveta glanced around, hoping she had made a good decision.

Denis raised his hand to summon a waitress who flashed a big smile at him as she came to the table. In fact, she leaned over and offered him a small hug as she reached him. While her low-cut dress revealed her well-developed breasts as she bent over, Sveta knew if she had nice ones like those, she would flaunt them also. Her eyes quickly darted over to Denis, who seemed to not be affected by them. That was a good sign.

"We'll have some Cuban sandwiches. If you can, please make the ones for my friends with only a little spice. For me, I'll take the usual. "He glanced at the girls. "Do you want beer tonight? If not, we can order margaritas."

Sveta answered almost at once. "Margaritas would be great tonight."

After looking over the group to analyze his friends, the

waitress offered an inquisitive smile and left.

"Tell me, how was the day on the ships today? Olya asked, as she smiled. "From what I understand, handling freight is hard work. You two must be tired."

"Some days can be worse than others. Today was a usual day with nothing special happened." Andrew cleared his throat. "We actually work for the government, and our jobs are to check on smuggled goods and contraband. If we suspect anything, we have to unpack and repack. That can be hard work."

"I see, your work sounds like an intriguing job. And I'm sure you have some stories to tell."

Denis spoke first. "We have many, but unfortunately, we can't discuss them. These jobs were too hard to find."

"We understand." Yes, Sveta fully understood.

The bandleader came to the front of the stage, and announced, "We're so glad to see you on this Wednesday night, and we hope you can welcome my group of Cuban misfits, as we have some fun tonight. We want to see all of you on the dance floor."

As he turned around, he introduced the band behind him. With the people in the club applauding as they were introduced, the seven-member band looked like old friends who were on stage to have a good time. Finally, the bandleader turned and pointed to the conga player in the center of the group who exploded into a rhythm needing no other instruments to make the place come alive. His magic filled the place and made the crowd want to click with the music. He played for a full five minutes, as the rest of the band waited patiently for him to ask them to join him.

"This drum player is known as the key." Denis said, as he leaned over toward Sveta. "It's his job to keep the beat of the music on pace all night."

"I see." Sveta could not think of any other questions to ask, since all of this remained so new to her.

Soon the other two drummers joined in to harmonize with the first, but they remained distinctive. As the music became more exciting and lively by the minute, a large bass player joined in to add another layer of composition, making the depth of the music quickly become more and more astonishing to witness.

When the two horns came into play, the music electrified the casino with excitement. Everyone moved with the music to engage with the band's exhilaration. All over the room, she saw people swaying to the music with a definite salsa motion.

The bandleader, who also was the lead singer, stood tall as he moved forward. With his microphone in hand, he used it to indicate that he wanted to see everyone dancing. When he started singing, and the first wave of dancers hit the floor, the guys quickly stood and pulled their dates to the floor.

Sveta and Olya looked at each other, as if to say, "Here goes."

Denis started solo dancing for a few seconds to kind of demonstrate to Sveta what the dance should look like. His movements looked impressive, but something she knew she would need to learn, to be able to compete later. Denis, however, soon moved in closer and started moving with the basic steps. His movements felt easy for Sveta to follow as the music became so intense the beats easily controlled their tempo.

Sveta turned on a small twirl to be pulled in close to Denis. He lingered, inches away, as his eyes penetrated hers. The presence of his firm, well-toned body pressed against hers sent flurries of exploding fireworks throughout her body. She had little experience with men since she had dated so little in her life.

On the next round of beats, Denis stepped to the side, and pulled her around into another twirl. Each time she stood in front of him, the intense meeting of his eyes with her eyes became more piercing and haunting. With each new move, she had to concentrate, but it became harder and harder to do so.

After a while, she became tired and while she would love to rest for a minute, Denis continued to lead her, and teach her new steps. In Latino music she noticed that they never stop to give you a chance to go to the table. On one step, she almost fell. "Here, I think you need to rest," Denis said, as he escorted her to the table.

Their waitress was placing their order on the table as they approached it. When Denis smiled at the waitress, she offered some salsa moves of her own, as if to tease Denis.

Denis leaned over to Sveta and said, "I know you're tired. Since this is an old friend of mine, is it all right if I give her one dance?"

"Sure, I understand." In fact, it would be great to understand what he could do with a good dancer. "It will be fun to watch you dance."

"Thanks, I'll be right back." He turned to the waitress, and led her to the dance floor until she rushed ahead of him and entered into the rhythm with her hips churning away at the music.

"Wow." Sveta felt amazed at how in tune with the music she danced. It was as if she could feel the music and became one with it. When the bandleader noticed her, he transitioned into a new sound filled with a lot of emotion in it. His focus became very obvious as he tailored his music to them.

Sveta suddenly noticed how the floor had cleared for them to dance. For the next ten minutes, they put on an amazing demonstration of their dancing skills. The patrons of this club must have watched them dance before, as all locked into their every movement. The dance floor belonged to them, and they used every meter of it as they expanded their dance, much to the delight of all who watched.

Finally, she did a double spin into his arms before immediately falling backwards into a full backward dip. And one where he floated her from left to right before snapping her straight into his arms again. With her fluid body completely under his control, he dipped her again and again. She finally dropped into a full split on the floor as he raised his arms in the air. This definitely depicted a move professionals would do.

After lifting her again, the two came back over to the table, where she turned to thank Sveta for letting him dance with her.

"You're welcome." Sveta leaned forward. "I really enjoyed watching you dance. I would love to learn to dance like you."

The waitress offered a huge smile. "You have one of the best teachers, but keep an eye on him—he has many admirers."

Denis started to protest as he raised a finger to his lips. "Please, help me keep a few secrets for later."

As the floor started to fill again, she noticed Olya and Andrew heading for the table. Since Olya struggled to stay in good physical shape, she had to be tired. However, she had danced some salsa before, and she seemed to be having fun on the floor. It also looked like she was hitting it off nicely with Andrew tonight.

Sveta glanced over at Denis. "How did you learn to dance so good? Do you have some Latino in you that I need to know about?"

He grunted. "I don't have any I know of, but you aren't the first to ask me. I fell in love with this dance a long time ago, and I go out dancing every chance I get. Sometimes my work interferes with it, but I love to dance, and this music is fantastic."

"I can tell you like dancing salsa, and you have many friends."

"Yes, you'll find friendly people in most of the dance clubs." Looking directly at her, he moved closer to her. "Why did you decide to learn salsa?"

Somehow, she had known she would be asked this question, and that she would definitely have to lie about it. She felt lucky to have a friend like Olya to blame the late night dancing on. "My friend here. . ." She pointed to Olya, arriving at the table. ". . . dragged me into the club where we met last Saturday. I didn't know if I would like salsa or not, but I'll admit I'm enjoying it, and I would like to learn more. In fact, I also met a dance instructor and his wife last Saturday, who have offered Olya and me a free lesson."

"Great, it sounds like I'll soon be watching you perform in front of the crowds, and who knows, maybe even win in one of the local competitions. This way, for at least one night, you could be the queen of the dance floor."

"I don't think I'll ever be good enough to compete, but I want to have a good time and learn."

"Trust me, this music gets under your skin, and it will soon take over your life if you let it."

Olya fanned herself, trying to cool off as the temperature became hotter in the club. Noticing the drinks in front of them, she lifted her glass, and waited for all the others to raise their glasses before she offered a toast. "To salsa and great friends."

They all repeated the toast as they tapped their glasses together in the center of the table. The Cuban sandwiches became the next event to attract the group's attention. The guys managed a large bite while waiting for the girls. After a slow, apprehensive look at each other, the girls lifted their sandwiches and tried a bite. It tasted spicy, and extremely hot!

Both girls laid the sandwiches on the table, and raised their glasses to wash down the heat. Sveta breathed in fast. Damn, the spices were hot.

"I'm sorry," Both men spoke at once.

"Perhaps we can order some pelmini for you. Would you like some?" Andrew asked.

"Yes, pelmini would be much better, or maybe a salad would be good." Olya still showed signs of wanting more drink to quench the spicy sandwiches.

The night advanced with many hours of dancing and learning the various steps on the floor. Many friends stopped by to say hello to Denis. He always had a way of making everyone feel good, and he often purchased drinks for others at the bar. It seemed he had money for spending that many people didn't have. He must be making much more than she assumed at the government job, which was strange, since she knew the job usually didn't pay too much.

As they left the club, they had to wait a minute to let their eyes adjust to the outside light. The sun was still shining slightly above the horizon as they walked together for a while, and passed over the bridge just minutes before it was time for it to be raised.

Sveta stopped when they reached the place where Olya and Sveta normally departed to make their way home. "Listen guys, we had a great time tonight."

"We can take you all the way home," Andrew said, as

he lightly placed his arm around Olya's waist.

"I'm sure she'll appreciate it, but I need to wake up tomorrow morning and go to work early. I also live with my mom, and I'm sure she's already in bed. You do understand, I hope," She said as smiled at Denis.

"Sure, but you'll have to introduce me to your mom later."

"I'll be glad to since I'm sure she'd love to meet you also."

Denis pulled her over to him, hugged her, and focused on her eyes. "I had a great time tonight, and we'll have to do it again." He appeared to be studying her lips as he looked down at them, but he never moved forward to kiss her. Sveta wished he had, but she didn't want to rush things too much. He smiled at her instead as he let her go and headed back toward the bridge.

Olya and Andrew waved a short goodbye as they headed toward her place. Sveta would have loved to join them for more conversation, but she knew they needed time together also. She looked forward to talking to Olya later to see what happened during the night.

CHAPTER 9

The smell of fresh tea floating across the room forced Sveta to open her eyes.

"I knew you felt tired from the night before, so I decided to let you sleep later this morning," Her mom said as she walked over to her sofa.

"Thanks, I appreciate it, but I need to arrive at the gallery to access the computer before everyone comes in and starts looking over my shoulder."

"I had a dream last night. Your papa came here, and had dinner with us. It felt as if he had never left us." Her mom had tears dripping down her face.

"Mom, I know how much you must have missed him all these years and remember how I've been here with you all this time. Not a day passes that I don't wonder what happened to him. The last few days have been so hard on me since I can't understand the reasoning behind the letter. After seeing people salsa dancing last night, I realized just how hard it will be to dance professionally in such a short period of time."

"I understand. The letter has to be some kind of sick joke." Mariya smirked, but still appeared to hold on to some kind of hope.

"Mom, I have so many things to tell you, but I don't have time now." Sveta hurried to the bathroom to get ready. Since her hair would be too much for her this morning, she decided to tie it behind her head in a long ponytail. This would have to do for today.

"Goodbye," Her mom whispered as she kissed her on

the cheek before she left.

After hurrying out of the building, Sveta headed for the park to catch the metro, but within fifty meters of the building, a man rushed to intercept her. At first she didn't recognize him, but she did when he moved closer. He was the man she thought had been following her lately. She tried to ignore his presence at first, but suddenly he called out, "Sveta, I need to talk to you."

She stopped dead in her tracks; he knew her name. She turned slowly and asked, "Do I know you?"

"No, I don't think we've ever met before. I mean you no harm, but I think it will be good for us to talk for a minute, if that's okay with you. We can talk on the way to the metro."

"What do you want to talk to me about?"

This man kept a polite distance from her, as if he knew her anxiety level was high. "I have some news I think you'd like to have. If I were in your shoes, I would want to know. This information is strictly off the record, and only for you."

"What are you talking about?" she asked, as a nervous chill ran down her spine.

"A man by the name of Pavel Pavlovich Lisin was murdered a few days ago."

Sveta studied this large man with new interest. "I saw the article in the newspaper the other day, but read almost nothing about it in the paper since then, and I've seen nothing on the TV evening news at all either."

"It was a situation that needed to be handled quietly. A week ago, Pavel had too much to drink, and he admitted to throwing your father off a bridge in New York City many years ago. The story the Americans told about your father being murdered appear to be true."

"So . . . you're telling me Pavel is the one who killed

my father?”

“Since the body was never found, we assumed the story was false. I’m sorry to have to tell you this, but I assumed that telling you this now would be the right thing to do.”

Sveta stopped and forced her hands over her eyes. The nightmares she had had all her life were true. Her papa had been murdered. Glancing back at the stranger, she had to ask one question. “Why?”

“I knew you would ask this question, and it isn’t an easy one to answer. A large collection of priceless paintings were stolen from a gallery days before the trip to America. Many people still believe the stolen items were smuggled to the United States. As I’m sure you have heard, one of the paintings was discovered in your papa’s room after he was killed.”

“Are you saying my father was involved with the theft?”

“That is one question I think might not ever be answered, and especially since the only one knowing the answer died a few days ago.”

“Why are you telling me all this?”

“Since someone didn’t like Pavel admitting he killed your father, I think someone still has an interest in this case and wants it to remain quiet. That someone has enough political clout to hide this story, as you know already. Ivan Lisin has always stated his family hadn’t anything to do with the theft. I think he’s mistaken, and his brothers did this without his knowledge or consent, and they will never admit the involvement to him later.”

“I understand.”

“I would like to offer you some protection; however, I can only do so much. If you hear anything concerning this, I would appreciate you letting me know.”

“How do I do that? You haven’t told me who you are.”

He offered a low rumbling laugh. "We do know each other, but we've never met in person before. If anyone contacts you about your father and starts asking questions you need to be cautious. The man who killed Pavel is still looking for answers. Also, as you might suspect the Pavel's family is looking for his killer."

Sveta shook her head while attempting to concentrate. "What do you mean we know each other?"

"I'm probably your biggest client. By the way, the painting from Italy was the best work I have ever seen from a contemporary painter. Thank you for handling the purchase for me." With this he offered a wave of his hand before turning and walking away.

"Ohmigod," she muttered under her breath; she had been talking to Yuri Zotov.

###

While hurrying to the gallery, her mind raced through every possibility she could imagine. She thought Pavel may have been killed because of her father's death, and in a way, she felt happy he received what was coming to him. On the other hand, if her papa was dead, who had sent her the invitation?

She also shuddered about the prospects of being in danger. Pavel had been killed recently by someone who apparently had connections, and Pavel had family members who would surely seek revenge. She didn't want to get in the middle of this.

As she expected, no one had arrived early at the gallery when she walked in. As in the previous few days, she headed straight for her office and locked the door, but her head hurt too much for her to concentrate on doing research.

While attempting to clear her head, she decided to play with the computer where she flipped from site to site until she remembered the site of the American salsa dancer. After taking a deep breath, she entered the address and clicked on the enter button. With the site much as she remembered it, she clicked on his personal chat site out of curiosity.

When the site opened, she noticed only one person in the chat room. Looking at the user name, she noticed that it was Salsaking. She waited for a long minute before she entered the site as the dance princess.

Her name registered in the column of those active in the site. "Now what?" she thought. While deep in thought, she wondered what she should say. She typed in English, "Hello."

She waited for a long time, but nothing happened. When she finally assumed he had left the keyboard and was now off line, she started to close the window, but the screen flickered and a reply materialized. "Hello, how are you?"

Sveta replied with new curiosity. "I am fine. I saw you in the chat room and I would love to chat with you. Are you busy?" She typed the words with quivering fingers, hoping to not make a mistake.

"I have just returned home and was getting ready to go to bed, but I am fine."

"What time is it in America?" Sveta asked. She didn't know the exact time difference.

"It's fifteen minutes after two in the morning. Where are you from?"

"Wow, I am sorry. I didn't realize the time was so late in New York. It is almost eight in the morning here."

"I see. You must already be at work."

"Yes, I am at work. I live in Russia."

"Wow, I never chatted with anyone from Russia before. How did you find my site?"

"It was posted on a salsa dancing web site. Are you a good salsa dancer?"

"Salsa is my favorite dance. I returned to my place a few minutes ago. That's why I'm up so late."

"If you need to go to bed, I understand. I can chat with you later."

"No, don't leave. I don't have a chance to chat with many people from Russia. Which city are you from?"

"I am from St. Petersburg." Giving the information made her nervous, but she felt compelled to do so.

"I understand St. Petersburg is a fantastic city. How did you learn English so well?"

"We are taught English from the third grade, but I don't think my English is too good."

"I think your English is good."

"Not really. I located many sites on salsa dancing in New York City. It must be popular where you live."

"We have many dance clubs and different kind of dances, but salsa is my favorite form of dance. Can you salsa?"

"I am learning, but I am not too good at it." Sveta felt her palms sweating.

"Do you have many salsa bars in your city?"

"Yes we have some, I do not know how many. I have only started to learn. Salsa is exciting." She glanced around, still feeling nervous.

"I would love to see how different the salsa dancing is in Russia."

"Yes, I guess. It would also be great to see how salsa is danced in America." She typed slowly to make sure she made no mistakes.

"Can I ask you how old you are?

"I am 28. How old are you?" She paused before she answered but decided it would be no harm in telling him her age.

"I'm 26. I enjoy chatting with you. Do you have an e-mail so I can chat with you later when it isn't so late?"

"I have one, but I'm only supposed to use it for business, or I'll be in trouble."

"Why don't you have a personal one?"

"I only have a computer at work; it's too expensive to buy a computer and to pay for internet service at home." She felt embarrassed, but what could she do about it. The hourly rate would cost too much.

"I know of many free e-mail services you can use. I'll be glad to help you obtain one."

"I think I know how to find one. If I do, I'll let you know." Sveta made a mental note to check on this.

"That will be great. My e-mail is on my site. I enjoyed chatting with you, and I love making new friends."

"I do also. It is late for you, I know. When will you be back in your chat room?"

"I have no particular time I visit the room. It isn't used much, just when I normally want to chat with several people at one time. Let me know when, and I will try to check in at the same time."

"I can do that. I hope you have a good night sleep, and it was great to meet you." She wanted to talk to him more, but still had a flutter is her stomach, and hoped she wasn't being monitored.

"I enjoyed meeting you as well. I hope to see you again soon."

She watched him sign off before she glanced around. She had made a very important contact, she knew it.

CHAPTER 10

Sveta stayed busy with the constant flow of clients coming in during the day, and even sold a few paintings. She felt good to have her mind active with work and not the constant agony of not knowing what was going on with her papa's letter, or the murder of the man who had killed him. But again, he might still be alive; his body had never been found. She still had hope she could hold onto.

At five thirty, Olya entered the gallery. Sveta looked at one of the clocks on the wall, and realized just how much time had slipped away from her. "I'll be ready in a minute." After waving at her friend, she went to tell her boss goodbye. He had reluctantly agreed to let her off early, but he had always been kind to her, almost like a second father.

As they left, Sveta looked at her friend who looked so fresh and full of energy today. Olya had styled her hair and used a little makeup—something she seldom used. "So how did your date go last night, Olya?"

"It went well, actually. He's a nice guy, and he asked many questions. It's always good to have someone show interest in my work."

"I'm glad to hear it, since I was concerned about how a blind date would go for you."

"He told me about some of the places they go dancing and on which nights. I think they like to go dancing somewhere almost every night. He also asked me many questions about you and he thinks you can become a great salsa dancer."

"What makes him think I can learn salsa as good as they dance?"

"He said with your background in ballet you'll have a natural ability to learn movements and various steps. He was also interested in your father and if he had taught you anything in dancing, but I told him you were a baby when he disappeared."

"How does he know about my father?"

"I don't know. I assumed Denis told him, or you did."

Sveta raised her head, and looked at the blue sky above them. She could not remember telling him anything about her father, but they did have a lot of beers the night she met him. She did remember talking to Dima and Natasha, who knew her mom, and had heard of her father. Perhaps he had overheard the conversation, she thought. "I don't think so, but maybe he heard me talking to the dance instructors." She wanted to tell Olya many things, but knew it wouldn't be good.

Walking quickly, they finally located the entrance to the dance studio where the overhead lights reflected on the floor and music played as they entered. The instructors were working with an older couple, teaching them a ballroom-style dance. She noticed how wealthy they looked as they practiced a waltz.

Sveta looked at her watch. Since they had arrived five minutes early, she decided to have a seat and read some of the material by the desk. After reading about their studio and various events they sponsored, she noticed a list of dance competitions around town. While filtering through them, she searched for a salsa competition scheduled for the first of October. "Here you go, Olya, we have several months to prepare for this. What do you think?"

"Me—dance in a competition? I think you must be crazy. You're the one with the ability to be a great dancer, not me."

Natasha walked over after the lessons ended and Dima finished saying his goodbye to his students. "It's good to see you this afternoon. Are you ready to learn some new dance steps?"

"We went out again last night and saw some really flashy dancers. The guys who invited us were also awesome. I would love to at least learn the basic steps and not be so awkward on the floor." Sveta glanced around the room nervously.

"We can help you learn to be as good as you want to be, but it's up to you to decide how far you want to advance. Some people want to make it through a social event, like the couple leaving here who just want to dance at their daughter's wedding. Others want to be able to dance in competitions and we love to help those with such ambition."

"Do you dance much in competitions?" Sveta asked.

"Dima and I, as well as most of the instructors here, love to compete. We also have many students who compete. The competitions are divided into various ranges of ability, from those just starting to those who are professional. As you can see from the flyers, the competitions cover all forms of ballroom dancing, including the salsa and mambo."

Another guy crossed the floor after he emerged from the office. He quickly extended his hand, as he approached them. "Hello."

"This is Vadim. He's one of the instructors, and he will be giving one of you a lesson today, along with Dima."

Vadim extended his hand toward Sveta. "Please call me Vadik."

"My name is Sveta, and this is Olya." She glanced at her friend.

Natasha paired Vadik with Olya, and escorted Sveta over to Dima. "I'll assure you that you're in the hands of an expert." She left them together.

"I'm glad you decided to come today." Dima smiled. "Being the daughter of one of the great Russian dancers, I think you'll do extremely well. It's going to be a pleasure to teach you, and I hope you enjoy it."

"This is different for me." Sveta confessed. "I feel like a child in a new class. Salsa dancing is so much more exciting for me than ballet. I love the music, and I never thought I would say that."

"We teach many more styles than simply salsa, and it would be good for you to learn the basis of them so you can see for yourself."

"I understand, and I may later. As I said, I don't have much money to spend, and I need to concentrate on salsa . . . if that's okay." She would love to do other types of dancing, but the cost of lessons remained out of the question.

"Very well then, let's learn the salsa. I'll teach you the basic step, the one originating from Cuba. It's also called the on-one method, or the casino method. When you go out dancing, don't be surprised to see many freestyle salsa moves also. One of the great things about being a lady is that your job is basically to follow your partner's lead. It's the man's job to show you off, and make you look beautiful."

"Where did you learn to salsa?"

"My parents learned in Cuba many years ago when they attended school there as students. In the parties they went to, they saw the locals dancing, and they learned from them. Later, they danced the same when they returned to Russia. They found other friends here who loved Latino-style dancing. Somewhere along the way, I learned other ballroom-style dances, and decided to open this studio."

"Do they dance salsa differently in other parts of the world?"

"Yes, the step we're working on is called on-one. In America, many people dance on-two. When you go to the international competitions, you'll see many different styles."

"Do they have any international competitions?"

"Yes, and they are offered in many places by many different organizations. They actually held one here in St. Petersburg recently," he said as he led her through the basic moves over and over, letting her feel the beat as she practiced the steps. "Many people overdo the hips, which makes the movement look awful. To produce the proper look when you extend your leg, shift your weight on it and make the leg straighten. This automatically makes the hips respond correctly."

"From the dance clubs, I see some of the dancers with this natural rhythm in their body. I'd love to move like them."

"Salsa takes practice and you'll understand it more and more as you start to feel the music." Dima hesitated. "Do you mind if I ask you a question?"

"Sure, what do you want to know?"

"I've heard your father's name mentioned so many times. Since he was considered the best during his time, why didn't you follow him and learn ballet?"

"It hasn't been easy to be known as Nickolay's daughter. His name was associated with the theft of many priceless painting belonging to Russia. I've never believed the stories, nor has my mom. Still, I've had to live with the constant reminder that I have no father. It's been hard on my mom and me."

"I am truly sorry." He leaned forward and flashed a sympathetic smile. "Perhaps salsa will give you a new life in the love of dance. You really are a good dancer and know a lot about movement, so the steps should be easy for you to learn."

"The only dance instruction I ever received is from my mom who has taught ballet all of her life. The government doesn't pay much, but it's something she enjoys doing."

The hour disappeared fast as they danced, but she learned many new steps, and most importantly how to keep in step with the fast pace-change of dance partners. Looking over at her friend from time to time, she also knew Olya had a great time. With about six or seven minutes remaining, the two walked over to a table where Natasha waited for them. "How was the lesson?" she asked with a big smile.

"It was fantastic!" Olya leaned forward.

"I am so glad. Let me show you what we have to offer at the studio. To get you started, we have a beginner package consisting of four lessons. This will teach you the basic steps of the most popular dances."

"What if I only wanted to learn salsa?" Sveta asserted.

"If salsa is what you want to specialize in, I think we can make an exception. I see you've taken a liking to salsa." Natasha glanced at the paperwork in front of her.

"Yes. I know I can't afford much." Sveta grinned.

"I think you'll like this package. The four lessons you can receive as an introductory offer for only two hundred rubles."

Olya spoke first. "I'll have to think about it, but it sounds like a good price."

After Sveta remained deep in thought for several minutes, she finally agreed. "I made some extra sales today and while it's a lot of money to me, I think I'll do it, that is, if I can just learn the salsa."

As Dima walked over to the table, Natasha glanced at him and said, "She's interested in dancing salsa and nothing else. What do you think?"

"If she really wants only salsa, we can do it for her, but since we have the group practice lessons in a few minutes, maybe she'll change her mind when she sees some of the other dances."

"We'll see." She had to hide her reasons, but appreciated their efforts.

"Give us a few minutes. We have to prepare some refreshments for the dance. I hope you both enjoy it." They hurried to greet some of the others walking in.

Over the next hour Sveta and Olya danced with many other students and occasionally one of the studio instructors working at the studio. The dances varied from the waltz, to the mambo, and many variations in between. While the salsa held her interest, she would admit the cha cha cha felt like fun, and especially since the best-looking student danced with her for that one particular dance. This dance also generated excitement, much like the salsa.

When the music stopped at the end of the hour, Dima walked forward. "Tonight we have a special performance by one of our students. She's been working hard and wants us to see what she's learned." A tall girl with short, sassy hair moved to the middle of the room. She wore a flashy, yet elegant outfit produced from a sheer black material. "This is a dance she'll be doing next month in a cha cha cha contest." Dima bowed to her.

Natasha started the music as the two moved to their positions and exploded into a rhythm of dance which looked professional. While they were obviously having a good time, she looked so—polished. Dima constantly added steps to the dance which helped his partner look stunning. While it was his job to make her look great, he excelled in doing his part. The girl radiated smiles as she maneuvered through some complicated steps with ease. She must have practiced this dance a lot to make each step look that perfect.

When they finished, the group rushed in and congratulated her on a fantastic job. She had performed great. Dima raised his hands to have a chance to speak. "Would you believe this is how good you could dance . . . and just after four lessons?" The crowd turned silent—she had become this good after four lessons? Suddenly, the crowd realized he was kidding and started laughing at being fooled so easily. "Okay, maybe a few more." He added a mysterious smile by arching his brow.

Natasha joined him and added, "For those who are new to the studio, we have a special package consisting of four lessons which only costs . . . two hundred rubles. For those who brought guests that sign up tonight you'll also be given one free lesson. We always encourage you to bring someone with you on Thursday nights to the group practice dance as a guest."

As the crowd started drifting around the tables, Sveta decided to sign up for the lessons. Somehow, she would make her money stretch. She knew she needed the lessons, and she owed her papa this much.

CHAPTER 11

Sveta lay awake on the sofa, enjoying her Sunday morning where she didn't have to rush to the gallery. Last night had been another late night of dancing. The four weeks of lessons had helped her improve tremendously, and she had made many new friends at the studio and in the salsa bars. She thought of the studio and the next package of lessons—they were not cheap. For the next package of ten lessons, the price jumped to over three thousand rubles.

She looked over at the box she had received at the studio the day before. The gift had her awake all night. It felt like someone might be playing with her, and giving her little bits of information to let her know her papa was still alive. She opened the box and looked at the new dancing shoes inside, which had to cost much more than she wanted to imagine.

She remembered how Dima had called her on Friday and wanted her to come by the studio to see something he had for her. It was Saturday before she could make it to the studio to receive a surprise she wasn't ready for.

Dima had the box sitting on the table when she walked in. "These came for you yesterday. I'm not sure who ordered them for you, but I know they're for you." The note on the side of the box read, "To the little lady Sveta."

Someone had purchased her some new dancing shoes! Dima denied knowing anything about them and she couldn't imagine who would buy them for her without telling her. She studied the tag again addressed to "Little lady" and how her papa had called her by that name. After crying, she had thanked Dima for the shoes and left.

Was her papa alive? She had talked with her mom late into the night after she returned home from dancing, discussing the shoes. The hours of agonizing over the possibilities had drained both of them.

Suddenly, she remembered she had promised Danny she would go to the gallery to chat with him. Over the last four weeks, they had chatted more and more and she had even opened an e-mail account she hoped would remain secure. Early in the mornings, she could send him long letters and even during the day, she ventured to her office more and more to be able to chat with him online in his special private chat room. With no one at the gallery today, she felt like she could leisurely chat with him with no interruptions.

On the way over to the gallery, she stopped to purchase some coffee before glancing at a paper where she read the headlines: Ivan Lisin under investigation for smuggling. While the Lisin family had been famous for involvement in the Old Russian mafia, they often tried to convince the public they wanted to become respectful businessmen who were now in the import and export business. She rolled her eyes at the very thoughts of such a lie, but decided to purchase the paper anyway and read the full article in detail later.

As soon as she reached her office and connected online she noticed Danny waiting for her. She had never seen a photo of him before and she'd always wondered what he looked like. She hoped to trade photos with him today. "Hello," she quickly typed as soon as she logged into the site.

"Hello, I'm glad you're here. I've been waiting for you."

"Sorry, I slept late and have just arrived at the gallery."

"I see. How's the weather in Russia?"

"It is warm today. How is your weather in America?" She had felt herself becoming more and more interested in knowing more about where he lived.

"It's raining outside and a good day to stay in and read."

"What kind of books are you reading?"

"Don't laugh at me if I tell you."

"I promise. Tell me." She felt intrigued.

"I'm reading screenplays from the internet and acting as if I had the part in some old movies. It's good that no one sees how bad I am."

"I bet you are good. It would be good to hear your voice and see what you sound like." She lied slightly, she felt scared about her English being so bad.

"Well, perhaps I can give you a call."

"Well, one day I might give you my number." While she decided to mock him, she hoped that they could talk one day.

"I see you're still a little bit unsure about the internet thing."

"Well, you never know what kind of bad man you might be." She hoped her teasing might hold his interest.

"Yes, and who knows, you might be some guy from Brooklyn I'm talking to."

"You never know." Yes, she liked this teasing game.

"Is Sveta your real name?"

"No—it is the name all of my friends call me."

"What's your real name?"

"It is Svetlana."

"I'm not sure I'm pronouncing your name correctly, it's an unusual name for me."

"Do you have a photo of yourself?" Here goes nothing,

she thought, since he would surely want to know what she looked like also.

"I have many of myself. Would you like to see some of me dancing?"

"Yes, that would be great."

"Okay, give me a few minutes to pick some from the files and I'll send them to you."

"Thank you. Only one thing, if you can reduce them so they will not be so large. I do not want to cost the gallery so much on the transmission."

"We talked about the cost of the internet before and I understand. Give me a minute. And by the way, do you have a photo of you? I'm dying to see what you look like, as long as you don't look like some guy from across town."

"As a matter of fact, I do have a photo for you that my friend, Olya, made the other day."

"In such a case, I'll hurry and find mine. I'll be back in a minute."

"Take your time and I will read the paper for a minute."

Sveta placed the paper on her desk and started to read the article. An international investigation was being expanded into smuggling that had been going on for a long time. Many of the strongmen in the family organization had been indicted, and others were turning state evidence to save their skins. The lower part of the article mentioned the murder of Ivan's little brother, Pavel. The article suggested he had been killed by insiders before he had a chance to talk too much or say the wrong thing.

The article mentioned how the family was rumored to have been in the smuggling business since the time of the great theft of priceless paintings in Russia twenty-five years ago. The case had never been solved, and the paintings were still missing. Ivan Lisin addressed this one accusation in the article by stating that he had nothing to do with the theft or disappearance of the paintings. He felt like these items represented a part of Russia which could never be replaced, and while many people might have bad thoughts about him, he still remained a Russian and loved his country, traditions and culture.

Danny reappeared on the screen and wrote, "I located the photos I was looking for and hope you like them. They should be in your inbox now. Let me know what you think."

"I cannot wait to see them. Let me find them." She squeaked slightly, as the excitement built.

"Now, remember you promised to send me a photo of you. A promise is a promise."

"I will in a minute." She opened her e-mail and hunted for the one from him. When she located his e-mail with an attachment, she clicked on it and waited for the image to materialize. The anticipation built as she watched the photo materialize on the screen of him standing on a dance floor, where he had his hand raised in a motion indicating he was dancing. His posture was straight and his frame perfect.

She continued to type. "I see you now."

"And… what do you think?"

"You look nice and professional. Was this taken at a competition you danced in?" Wow, she recognized that he must be better than she originally thought.

"Yes, this photo was taken about three months ago."

"So, you are a talented dancer. How did you do in the competition?"

"We didn't win, but we didn't do too badly either."

Sveta fantasized about him dancing with someone else,

and had, believe it, or not, a jealous feeling surge over her. She felt slightly envious of someone who had the chance to dance with him, but at the same time she was also curious about this other girl. "Who was your partner in the competition?"

"Her name is Ginger. I noticed her dancing at many of the clubs, and we decided to try competing. It was a learning experience for both of us."

"Is she your girlfriend?"

"No… she's someone I dance with from time to time. She's good and has helped me learn to be much better."

"Do you still compete much?"

"I would love to, but I haven't. I would love to dance with you one night."

"Yes, I would like that. You could come to Russia."

"I could, but Russia's a long way from here. Maybe you could come to America."

"America is also a long way. Perhaps we can at least dream about it and you never really know where you are with the life."

"That's right—you never know. I would love to know more about St. Petersburg. I've heard it's a beautiful city."

"Yes, it is a great city. You should come and see."

"For one thing, I don't know Russian. I would be totally lost where you live."

"I could show you around. It is easy to find things here and St. Petersburg has so many beautiful sights to see."

"Maybe, but I think it would be easier for you to come to New York. You know English well."

"I can read English, but I have a hard time speaking it well."

"One day we can talk on the phone. I think it would be good to hear your voice."

"It would be good to hear your voice, too. I will think

about it." While she wondered if it could really happen, she knew to be careful.

"I understand, but you did promise me a photo, if you remember."

"Yes, I have not forgotten. I will send you my photo now." Sveta palms sweated again as she hit the send button.

CHAPTER 12

The nagging late night lights vanished as September made its presence known, but allowing Sveta to be able to sleep better. She felt like her dancing had progressed, but since no one ever admitted to buying her the shoes, she thought that this gift would remain a mystery forever.

"When is Denis coming by to take you out tonight?" Her mom asked as she finished her meal.

"He should be here anytime, I think." Sveta had worked hard on styling her hair. Her thick and shiny hair had always been her best feature. She had seen the other girls at the clubs use a lot of makeup, and had experimented with some. While she felt like the cosmetics made her look older and not as fresh and clean as she wanted to look she knew that Denis liked the way they made her look.

"I'll have to come watch the two of you dance one night and see how good you've become." Her mom was becoming more comfortable with her learning salsa.

"I would love to have you watch us dance. The salsa is an exciting dance, and the music is fantastic, but it's nothing like ballet."

Joining her daughter, Mariya lowered her voice and said, "It's only three months to the competition in New York, and it takes a while to obtain a visa. I hoped to hear from your papa by now to let us know what's going on. Have you discovered anything in all the research you've been doing lately?"

"I know the process of getting a visa, and a little about

New York thanks to my online friend from America, but other than the mysterious shoes, I have not received anything else. It's slowly driving me crazy."

"I understand. This guy you're dancing with seems to be a good man. It's time you settled down with one guy and become married."

"Denis isn't a bad man, and I'm sure he will make someone a good husband, but he isn't the kind of man I think I can settle down with. He loves to go out every night and dance with different women. He spends a lot of money, and I've often wondered where he gets the money he spends."

"It's still something for you to think about. Remember, you're not getting any younger, and you know what it's like to not have a husband."

"I know we've been through this so many times before." She lifted her hand in a manner to say she wasn't going to discuss it tonight.

Luckily, the knock on the door interrupted the conversation—Denis had arrived. "I'll be back later. Don't wait up for me since you know we'll be out late." She gave her mom a few quick kisses before she smiled on her way to the door.

Denis waited in the hallway, where he looked clean and sharp. With his endearing Swedish boy look and flashing eyes, he smiled at Sveta and her mom. "Hello."

Sveta didn't want to have her mom questioning Denis tonight, so she rushed toward him, hoping to leave quickly. "We'll be back later. Try to obtain some good sleep tonight and don't wait for us."

Denis, however, quickly waved at Sveta's mom before he closed the door and they left the flat. They walked toward the metro while they discussed what they had worked on during the day. Over the last two months they had become close friends and their joy of dancing had kept them together. Sveta knew he dated other girls, which it didn't bother her too much. She still wasn't ready for one guy, even if her mom pushed. While she always noticed something strange about Denis, she couldn't put a finger on it.

"I'm glad we're going to arrive at the club a little early tonight. I wanted to see if we can learn some new steps before the others arrive. The owner will let us use the dance floor." Denis paused. "Are you still thinking of entering the dance contest at the studio where you had lessons?"

"I don't know. The reason I'm thinking about entering is because only those who are new to the dance can enter. You can have an experienced partner, but his dancing doesn't count, only the one who is just learning now. The contest could be lots of fun."

"I would love to see what your papa thought of your salsa dancing. From what you've told me, he was a fantastic ballet dancer." Denis always seemed interested in her father's dancing. He never pried, but always had an interest in him. However, this was one subject that Sveta never expanded on too much.

They soon arrived at the club where the atmosphere remained quiet as the dinner crowd finished eating and the workers started preparing the floor. Denis removed a miniature cassette player from his bag and clicked the start button as a familiar salsa song started to play.

"This will have to do for a while until the band starts." He slowly pulled her over to him and went into teaching her some moves he had on his mind. They were much more seductive than ones he had ever taught her before. In fact, his actions became too much for her, and she had to pull from him and his advances several times. She didn't like his hands on her butt, or being pulled in so tight to him that she could feel his manhood. The more he tried to work with her, the more she resisted.

He suddenly stopped the music as he acted totally frustrated. "That's fine; we'll dance like a couple of old people." He strolled toward the bar and ordered some drinks.

She slowly joined him. "I'm sorry. I've never dated much and I'm not used to this."

He flashed a big smile. "This isn't dating, it's dancing." He glanced away for a moment before staring directly at her. "Don't worry about it."

She could see the frustration on his face as he walked over to talk to some of the band members setting up. She decided to walk to a table and wait for him there, but he stayed at the stage and helped them until the other dancers were coming in and getting tables.

After he had completely disappeared, and the free lesson had started, she walked onto the floor alone. While the instructions reverted to the basic moves again, she needed all the practice she could get. While several guys came over to dance with her as the lesson proceeded, Denis never returned.

Eventually, she noticed him at the bar talking to the waitress he had danced with before several times. She was flirting with him heavily and had her arm around his waist. Since it felt strange seeing him with someone else, she tried not to stare, but damn it, she couldn't.

An older man came over to her to ask her to dance and on any other night she would have told him no, but tonight she needed to get out of her seat and not just sit and wait. "Sure, I'd love to."

While he looked much older on the floor, he danced well, and the dance did help to relieve her mind of the problems she had with Denis. However, as life would have it, she watched Denis and this girl walk onto the floor where their eyes locked into each other intensely. While he normally had great posture, he leaned slightly forward to connect with her as her hand wrapped around his head and seductively played with his neck and then his face. The movements flowed so smooth and slow until she would abruptly break away only to be wrapped back into his arms. Their movements made Sveta feel like she was watching a play where a complete story was condensed into a single dance.

"You're a good dancer." The man's voice slightly broke her out of the trance she had entered.

"Thanks." She glanced back at her dance partner for a second, but when she looked around again for Denis she had lost him in the crowd. After quickly dancing around the older gentleman, she saw them again on the other side of the room. He had his hand covering the girl's butt and maneuvered her around in several dips. She felt almost like she was watching someone have sex on the floor. The erotic sight made her nauseous as part of her fought the urge to leave and another part of her felt intrigued by the dance, in spite of being ignored and hurt. She knew she was falling for this guy and she knew better. He would only break her heart.

Finally, she could not watch any more as she smiled at the gentleman and asked to go back to her table. After he followed her to the table he acted like he wanted to have a seat. "I'm sorry. My boyfriend will be back in a moment." She, at least, hoped so.

"I see—I didn't know you were with someone." He turned and left. Boyfriend—that's a word she never intended to use.

Eventually, Denis walked over to her table without

offering a smile. "Would you like anything to drink?" He stared intently at her.

At first she thought about telling him no as she closed her eyes for a moment to concentrate. "Yes, I think I will have something tonight."

"What do you want?"

"Something good—I think I need something strong tonight." Her voice sounded cold, and she knew her face definitely reflected no emotions. With a small grin, he headed for the bar. She felt upset, but she didn't want to get into a fight. Yes, it would be a good night to have a strong drink.

That one drink led to several more, and they finally started laughing over a few stupid jokes. With him paying her attention again she soon enjoyed their time together. Finally, he asked her to the dance floor again. He started slow with basic movements and then helped her through several more. She had to admit that she enjoyed the time dancing with him.

Her head felt dizzy as he leaned forward, seducing her with his eyes. He came close enough to kiss her, but he hesitated as he often had in the past. She froze, looking into his eyes as time almost stopped while he held her tightly and seductively in his arms. At first she didn't notice how he grabbed her butt and pulled her closer and closer to him on the floor.

She closed her eyes for a minute to enjoy the rush of heat going through her body. She wanted to say no, but how could she when she opened her eyes and saw him looking at her only inches away. However, unlike so many times before, he let his lips touch hers in a slow, gentle kiss.

Wrapping her arms around him, she whispered in his ears, "Thanks." She was falling for him, and knew she had little power to resist him, but somehow, down deep, she knew she had to. As she pushed away from him, she tried several moves she had seen other girls make, and hoped he wouldn't know how much she tried to act like she wasn't totally falling for him.

CHAPTER 13

October finally arrived, putting an end to the hot weather and long days. The leaves looked beautiful, but the rain and winds cast a far different scene as Sveta needed to start wearing warmer clothes. The dancing around town had given Sveta a full appreciation of salsa and she had many new friends now. In two days she would be entering her first dance competition at the studio where she had taken the lessons.

Thinking back to three weeks ago, she remembered the call from Dima at the studio. He had a student who wanted to compete in the competition and was interested in finding a salsa partner. They would be placed in the novice category, and most importantly, this student would pay for her entry fee.

After refocusing on the present, Sveta glanced at her mom. "I'm leaving for the studio to practice with Alex. If we finish early, I might stop by one of the salsa clubs, but I think I'll come home soon tonight."

"I hope you have a good practice. Where's Denis tonight?"

"He's out with his friends. I don't know if he's coming to the competition tomorrow night or not. I think he would rather be with his friends. He acts like he likes me, but his friends do take most of his time. Mom, Let's face it, when you're as good as Denis you can have any girl you want at the clubs and that's not really the kind of man I want."

"Sveta, I know you have deep feelings for him, and I think in time he'll come around. We'll see."

"Yes, I guess we will, but don't wait up for me. You're still coming to see the competition on Friday night like you promised, aren't you?"

"Yes, I'll be coming."

After leaving her flat, she walked instead of taking the metro so that she could relax and see the views of the city. The leaves on the trees were beautiful, and the evening air felt crisp and clean as people scurried around her trying to hurry home for the evening.

Her thoughts concentrated on Denis and why she let him have such an effect on her? She had known from the start he had many girls chasing him. While he had never forced himself on her or abused her, she felt like she at times she was attacking him most of the time. She hadn't slept with him yet, but if he really made a move on her, she knew she would be almost helpless to evade him. Maybe she should simply be happy he did take her out sometimes and at least he saw her more than he did the other girls he knew. Like her mom said, maybe in time he would come around.

As she started to get closer to the studio, she also thought of the invitation to the American salsa contest. Since she had received no more instructions from her dad, she and her mom both thought that maybe the trip wasn't meant to be after all.

After walking through the entrance to the studio, she saw several couples on the floor taking lessons, but didn't see Alex anywhere. Since everyone was busy, she decided to take off her light jacket, walk over to the far side of the floor, and work on the basic step. The music played in a cha cha cha rhythm, but provided a beat to keep steps with. She had learned many steps now and she hoped she would continue to become better and better.

Dima soon finished with his students and walked them

to the door. With a big smile, he said, "I'm glad that's over since it's been a long day. How are you?"

"I'm doing fine, thank you. The walk over here tonight felt great. I love this time of year. Have you seen Alex?"

"Not yet, but he'll be here soon. He's really glad you decided to accept his offer to dance with him. Have you decided what to wear in the competition?"

"Yes, my friend has found me something I think will look good. What do you think my chances are of winning this one?" She knew that she had to do well.

"You never know—the main thing is to have fun and enjoy yourself. You'll learn much about competitions by entering them. Remember Alex has only been dancing for a short time, and he is nervous—just like you."

"I know, and I'm so thankful for his invitation. How hard is it to prepare for a major competition in salsa?"

"The competition depends on which one you're talking about. Some can be fierce, and the dancers are professionals who dance all day. Why do you ask?"

"It was a curiosity question. I've been going on the internet and watching clips of professional dancers, and like wow . . . I would love to be so good."

"I understand. While we're waiting for Alex, let me put on some salsa music and see how good you are now." He crossed the room and loaded a CD into the player. The music sounded exciting as always. With a big smile he turned the volume higher and the room came to life with the beat of drums echoing off the walls and floor.

They had danced for about five minutes when Alex entered the room, flashing a smile and indicating that he felt happy to see her. As he approached them Dima said, "Alex, you're a lucky man. I think Sveta has improved dramatically in the last few weeks. It's going to be good to see you win the competition on Friday night. If you want,

I'll be glad to work with you tonight at no charge, since I would love to see you two win. After the lesson, you can stay as long as you wish to practice."

Alex grinned, as he said, "That will be great! We would appreciate it."

As the lesson progressed, Dima forced them to perform the dance they planned to do for the competition over and over, and each time he stopped them briefly to make adjustments in their style. While the steps were much rehearsed and could not be changed at this late date, he indicated that they had many things they could add later. The most important aspect was to act like they were one during the competition, and that they enjoyed dancing.

Dima soon left them on their own, and went to his office to do some work. They went over the dance again and again, as they knew this would be the last chance they had to practice for the competition. Alex always acted kind of quiet, and she knew that he had taken the lessons to mainly help him with his social skills. Sveta had always wondered why he had decided to learn this kind of dance, but she was glad that he did. She knew that Alex didn't go to the clubs at night, and had wanted to wait until he learned to dance better. He had even mentioned to her that he felt girls wouldn't want to dance with him. Perhaps she could talk him into going to one later tonight.

Sveta knew that it was this shyness that caused problems with their dancing. He didn't control or command her attention like Denis did on the floor, and this, unfortunately, might create problems during their competition. As she summoned her courage, Sveta whispered to ask him, "How would you like to go out dancing at a salsa bar?"

"Do you mean tonight?"

"Yes, I think it would be good for us to see how we do

with some different music. I know a place not far from here."

His quick reactions indicated he would agree. "Sure. I'd love to see one of these places, if you don't mind going with me. I know you have some friends you go with often."

"I have one guy I have been dating, but he dates other girls also, and we're simply going for a few dances. We'll have fun. What do you think?"

"Sure, but we need to let Dima know we're leaving."

They soon walked into the club, and while she did have some misgivings about seeing Denis dancing on the floor with someone else, she knew he could be anywhere. After all, they weren't strictly seeing just each other. In fact, she had seen him dance with other girls many times. As they entered the salsa bar, the inside looked dark and crowded for a Wednesday night. While she recognized many of the regulars as they approached the floor, she saw no tables available anywhere. The bartenders, as expected, stayed busy preparing many drinks for thirsty patrons at the bar.

"Let's go dance since I see nowhere to sit right now." She pointed toward the occupied chairs.

"Are you sure?" He shifted uneasily, acting unsure of his dancing ability.

"Yes, that's why we came. Come on, you'll do fine."

While pulling him by the arm, she entered the floor with him. Rather than giving her his full attention, he constantly glanced around at the other dancers, as if they mystified him. This truly must be his first time dancing in a club. Finally, however, his lessons finally paid off when he started to move through the basic steps with her, and they began to synergize to the music. The smile on his face indicated how much fun he was having.

As she completed one turn, her heart raced as she saw

Denis on the far side of the floor with another girl. They gyrated in a close embrace with this girl's arms wrapped around him. He was totally engaged with her and locked in eye to eye. As the movement quickly turned slower and more seductive, it was much too intent for Sveta to handle. She felt her heart breaking; she had to leave—now.

As she turned around to Alex, she suddenly had another thought. Perhaps she could return the same favor. She had to plan this quickly and properly. Thinking fast, she moved in close to Alex. While she had never had any practice at acting like a sexual goddess before, tonight she decided to give it her best shot.

Her hand gently brushed upward against Alex's chest before the back of her hand caressed his right cheek as she moved her fingers over his head and down the other cheek. While she had watched other girls do this many times, it was the first time she had tried to be seductive. Although the move felt strange for her, she poured her soul into this dance.

Alex appeared to have no clue what had happened to her, but appeared to be intensely enjoying the dance. He also had no idea as to what he should be doing, but he pulled her close and kind of grinded with her movements. When she felt him rub close to her breast, she pulled apart from him for a moment and did a quick turn before rushing back into his arms again, and this time even closer. The turn happened too fast; she didn't see anything. She needed to know if Denis had seen her.

Chancing another turn, she pushed out and proceeded in a slower spin. The spot where Denis had danced was now occupied by someone else—Denis was gone.

CHAPTER 14

Sveta's mom shook her, letting her know how late she had slept. Last night had been a nightmare. She had been bad the night before. How could she have led Alex on so? He had acted like such a nice guy. The attempt to make Denis jealous had backfired on her. Now Alex thought she had a passionate love for him. She didn't know how to handle this, but would have to think of something since the competition was tomorrow. She knew that after the dance, she wouldn't see Alex anymore and she needed to let him down easy. As far as Denis was concerned, she knew she would see him on Saturday night when he was supposed to take her dancing. The image of his dance partner had haunted her all night. It felt terrible for someone to have such an effect on her.

"Okay, okay, I'm getting up." Sveta finally acquiesced with her mom's attempt to wake her.

"I hope so, it's late. You'll not get to the gallery early enough to chat or check the internet if you don't hurry and I also have some things I want you to check on this morning. I saw a paper yesterday and many members of the Lisin family are still being investigated. Something is going on and I'm not sure exactly what to make of it."

"I'll check on this report as soon as I get to my office. Did you save the paper?"

"No, I was looking at someone else's on the metro last night."

"I see. I also promised Danny I would chat with him this morning. He's been so supportive of my upcoming competition." She stretched on the couch. The baby doll-style nightshirt she wore felt light and comfortable, but not much to keep her warm on a cold morning. She quickly wrapped in a small robe and headed for the bathroom to have a shower.

"I don't know why you keep chatting with the American. Do you think he could help you?"

"Yes. If I ever go to New York, he could be a big help."

"I don't think it's possible for you to go. We haven't heard anything since we received the invitation."

"I still have to believe something will happen. We did receive the shoes."

"We'll see."

In a short time, Sveta had transformed herself into a professional-looking saleslady again. "I'll let you know what I find out. Have a good day, Mom." She went out of the door before her mom could say anything else.

She soon rushed into her office at the gallery and waited for the internet connected while she went to make some fresh tea. It had become a habit of hers to make tea for everyone and have it ready for them when they arrived.

On the internet, she soon located many stories about the Lisin family and commentaries by numerous sources. Many suspects had been taken in for questioning and the police had promised further investigations. Ivan Lisin, the oldest brother, denied any wrongdoing by insisting that he operated as a legitimate businessman and that someone was trying to frame him for smuggling. He openly requested a full investigation by promising his full co-operation.

She suddenly noticed the flashing icon on her computer, letting her know Danny waited in the chat room for her. This brought a big smile to her face, since she enjoyed chatting with him, and the things he did in his normal day were so unusual for her.

"Hello." She typed the letters in English making her have to hunt for the symbols on the keyboard.

"Hello, how are you today?" He responded immediately.

"I am fine, but a little tired. I worked with Alex last night for a long time, and I hope we are ready for the competition tomorrow night."

"I'm sure you'll do great. I want to hear how you do as soon as you finish. I am sure you will win this competition, but then you'll be hooked for life."

"This one is for beginners and you would probably laugh at me if you could see it."

"I don't think so. I would love to dance with you someday."

"I think I would like to dance with you also." She had, in fact, secretly dreamed of them dancing together one day.

"Is there any way you can come to America to visit?"

This question she wished she could answer, but she knew it was impossible for now. "The cost is too expensive and I would have a hard time to leave work for so long."

Then, she saw the unexpected. "I understand. If you could find a way to get off work, I could pay your way to come here."

Her heart started to pound wildly in her chest. "You would pay my way! I am sure the cost is expensive."

"The cost isn't too bad. I've already checked on the price of plane tickets, and on how much it will cost for a visa. I can afford it, if you're interested."

"Your offer is extremely generous, but I would have also living expense. I understand it is expensive to stay in

New York."

"Yes, it costs money to live here. If you come, you can stay with me. I have an extra couch I can sleep on while you're here. I promise I can be trustworthy and not bother you."

"I think I have heard guys say that before (smile)."

"I'll make you that promise. It will be one you can rely on and never doubt. While it's a decision you need to make, you don't have to answer right now. Just let me know."

"I'll do that, and I really do appreciate the offer. Making arrangements will be hard, but I am definitely interested. Are you sure I can trust you (Just Kidding)?"

"Yes, I know you can. It would be so great to dance with you. If you can, please check on what you have to do to come—I assume you know how to obtain a visa."

"Yes, and the visa will only be the start. I will be honest in that I have also completed some checking on what is involved. The process isn't easy."

"I'm glad. I'm going to give you my phone number. You can call me from any phone collect and I'll cover the cost of the call. All you have to do is tell the operator you want to make a collect call. I would love to hear your voice after you win the competition tomorrow night."

"I am not sure I can do this, but I will try. Are you sure the call will not be too expensive?"

"Don't worry. It won't be a problem."

"Okay, I will try. It is getting close to opening time. I will check with you again tomorrow morning. Have a good night sleep, and I will start my working."

"Okay, bye for now."

"Bye." As she disconnected, she fought a squeal fighting to escape her lungs. Instead, she walked to the kitchen, poured some more tea, and strolled to the main entrance where she saw her boss standing there, talking to two men. While the conversation sounded harsh and heated, she couldn't make out exactly what the conversation concerned.

After seeing her enter the room, one of the men called for her to come over. "You must be Sveta." A tall, lanky man in his late fifties, or early sixties said as he glared at her.

She didn't know exactly who they were, but knew they must be important since they wore expensive suits and gold Rolex watches. She studied the anger on the face of her boss as he said, "These two men are Boris and Michael Lisin, who apparently have forgotten that I am under the protection of Yuri Zotov." He waited for their reaction.

Boris spoke first. "We fully understand what you're saying and we wish no problems. This is just a friendly call. Since many people are talking these days, I think it would be good if we talked for a minute. I'm sure you read the paper."

"I do, of course and I understand you have some problems needing to be taken care of, but I don't understand how your business could affect me."

Boris continued, "You do a lot of importing and exporting, like we do, and we would be glad to have you keep an ear open for us. Someone is singing, and we will find out who that rat is soon. I'm sure you understand that it will be good for us to handle this as soon as possible."

"I know nothing that might be of use to you. If I did, I would tell Yuri. Have you talked to him?"

"Not yet, but we will soon. He doesn't want to dirty his hands. He's much like my older brother, Ivan."

"I read the news about Pavel. Please send my condolences to the family." Her boss lowered his head in respect.

"I'm sure they will be glad to hear it. He was running his mouth too much, and that is what happens. While he could have caused problems for the whole family, his death has sent a message loud and clear to others."

Boris turned to Sveta. "I've heard rumors circulating concerning your father being alive and behind all the problems we're having."

"My father . . . ."

"Yes, your father's name has surfaced. It was Pavel who thought for sure your father was dead. He was convinced that your father had switched the shipping location on a shipment document and had hidden something that belonged to us many years ago. His death was an accident—he was being asked questions about what he knew when he went over a railing and into a river below. While his body was never recovered, he carried with him, we believe, the information on where the shipment was sent. Our property has never been located."

"So, you're admitting that your brother killed my father!" She felt the muscles in her fingers controlling her nails tighten.

"His death was an accident."

"My father was a dancer. How could he have done something like this?"

"We're still not sure, and I think we'll never know now."

Sveta held much better than she thought she could have—after all she had just learned her father was indeed murdered.

"We hate to bother you, but give our respects to Yuri, and please let us know if you hear anything." Michael glanced over at Sveta. "I know you're upset and I would be also, but it was simply business that had to be taken care of at the time. For what happened to your papa, I'm so sorry to have to tell you this."

Sveta looked at him in shock. It was a good thing she didn't have the ability to attack these men because if she had the opportunity, she would. "You knew all this time and never said a word. You let me and my mom live in hell all of this time!"

"That's life, honey." Boris said as he leaned forward with a sly, wicked smile.

Sveta nearly came after him, and would have if Gleb hadn't stepped in front of her. "One day you'll receive yours," she murmured softly under her breath, but still loud enough to be heard.

Boris chuckled. "You have some spunk in you, but you have no idea what you're asking for." His glanced slowly over at Sveta as he approached her. "I could strip you and lean you over the table right here and have you all day if I wanted to. Make you scream like a little girl. What do you think about that?"

Her face flushed with anger, but what could she do? She stumbled backwards when Boris approached her. Thankfully, her boss stepped forward and aggressively asserted that she worked for him and as such was also under the protection of Yuri Zotov.

The two men grinned at each other, as Boris leaned forward. "I don't think Yuri is interested in one little lady in a gallery."

"Perhaps you should ask Yuri. This is the lady he constantly works with to search for his personal collections. He's very fond of her."

Not sure what to think of this, Michael said, "Forget it, Boris, she isn't worth it. Look at her—she's nothing special."

Boris lifted a finger. "You need to show some respect,

little woman. Next time I won't be in such a good mood."

The two turned around and headed for the door. "You know how to reach us. We'll talk again, I'm sure." Michael said as they left.

Sveta looked at her boss for answers as they left. She had so many questions, but she also felt sick, knowing that she had just talked with the men who were responsible for her father's death. "I don't feel good." Her voice trembled.

"I understand. If you want, you can have the rest of the day off. We can handle things for the rest of the day. Your father was a good friend of mine." He had tears falling down the sides of his face. After they offered each other a big hug and comforted each other for a moment, she had no way of knowing what would happen to her in the future. "I need to call Yuri Zotov and let them know we had visitors—he'll want to know." Gleb glanced at his watch.

"I think we're lucky to have him looking out for us."

"Yes, but the coverage isn't as big as I suggested. Since they don't know that, they won't be back for a long time you don't have to worry about them."

"I'll have to tell my mom since she should be told the truth. This news will be hard on her. Life's been tough on her all these years by not knowing what really happened to him."

"I understand. You haven't had a vacation for a long time. Maybe you should consider taking one. A break would be good for you, I think."

"I don't have any money to go somewhere for a vacation, but it's nice of you to offer it to me."

"Well, think about it. I want you to know I'm willing to help you any way I can and as far as these two who came by here, I think they might soon be in jail. The news on the investigation is generating a lot of pressure on them. I have no doubt they're trying to find out what's happening to their organization. They're so different from Ivan, their older brother. He's the only one, I think, who's really gone legitimate over the years. It's too bad his younger brother runs things behind his back."

"You seem to know a lot about what's going on. I never have really thanked you for taking care of me the last several years. You mean a lot to me and my mom."

"Thanks. Now go on home for today and we'll take care of things here. And remember; think about taking some time off."

CHAPTER 15

Not only did she take off the rest of the day on Thursday, but she only worked for half the day on Friday. Her boss insisted she go home early to prepare for the competition. To her surprise her mom showed a lot of interest in watching her dance, and Olya had promised to help her get ready. While she wanted her hair styled on top and looking professional, her thick, blonde hair would take some time to do right. She also had to work on her makeup, which was something she didn't use much, but she knew she had to use tonight. She glanced at her new dress which had the perfect Latin look to set the mood of the dance.

On Thursday, she had cried with her mom all day over the news of her papa's death. The news opened old wounds, which even after twenty-five years had never fully healed. While they, at least, had a few more answers now, they still didn't know how to explain the invitation or the new shoes that had arrived. It did feel nice to know that two things had been working out. If she went to New York she had a place to stay now, and the prospects of getting time off from work would be easy.

Olya brushed her hair as she said, "I wish I had hair like this."

"You only think so." Sveta frowned. "Come on, you know how hard my hair is to work with. I keep thinking of cutting it all off one day and wearing it short."

"Well, if you decide to cut your hair, save it for me. I'd love to have it," Olya teased. "Do you think Denis will be there tonight?"

"I asked him once, but he didn't answer me. I don't think this is exciting for him. He'd rather be out dancing in a club somewhere. After the other night, I know who he really wants to dance with."

"It could be you read too much into his dancing. Sexy is the way he likes to dance and he really gets into the music and the mode of the salsa. Remember that salsa is a very erotic and seductive dance."

"I understand, and I'm not sure, but I have this gut feeling he really enjoys the company of some girls too much."

"Have you heard from Alex since the other night?"

"Yes, he called to check on me at work, and when they told him I wasn't working he called me on my cell phone. He's a kind and gentle guy, and in fact, he's too much so and he knows it, but it's just him."

"At least you have a partner for tonight and it will be so good to see you dancing on the floor." She pouted. "I wish I was dancing in the competition, but no one asked me…"

"I'm sorry, but you're right, you would be much better than me. We should have asked if he wanted to dance with you so that he would have a much better chance of winning."

"I think Dima likes you and wants to help you a lot. He appears to have a special attachment to you because of your father. I wonder if his parents will be at the competition tonight since they're the ones who knew your father and had danced with him earlier."

"I never considered asking him, but I would love to talk to them."

After hours of work and preparation, the final product didn't look too bad. They both glanced in the mirror one last time to make sure all was perfect before they hurried to the metro to make the trip over to the studio. They entered just in time to watch the other competitors in her classification arrive. It would be so good to see what the other eight couples looked like.

Alex had already arrived since he had promised to help with some of the decorations. He hurried over them where he stopped to study Sveta. "Wow, you look beautiful tonight. You've been on my mind all day."

Sveta blushed slightly, as she felt the heat radiating. "Thank you. You also look good tonight." He had on new Latin-styled clothes, making him look slim, and in a good, firm shape for a dancer. With his black hair now cut short and stylish, he seemed to radiate with a newfound confidence. "Have you seen the competition yet?"

Alex glanced around. "Yes, some of them are here already. I think many of them are new to dancing, but it will be interesting to see them on the floor."

As she watched him grinning at her, she reached over closer to him. "I'm so sorry about the other night. I never meant to lead you on or anything. It was bad of me to dance like I did."

"Don't say a word, I loved dancing with you. It meant a lot to me to have you dance with me, and I didn't know you liked me that much. Now that I know different, I hope I can keep making you happy." He winked at her quickly before he left to help with some more decorations.

Much as she had feared; he had the wrong idea in his head. While she would have a hard time letting him down easy later, the new confidence in him might be the one thing they needed to win.

Her mom soon walked through the doorway and looked very stunning tonight. She had also fixed her hair and dressed in her best clothes. As a dancer she had developed a certain style and elegance which Sveta felt proud of.

"Mom, come here. I want you to meet some people. This is Alex and he'll be dancing with me tonight."

Alex quit working on some candles. "Hello." He smiled broadly as he had mentioned several times how much he looked forward to meeting her mom for the first time. "You have a great daughter." He glanced at Sveta.

Sveta turned to the side to avoid further connection with Alex. "And these are the dance instructors and owners of the studio," Sveta announced as Dima and Natasha came over to meet her mom.

"I've heard so much about you." Mariya said as she reached out to take Dima's hand. "I'm curious to see what you've taught my daughter."

"I hope you approve, but it isn't the same as ballet. My parents have told me so much about you. I'm glad to finally meet you."

"Are your parents going to be here tonight?"

"Unfortunately . . . they aren't." He said as he lowered the focus of his eyes.

"If you would, please tell them to call me. I would love to see them again. We have a lot to catch up on these days."

"I'll be glad to." His smile returned. "I hope you enjoy the competition tonight. Your daughter has become a very good salsa dancer in a short period of time."

The place soon looked great with many people packing the studio. Sveta knew that they would all eventually have to move off the floor to let the dancers on, which would also make standing room crowded around the edges. Many of the dancers acted excited which reflected in their fidgeting mannerism. It would soon be time to start. While Dima and Natasha stayed busy meeting people, and making introductions, Sveta realized that these people were why they offered the competition. They made contacts and obtained new students at these events.

After walking to the center of the floor together with his wife, Dima raised his hands and yelled in a loud voice for everyone to pay attention. "We need to begin, and I'm going to ask our visitors to go to the side of the floor to give our performers all the room they'll need. I'm so thrilled to have so many of you here to watch the competitions tonight. I think you'll see some great dancing."

Natasha retrieved a microphone since the noise continued to be too loud for those in the crowd to hear them without it. "Before we start, we've some special guests tonight who will give us an exhibition. They're from the international salsa club in Moscow, and they have ranked at the top of the world year after year."

A couple entered with perfect poise and a style hard to describe in mere words as they floated across the floor. As they met in the center of the floor, the music started with a lone conga player. They locked into each other and waited for the full band which soon exploded into a salsa rhythm that vibrated every corner of the studio. Their performance was awesome. Sveta drifted into a total trance as they finished, thinking how exciting it would be to dance anything close to their level one day.

As Dima introduced the various couples, they had a chance to show what they had learned. While some weren't good and simply went through the basic steps, a few performed very well and had added some special steps for the competition. These were the ones she could tell had been coached by professionals.

When their time to dance arrived, she felt Alex give her hand a small squeeze, as if to let her know all would be good. She felt uptight and nervous, but ready to do her best. She looked around the floor one more time to see who else had entered the audience. Suddenly directly across from her, she saw Denis. Her breathing stopped; she hadn't been sure if he would come or not.

Dima walked onto the floor and placed the microphone in front of his mouth. "Please welcome Sveta and Alex to the floor next. For those who don't know, Sveta is the daughter of Nickolay Panov, one of the best dancers Russia has ever produced. We're also proud to have his wife, Mariya, here tonight as well. She's also a fantastic dancer and still teaches ballet."

Sveta didn't know Dima planned to say this, but it felt nice to have her parents talked about in such a flattering way. She walked to the center of the floor with Alex and found their starting place. She suddenly thought of Denis again, and looked around to try to find him in the crowd. While she didn't see him, she assumed he was in the crowd somewhere.

The dance started as they had rehearsed many times, with the timing executed perfectly, and each movement proceeding as planned. She had to concentrate, even if she wanted to search for Denis' face on each turn. The dance almost ended when Alex suddenly varied the dance to include a few double turns. Next he let her spin directly into his arms before pulling her close to him. She knew he was trying to show the sexy side of salsa they had experimented with at the salsa club the other night, but that had been at a salsa club and this was competition. He had definitely received the wrong message the other night. When she moved away from him and executed a perfect walk-away step, as if in a comical move to add humor to the movement, the crowd loved the move and clapped. She slowly relented and spun into his arms for a fantastic close.

As they exited the floor, they received congratulations

from many people. Only two more couples remained and the results would be known thereafter. She finally had time to look around the room again, but the floor remained too crowded to see everyone.

When the last couple finished, Dima walked forward. "It will take us a few minutes to analyze the results. While we're working on the scores, we have some refreshments that we hope you'll enjoy. We'll be back in about five to ten minutes." He left the floor with his wife and several judges who followed them to his office where they could talk in private.

After someone tapped on her shoulder, she turned around to see her boss staring at her with a large grin. "You were fantastic! I never knew you could dance like that. This salsa is an exciting dance. I think you'll win."

"Thank you for coming. I doubt we'll win since I saw some good couples competing tonight, but I had fun competing. The competition gives us a reason to practice and dance better. This competition dance is a lot different from the clubs, which is where the locals seem to enjoy the music. You'll have to try it some time."

"I think I need to stick with the waltz—it's more my speed."

The judges came out of the door. The evaluations hadn't taken as long as she thought for them to make a decision. Dima and Natasha followed them to the center of the dance floor. He raised one hand, and Natasha handed him a microphone. "We think we had some fantastic dancers here tonight. It's hard to judge a competition like this, but this is what the judges have decided."

From across the room, Sveta saw Denis again, staring at her. With all her attention on him, she didn't hear anything else that Dima said. While he studied her, he made no attempt to come and join her. He had dressed in nice clothes and had combed his blond hair straight, making him look extremely charming.

Alex grabbed her hand and pointed to Dima, who motioned to them to come to the center of the floor. "What?" Sveta felt embarrassed at not listening to Dima.

"Didn't you hear? We won the competition!"

Sveta felt humiliated since she hadn't heard anything at all and quickly smiled. We won! She walked to the center of the floor as Alex raised her hand with his in a victory walk. At the center of the floor Dima offered her a big hug while Natasha hugged Alex. Minutes later Dima handed each of them a trophy for winning and everyone pushed forward to give their congratulations. Her head continued to spin as she tried to talk to all of them at once. She had won and the victory created such a great feeling, one she hadn't experienced in a long time.

After turning around, she saw Denis in front of her. She stopped breathing, unable to speak.

"Hi, you did great tonight. I'm proud of you." Denis formally reached over and kissed her hand. He acted like a gentleman, and not like the guy known to be the life of the party all the time. His behavior represented a different side of him, and only intensified the feelings she had for him. "I know you have many friends you want to see here, and I won't keep you. However, I really want to see you later tonight, if you want. I'll be at The Salsa Connection in a few hours, and I hope you'll come."

"I may be able to, but it will be a while. My mom is having a party for us tonight. You're welcome to come."

Denis looked over at Alex, and said, "I think it will be better if I see you later. Have a good time at your party." He turned and left.

Alex acted like he didn't know how to handle Denis, and how he had controlled Sveta's attention, but tonight he had won a dance contest with her.

After a little time passed and the crowd had started to thin, she knew she needed to hurry to her place and prepare for the party. Her mom had already left to get things prepared. Before she could leave, however, a deliveryman carrying a box approached her. "These are for you, but you need to sign here for them." The deliveryman handed her a pen.

After signing, he handed her a small envelope before she opened the box and saw five red roses inside. "Wow, I have roses." She quickly placed the envelope in her bag since she didn't know for sure who the flowers were from. It would definitely be best to open it later.

When Alex soon indicated that it was time for them to leave, she smiled and waved goodnight to the crowd as they left the studio. On the way home she remembered her promise to call Danny, but it would be impossible to do with Alex next to her.

He offered his arm. "I see you have roses."

"Yes, the flowers were very thoughtful." She didn't elaborate on them, but knew they probably didn't come from him. They walked in silence on the way home. She wished she could avoid having to tell him she had fun, but was dating someone else and the night they had gone out was just for practice. She could tell he had other ideas. While he kept trying to hold her hand, she would simply let his go and place her hands in her pockets.

They soon arrived at her flat, which was packed full of people her mom had invited to the celebration. The table in the kitchen had been moved to the large room, and was now full of food and drinks.

"Wow—that looks great." Sveta smiled at her mom. "I didn't know you were going to prepare all this."

"I prepared some things, but most of the food was

prepared by our guest." She moved around the table, retrieved a bottle of champagne and handed it to Alex. "Please, help me open this so we can all toast the two of you on a great victory tonight."

Alex quickly opened the bottle and started to fill the many glasses in front of him. As he finished, he raised his glass and said, "To all our friends who are here with us tonight."

All joined in with him as the night continued with many toasts which lasted for a long time. When all had left but Alex, she moved toward the door to indicate that he needed to leave also. He stopped in front of the door and waited for her as if he expected a kiss or something. Instead, she backed away and looked at him without saying a word. "I would like to go dancing with you some more. The other night was a lot of fun."

When he leaned forward as if to try again for a kiss, she backed away. "I agree that the dancing was good, but it was only for practicing. You know I'm seeing someone else, I'm sure."

"Yes, I know, but he isn't dating you exclusively." He paused, as he tried to make a stronger eye contact. "I thought we had a good time. Think about it, and I'll call you later, okay?"

"I will and thanks for everything. You're a really nice guy."

He edged out the door with his head lowered. He apparently knew he wouldn't be seeing her again.

With the door shut, she went over to the couch, and collapsed for a minute. While she felt exhausted, she remembered the envelope in her bag and retrieved it. She studied a simple message which read, "Congratulations on your competition. I hope to see my little lady at the next competition." It wasn't signed.

"Mom!" She yelled. "You better take a look at this."

As her mom quickly attempted to read it, they both knew the note offered a follow-up to the letter from America. "It looks like we've received another sign that he's alive," Mariya whispered with tears in her eyes.

Sveta had more questions as she began to shake. How did he know that she was dancing in a competition? Also, what if someone else had seen the note? Still, she had more information to give her mom. "Mom, I haven't told you yet, but I may have a way to go to America."

"How?"

"The American guy I've been chatting with told me he would love for me to visit him. He said he would pay all the expenses, and that I can stay with him."

"How well do you know him?"

"We've only chatted on the internet, but he seems nice and friendly. He wants me to call him collect to let him know how I did tonight. I'm going to call from a pay phone—this way he won't have my number, and I will feel safer. What do you think?"

"I think you need to be careful, especially since men on the internet generally can't be trusted. I don't believe in it."

"I understand, but I have many friends who chat all the time online and have made great friends. Some have even discovered their husbands there."

"I'll go hide this note with the others at the garden tomorrow. You know it won't be long until we have to close the garden for the winter time."

"I understand, and I'll try to help, but the evening is getting late, and I need to make it to the club to meet Denis before the time gets too much later. I'm going to stop and call Danny on the way, however, since I promised him I would."

Her mom glanced at her as she left. She appeared to understand how Sveta had a mind of her own and would do things in her own best way. "Please be careful, Sveta."

CHAPTER 16

At the metro stop, Sveta saw a store with a pay phone on the wall. She walked in, and looked around, but saw very few people inside. After taking this as a good sign, she opened her purse, located the phone number, and started to follow the instructions she had been given. Since calling collect was something new for her, she hoped the instructions Danny gave her would work.

As an operator answered the phone and she started to put the call through, her heart raced. She knew her English wasn't too good, but she wanted to make a good impression.

Finally, he answered the phone in a sleepy sounding voice. Apparently, he was still sleeping, but when he heard the operator talking to him and that the call was coming from Russia, he started talking much faster to the operator. Sveta wasn't sure exactly what they said until he finally paused and said, "Hello."

She replied immediately, "Hello, this is Sveta from Russia!"

"Wow—you called me! I wasn't sure whether you would or not. I've been waiting for you all night."

"I see. My mom had party for me, and I just now had time to locate a phone. Are you sure it's okay for me to call you like this?"

"Yes, I wanted to hear your voice. I love your accent."

She hoped he was telling the truth, and not just telling her that she spoke badly. "Thanks—you sound good also."

"How did you do in the competition?"

"We did great! We won a trophy for first place." She continued to feel nervous.

"Wow, that's fantastic. I'm so happy for you."

"Did I wake you this morning? If you want me to, I call back later."

"No, I want to talk to you. I've been thinking of you calling me all night."

"My English isn't so good. Is this call expensive for you?"

"The call isn't cheap, but it's okay. I can cover the cost."

"I think I'll be lost in your city. Do you speak any Russian?"

"I've learned a few words, but it would be embarrassing for me to try. You wouldn't be lost in New York. I would love to show you around."

"I know this is expensive, but I wanted to hear your voice and let you know . . . I won tonight!"

"Thank you for calling me. I would still love to call you and talk to you longer. If you give me your number, I can call you on my phone. I have special rates I can use."

Sveta listened intensely, but didn't understand everything he said. His accent was hard to follow, and he talked too fast for her to translate in her head. "Can you repeat what you said, and say a little slower for me?"

"I said that I want to call you again later, and I would like to have a number where I can call you."

Sveta understood some of his English. Her palms sweated, as she became more nervous, and her stomach fluttered. "I will think about coming to America. I am still not so sure about everything."

"I understand—I want to talk to you some more."

"My English isn't so good. I love chatting with you on the computer. On it I have good dictionary I use."

"I know, but please think about my offer."

"I will. And I think of your present to come to America. Such a trip is scary for me. I have many things I need to do to come."

"I understand. Anything I can do, you know to ask me."

"It is going to be expensive. Are you sure?" Her heart continued to race.

"Don't worry about the money. I make good tips at the restaurant where I work, and I think I have a part in a play which will pay me some good money."

She breathed easier. "I let you know. I love hearing your voice. Thank you for talking with me."

"You're welcome. I look forward to talking to you again."

"Goodbye for now." She waited for a response, but received none.

Sveta replaced the phone, ending the call. The conversation had drained her. She hadn't realized how bad her English was. She would have to check on getting some English lessons quickly, and especially now that she had someone to talk with. She hurried outside, and felt like no one had overheard her conversation. She knew she was getting into something she had no knowledge of how to handle. She had to be careful.

The metro wasn't crowded, and she was able to quickly find a seat. She hoped she would find Denis when she arrived at the club, but the night was already getting late. She had been so glad to see him for a minute at the competition, and was now wondering why he had decided to come. He had dressed in a casual suit and a white business shirt, and not in the usual Latin clothes he wore most of the time when he went dancing.

The walk from the metro to the club felt good for her,

and she now wished she had invited Olya to join her tonight. The comfort of her old friend would have been good, but again, she wanted to concentrate on Denis tonight. She wanted to know what he had really thought of her dancing in the contest.

When she arrived at the door, she had to pay to get in. While it wasn't much, every ruble was precious to her right now. With so many people packing the inside of the club getting to the dance floor took some time because of having to work her way around the people in front of her. With the musicians playing very loud, she couldn't hear much of the conversations around her. As she reached the floor, she noticed even a larger crowd and assumed it would take some time to find him. However, when she started around the floor, she saw him standing next to the bar, talking with some of his friends. He immediately waved at her when she moved closer. "How are you?" he yelled over the music.

"I'm great. Thank you so much for coming tonight. That meant a lot to me."

"I'm so glad you won, and I'm proud of you. You did great tonight." He leaned over and kissed her cheek.

"We didn't do much. The competition was for novices, and it was the only reason we won. I enjoy dancing in it very much."

Denis glanced around. "Where's the guy you danced with?"

"He isn't here. I came on my own since you said you wanted to dance with me tonight."

"Yes, I do." With a big smile on his face he led her to the dance floor where they danced for a long time. She enjoyed Denis intensely staring at her and giving her his full attention. He didn't stop to dance with others. His complete interest transformed into everything she could have dreamed for and a fantastic ending to a perfect day. She wanted the night to last forever, but the dancing exhausted her and they finally had to rest for a minute.

After he ordered a drink for both of them, they finished the margaritas quickly. "Would you like to go for a walk?" He smiled, flashing his boyish charms.

"Yes, that would be great."

She walked out of the club where the cool late night air felt crisp and clean. The fall air reminded her of how much she loved this season. As he held her hand they strolled down to the Neva River where she saw a crowd of people milling around, but no one looking to be in any hurry to get anywhere.

After a long silence, she finally decided to start a conversation. "When I came to the salsa club for the first time, I thought it would be great to have a quick look." Sveta paused for a minute to think. "It's remarkable how the dancing has become so addictive. The salsa is on my mind all of the time now." The new experiences had added much to her life over the last several months. She kept holding his hand, and just knowing that he wanted to be with her presented her with emotions that she felt totally unprepared for.

Finally, Denis stopped and turned her to him so that he could look directly at her while he talked. "I saw you dancing with Alex, and have been thinking about you a lot the last few days. You've become much better at dancing, and soon many guys will be asking you to go dancing with them now."

Smiling at him, in a teasing way, Sveta asked, "Are you getting jealous?"

Blushing slightly at her reading his thoughts, he added, "I enjoy being with you so much. Seeing you dance with someone else did have an effect on me."

"But I see you dancing with other girls all the time."

"Yes, I have many friends who dance and I will always dance with them. I hope we can learn to dance much better. Maybe we can enter a contest in the future together."

"I think if you entered a real contest, you'd want someone much better than me."

"We'll see how things go in the future. I've been on my own for a long time, and I'm not sure if I can see just one girl, but you know I like you, and—"

"I understand." She lifted a finger to her lips to whisper. "I won't put pressure on you to do something you're not ready to do." The last thing she wanted was for him to become spooked and run.

"Thanks, you're nice to be with. I want to keep seeing you, and I'm looking forward to tomorrow night."

"I am also."

He shifted uneasily, as they walked. "In a few weeks I'm going to enter a contest held at another club. I've already arranged to go with someone else, but sine I made this date before I met you—I hope you understand."

Now she started to understand why he wanted to be gentle and slow with her. The news was something he had to tell her, and he knew the method of delivery would be hard to do. "Who are you dancing with?"

"I think you've seen her before. She's a waitress I dance with some at the Salsa Connection."

She remembered her, and how she had wrapped herself around him on several occasions. "I've seen you dance with her before. She's a good dancer. You should do well in the competition." Her heart beat fast, as she wondered what the real story was behind their relationship. Was he sleeping with her? Her heart sunk, but she didn't want him to know how bad she felt. She had been hurt before, and she could see another new disappointing love affair happening to her again. Perhaps this was a way of reminding her why she had never married. Every time she had become scared in the past, she had run.

He squeezed her hand tighter. "I don't wish to upset you. You're a very sweet girl."

"I'll be fine." Thinking fast, she added, "I also have a chance to learn to dance better."

"How is that?" He glanced at her.

"I've been chatting online with someone from America who's a great dancer, and he's invited me to come to New York to learn. He's a friend I made online. I don't know if I'll go or not."

With a funny look on his face, he added, "I think meeting someone online can be dangerous. How much do you know about this guy?"

"I've chatted with him for a while, and that's about all I know. He's crazy about salsa dancing. That's how I met him online. I found him in salsa chat forum where he seemed to be nice. I don't know why I mentioned this to you, but the idea of going to America is exciting for me. He said he would pay for everything, which is nice of him."

Denis shook his head. "I can't tell you what to do, but I hope we're good enough friends you'll let me know if you really decide to go."

"Of course, I'll let you know. I've always wanted to go to where my father died and place flowers in his honor, if I can." She had a hard time reading his reaction. He acted disturbed in some respects, she thought, but he appeared happy for her also. She felt confused and didn't know why she told him this since she hadn't totally decided if she would go or not.

"We should go back to the club and dance some more.

I feel much better after getting some fresh air." He acted troubled, and as if he wanted to change the topic. He held her hand and said nothing as they went back inside the club. They danced for a while and had a few more drinks. An hour later she saw the waitress, his dance partner, walking into the club, and knowing that this girl would be dancing with Denis in a contest felt more disturbing than ever.

While looking over at Denis, she noticed he had seen his dance partner also, even if he tried to act like he hadn't seen her. Maybe it was because of all the drinks she had consumed, but Sveta didn't want to see her talking to Denis later, so she leaned over and whispered to him, "I think it's late, and I need to go home."

He looked over at her for a minute before he said, "I know you must be tired. I'll see you tomorrow night." He reached over, kissed her on the lips, and escorted her to the door. She had hoped he would offer to see her home, but he didn't offer. Yes, like it or not, she knew he wanted to dance with her after she left.

CHAPTER 17

It had been a long night full of tossing and turning. Her head felt sluggish, and every move she made was in slow motion. As she walked to her office, she constantly considered her options. While her Papa had given her no more clues on how to travel to America, she did have this one option available with Danny. She wondered how her Papa knew she had won the competition so quickly. Did he have contacts in Russia? She had so many unanswered questions.

After arriving at the gallery she saw no one inside and the showroom looked quiet, as it usually did for a Saturday morning. It would be so good to see Danny online. As the excitement quickly intensified, she tried to decide how to tell him that she was going to accept his offer. She felt lucky when she connected to the internet and saw him in the private chat room. She entered the room, and quickly typed, "Hello."

Again, he seemed to not be next to the computer, but in less than ten minutes he answered. "Hello, how are you?"

"I am fine, thank you for asking. And how are you?"

"I'm at home, and working on some lines for a part I'm trying to obtain. It's a small part, but you never know where one small part might lead. How was your night of dancing?"

"It was a good night, but I had so much on my mind I didn't sleep much. I been thinking of your offer, and traveling to America is exciting to me."

"That's great! So . . . you're coming?"

"I am thinking about your offer, but I need to obtain many answers first. I don't know everything about getting a visa, and I need to get more information about you."

"I understand. I'm like an open book. What can I tell you?"

For the next hour she asked him one question after another which he answered for her. Finally, he asked her a question, "What made you decide to accept my offer?"

This question she had known he would ask at some point. "I think such a trip would be exciting and no one has ever offered me such a present before. I would love to learn to dance salsa better and I think you must be a good dancer."

"I see. And do you have any other reason for wanting to come?"

She thought about his question slowly before she replied. "I have a few more facts you should know. As I told you, my father was killed in New York City and I would love to visit the place where he died to place flowers, or if I have to, I can just toss them over the side of the bridge. I would love to give some kind of closure to his death."

"I understand. If it can be done, we'll find a way."

"There is one more thing." She tightened every muscle in her body before she continued. "Since I won a contest here, I would love to dance in another competition. Do you know of any where you live?"

"Yes, they have many here all the time. I'll be glad to check on them, if you're interested."

"I do have one last question. Are you sure this isn't going to be a hardship on you by paying for all of this? I know the trip will be expensive."

"It is expensive, but I'll be happy to pay for everything so don't worry about the cost. To get started, I know you'll need money for the visa and clothes to wear on the trip, etc. Since I don't know how far money stretches in Russia you'll have to let me know."

"I don't know exactly either. Do you want me to obtain some amounts for you?"

"Yes. I can send you money by Western Union. Do you know how their system works?"

"I have heard about Western Union for sure, but have never had a reason to use it."

"I'm going to send you some money to get things started. The instructions will be in an e-mail. Let me know when you receive it and the money."

"I have not told you I was definitely coming. Let me think about the trip a few more days."

"You're too late since I just sent you the money. You'll see it in your e-mail. Call me when you've obtained the money."

"What do you mean, you sent the money?"

"I sent it online—the process is easy."

Her heart beat faster than she could ever remember. He had sent her money! "I will check my e-mail in a minute, but I still do not know how long it will take to get everything completed. From what I know, I think that maybe it will take about six weeks to obtain a visa. If this is true, it will be either middle or late November before I can arrive."

"I see. How long can you stay?"

"I am not sure. I will have to talk to my boss and see how much time I can take. I think the visa is only good for ninety days."

"I will start getting information on flights, etc., and I will find out what I can. I am sure I can find a travel agency we can use."

"I will do some research here also. I cannot believe I

am doing this."

"If you're going to be here around Christmas, I know of one competition I've recently heard about that is for salsa and being promoted heavily. Many of the clubs are sponsoring the competition. You have to win at one of them to be invited to the final cut, and from this win to be invited to the grand finals. It will be good to see how we do in it. We can keep entering the local contests until we win one. I'm excited about attempting the competition."

This sounded like music to her ears. This had to be the one she had been told to enter by her father. She felt like telling Danny the whole story, but knew it was best to save the details for later. She still didn't know how much of her chatting the police might be intercepting. She hoped the communications remained clear, but in Russia she never knew for sure. "That sounds fantastic! Can you send me some information on the competition?"

"Yes, let me do it tomorrow. The time is late here, and I need to get some sleep. I hope to hear from you again tomorrow morning. I'll be up late, waiting for you."

"Thanks—and goodnight to you."

"And sweet dreams to you as well."

CHAPTER 18

As Sveta worked on her visa, the month of October quickly passed. She only needed to have her interview and all would be in order. The more she worried about what they would ask, the more nervous she became. What if they suspected me of trying to reach my papa? She knew the government had a large interest in this, as well as the Lisin family. It felt strange just thinking of about how these events had developed. As she drifted around the gallery, she had a hard time focusing on working. The traffic was good for this time of year and it would be so good to make some extra money for her trip.

Her boss soon found her, as he asked, "Are you nervous about the interview tomorrow?"

"I am a little bit. What do you think they'll ask me?"

"I'm not sure, but I'm sure they have records of your father, and they may ask you many questions. However, the process may be simple. I have no way of knowing. Are you sure you want to go? America is a long way to go to simply dance." He acted more like a concerned dad, than a boss.

"Yes. I'm nervous, but this trip is a chance of a lifetime. I'm still amazed that someone is willing to pay for my trip. He's so nice on the internet that I'm looking forward to meeting him."

"I hope the visa works out for you." He paused. "Have you seen Denis lately?"

"We still go dancing some, and I don't think he knows how to handle this trip of mine. While he constantly asks me about the trip and about this guy in America, he's also still dating the other girl he likes. Since the tension is driving me crazy, I think it might be best if I don't see him anymore."

"It's up to you, but I know you enjoy dancing. We have everything all taken care of when you're gone. If we can do anything else for you while you're away, please let me know."

"I don't know how to thank you for this. You've been like a father for me all these years." She had to fight tears from forming.

"Your father was a very good friend. I think I owe him this much." His sincere expressions quickly turned to a large smile. "By the way, the new painting is due to come in from Italy for Yuri Zotov and I've heard this painting is extremely impressive. The commission on this sale will be large, but as you requested, I'll give the money to your mom."

"Thank you so much since she'll need the money. I hope the painting arrives before I leave. His work is so fantastic." She loved his work, and would hate to never be able to see it.

"I . . . haven't told Yuri Zotov you're leaving and I think it would be best if he doesn't know. However, with his contacts, I'll be surprised if he doesn't know."

"Has he said anything to you about me since the day, you know, when we had the visit from the Lisin brothers?"

"No, but I think he made a few calls in regard to their visit, and I don't think they'll be back here any time soon. That's one part of your life you need to get behind you. I know you want to throw flowers off the bridge to honor Nickolay and I do think that doing so will help you finally give your respects to your father." He paused. "Let me know how the interview goes."

"I will, and if they grant the visa, I'll leave as soon as I can." She thought of the new painting as she walked back to her office. It would be so good to see this painting, but she knew the masterpiece might come in after she left.

CHAPTER 19

While the next morning arrived as usual for Sveta, this morning it was Olya who pulled at her to wake her from her dreams. Olya had agreed to spend the night and go with her to the embassy to have her interview. Sveta knew she could not go in with her, but she could be close by to help her if they turned her down.

"Come on, we need to get moving. You have to look great this morning and I know how long it takes to do your hair. Believe me, I wouldn't complain if I had hair as thick as yours, but let's get to it."

"We have plenty of time." Sveta started to plead. "What time is it?"

"Time to get started." Olya yanked the covers off Sveta.

When the cool air grabbed Sveta's attention as she lay half-naked, she quickly rushed to cover herself and walk to the bathroom. "I cannot believe it's so late. I think I need more sleep."

"Both of us do, and especially after drinking wine last night. It felt great to discuss so many things and believe me . . . I'm going to miss you when you're gone."

"I won't be gone too long."

"You never know . . . you might fall for this guy and never come back." She pouted.

"We're just friends, and he promised to be on good behavior. I believe him since he's never made any kind of disrespectful comment to me, or acted badly in any way."

Sveta's mom, who had been cooking in the kitchen,

suddenly entered the conversation. "You know my thoughts about Americans, and how I don't believe them. I've heard many stories of how girls have been lured over to America, only to become servants of the men there."

"Mom, you don't know that to be true. I hoped you would love me to see the United States. This trip will do a lot to increase my horizons, and as my boss said, the trip could be good for business by giving me more knowledge of the Americans who come to the gallery to buy things. He's been nice to me in all of this."

"I know he has. Anyway, I know you've already made your decision to go, and this Danny has already sent you a lot of money for this trip. I just want you to think about everything carefully and be smart in your actions."

"I am, Mom, don't worry." The trip to the embassy wouldn't take long, but they had to hurry to finish getting ready. Smiling at her mom, she reiterated, "Don't worry, all is going good. I'll be careful."

"I know you will, but please call me as often as you can while you're gone."

"You know I will. We'll be back as soon as we've finished the interview."

As they left the flat, Sveta felt so glad to have her friend with her. She hated to admit how much she had worried about this interview since the questions could be hard on her. "Thanks for coming with me. You've always been such a good friend."

"I wouldn't have it any other way. Just keep your eyes out for some good-looking friends of this guy you're going to see. I've heard my work will sell much better in New York than it does here."

After arriving at the embassy, they hugged each other as Olya looked over Sveta for one last time to make sure all looked good. "Take it easy—you'll do great."

"Thanks." Sveta said, as she turned to go inside.

A guard met her almost immediately at the front gate where she handed him some papers. He read them, and directed her to the next room, where the process started. She had to check in her purse to make sure she had all of the papers she would need. She went to a waiting room to wait for her name to be posted. Several hours later she saw her name on the screen. After she went to the proper window, and waited, an older man slowly looked over her papers.

Finally, on the other side of the window, he spoke slowly. "I see your name is Svetlana Nickoaevna Panova. I have a few questions for you, but first, how good is your English?"

"I speak some English, but not too fluent." She considered speaking in English, but waited to see if he would ask her anything in English. The thought of such made her more nervous.

"What is the reason you're going to the United States?"

"I have several reasons. First, I met a guy who invited me to come and see him. He is paying for the trip for me. I have learned how to Latin dance and I understand that he is a fantastic dancer. We're going to practice and enter a dance contest in New York."

"Do you have an invitation from him?"

"Yes, I included a copy in the application—if not, I have another copy."

Searching through the papers, he located the invitation and studied the words for a minute. "It says his name is Danny Martinez, is this correct?"

"Yes, that's his name."

"How did you meet?"

"In doing research on salsa dancing, I went to a forum on the internet and saw his name where we started chatting. We now chat every day, or talk by phone."

"The visa you're applying for isn't a fiancé visa. Are you planning on getting married?"

"We've never discussed marriage. We're just friends who love to dance."

"From the invitation, he states you'll be staying with him. I need to let you know you cannot convert the visa to a K1 after you arrive in America. The visa you applied for is good for three months. You do plan on coming back to Russia, I assume?"

"Yes, I have a job to come back to."

"What kind of work do you do?"

"I work at an art gallery."

He went through some more papers and raised his eyebrows several times, as if in deep thought. "Excuse me for a minute." He reached for his phone.

She could not hear what all he discussed on the phone, but he acted agitated and full of questions for someone. When he turned back to her, he paused before speaking. "I just saw a letter in your file which should have been at the front. A Senator Knighton has sent a letter on your behalf and you're being treated as a friend of the state. You should have been approved weeks ago. I think your friend has great connections. Please . . . enjoy your trip to America." He handed her some papers, and directed her to the window where she had to pay 3,000 rubles for her visa.

The girl at the window received her money and told her that the visa would be sent out by pony express and she should have it in a few days. Smiling broadly, she accepted the receipt for the money and headed for the front door to retrieve her purse. While this had been much easier than she had thought, she wondered whom the little man had called when he saw the letter from the Senator.

After exiting the front door, she saw Olya standing to one side, waiting for her. She looked upset at first, but burst into laughter when Sveta approached her.

"I obtained the visa!" Sveta tossed her hands above her, as she yelled. The two girls danced up and down. This was a dream come true for Sveta. It looked like everything was going great.

Olya stopped and pointed down the street where Sveta saw a man walking away. "That guy had stopped and talked to me while you were inside. He knew I would be here and asked questions about you."

"Who is he?"

"He never told me his name, but he looked like someone you just don't want to mess with. I'm still shaking from talking with him."

"Why, what did he ask you?"

"He wanted to know why you were going to America. I told him your trip was none of his business, but he told me it was his business and not to play with him. He acted serious."

"What did you tell him?"

"I told him you were going to see a friend. He wanted to know whom and I told him I didn't know the name. After he received a phone call, he told me he would see me later and walked off."

"I wonder if he is one of the men who works for Lisin. They came to the gallery a while back, but it's my understanding they're not to do that again. I'll let my boss know, and he'll take care of the situation."

"I hope so. He gave me the creeps." Looking over at Sveta, she changed her attitude again, and screamed, "I cannot believe it—you're going to America!"

CHAPTER 20

The next few days disappeared quickly as she started packing and making final arrangements. Her mom had become much more quiet and reserved as the time for her to leave approached. Sveta was her only daughter and she depended on her very much.

"I understand you'll be seeing Denis tonight, and I was wondering what you're planning on telling him?" her mom asked as she remained busy getting the kitchen cleaned for the big party the next night.

"I'm not sure how things will go tonight. He's been so quiet lately. I think it has been only in the last few days he really believed I'm going to America."

"Just remember only a few men exist like him who have not been married before. He has a good job and he could be a good husband for you."

"I'm not so sure of that. He has his good points, but many bad ones as well. He's a ladies' man, and he may never change his ways. He likes to go out all night and be with his friends, and . . . drink, as you know."

"Most men do. Perhaps he'll still be waiting for you when you return."

"I hope so, in a way. If the trip is meant to be, it will be. No one, and especially me, knows what their life will be like in the future."

"I know, but I'm still concerned about this American guy you're staying with. If anything happens to you while you're gone, I'll never forgive myself for letting you go."

"I'll be fine, Mom. While I've never met him, I feel

like I know him well since we've spent so much time chatting and talking on the phone. I think that we know each other's thoughts, and it's as if we've been friends for a long time."

"I hope you're right. You always were one to do things in your own way, and I trust you."

"Thanks for being so understanding and supportive. I'm not sure where all of this will lead. It's so scary but exciting, just thinking about the next few weeks."

"I know it is. I have to leave to go back to the school for a private lesson I promised one girl tonight. She wants to be accepted in a school in Moscow, and she's working so hard to make a good impression next month. I'll be home in a little while. Please don't stay out too long since tomorrow will be a long day with the party and all the preparations that we have to do."

"We're going out for a short time, and mainly to walk and talk for a while. He won't be here tomorrow night, and this will be the last time I'll see him before I leave."

"I understand, and I'll be thinking of you tonight."

After she offered her daughter a big hug and walked out the door, Sveta went to work on her hair. The style had to look good tonight and she wanted to try some new makeup she had purchased. She planned to wear some of her new clothes she had purchased with the money Danny had sent her for the trip. He had been very generous with his money and so supportive of her decision to come to America that she truly felt excited about meeting him.

As she finished, she heard the knock on the door which had to be Denis. Nervously, she walked to the door and opened it for him. He glanced around like a big kid before he offered her some roses. They looked beautiful and they were definitely something she hadn't expected from him.

"Wow . . . you bought flowers for me! You shouldn't

have spent such money."

"I hoped it would be something for you to remember until you return. I hope you like them."

"They're great! Let me place them in some water so they'll stay fresh. Please come on in, the weather is starting to turn cold outside."

He obeyed her and entered the foyer of the flat where he quickly removed his shoes and placed them on the floor behind the door and then removed his coat, placing it on a hanger.

Sveta motioned to some house shoes. "You can use these while you're here, if you wish."

"Thanks." He smiled as he glanced over his shoulder.

Sveta worked on arranging the flowers as he entered the kitchen. The room appeared in perfect order while looking comfortable and functional. The table in the kitchen, where Sveta and her mom spent most of their time, didn't have much extra room for items like flowers, but she made the necessary space for them.

"Have a seat." She slid into one herself, as she waited for him to comply. "How do you like our little place? We've been here for a long time."

"I like your flat very much. I can tell you and your mom have added your special touches to it." Lifting a bag he had with him, he added, "I also thought it would be good to celebrate a little tonight, and I hoped you might like this." He removed a large bottle of champagne from the bag.

"That's extremely thoughtful of you. I love receiving flowers and champagne as presents." She was going to miss him.

After he opened the bottle, he waited for her to find some champagne glasses. The champagne was cold, and the bubbles fizzed and sizzled as he poured each of them a glass. "What shall we drink to?" Sveta asked as she received the glass from him.

"Since I know this is the last time I'll see you before you leave, I think we should drink to us and to your trip. I know we've only dated for a short time, and I'm not one to settle down with any one girl, but you've made me do some thinking. While you're gone, I'm sure I'll do much more thinking."

While smiling at him before winking, she responded in a mood matching his. "I'm sure as soon as I leave, you'll be out on the town every night with a different girl."

"Going out at night may be the only way I can keep my mind off you all the time."

"And what makes you think you'll be thinking of me all the time, and not other girls?"

"I can see you're not going to make this easy on me." He offered a big beautiful smile. "Yes, you're growing on me, and these feelings are something I'm not used to. After all, you're leaving for America in two days to meet some guy. I still don't know how to take you going to see someone else."

"He's a friend. In many ways, he's like you. He loves to dance all the time."

"Like me. Now that's a comforting thought." His voice deepened in a cynical fashion.

She lifted her glass, and waited for him. "For tonight, let's enjoy each other and not wait for the future. It will be here soon enough."

He lifted his glass and accepted the toast. "Agreed."

"I'll be back here before you know it."

He poured another glass for each of them. "Let's go have a seat on the couch and relax since it's not often that we're alone. How long will it be before your mom returns?"

"She's working with a student tonight, and it may be several hours. I'm not sure how long she'll be gone, to tell the truth."

As they reached the couch, he offered another toast. "To a guardian angel that goes with you to protect you, and makes you happy on your trip."

Smiles beamed across her face as she enjoyed having him say good things about her trip. She was also happy that he didn't press her too much about this other guy. As they finished another drink, Sveta could feel the effect of the champagne in her system. The drink did feel good and warm which helped her to relax even more. She felt herself slide in closer to him and his muscular body. He felt comfortable with the connection feeling so natural.

He raised his arm and pulled it over her head to finally rest on her shoulder. Once in place, he pulled her closer to him. The warmth of his body felt great on a night which was turning colder and colder outside.

Moments later his weight shifted as he turned toward her and stared directly into her eyes. After his focus penetrated deep into her eyes, he redirected his stare slowly down her face and came to rest on her mouth and lips. "You have a great smile."

Sveta knew he wanted to kiss her, but he still hesitated, and as if he wanted her to agonize over what was going on in his mind. She closed her eyes and waited for him as she could now feel the breath of air he exhaled only inches from her lips.

She had wanted his love and affection for a long time, but he had amazed her on many occasions by keeping things under control. The idea of him making love to her and leaving her to make new conquests had given her the strength she had needed to resist him before, but would those doubts be enough to keep her under control tonight?

She wasn't sure.

The warmth of his lips touching her own sent sparks of energy throughout her body. With the moist and fleshy feel of his lips melting her layers of resistance away quickly she wanted more, and she wanted him now. Opening her mouth for him to use his tongue to explore the inside excited him she could tell, as his breathing intensified rapidly.

After enjoying the feelings and the effects of the champagne she almost didn't notice his hand working along her leg and finding the inside of her thigh. His strong hands felt muscular and provided a good massage as he worked his hand higher and higher. With one decisive move, he had his hand on her crotch where he explored her through her pants as best he could. She knew she was getting wet as spasms of excitement riveted through her body.

Since making out with this guy felt fantastic, she must be crazy to think of leaving him and going to America on some kind of crazy dream. "That feels so good," she moaned as he let her up for air for a minute.

"You feel so good to me also." He continued to play with her as he kissed her cheek and neck. His hand moved to her side where he went to work on her button and zipper. She attempted to use her hand to stop him, but he moved too fast for her. Perhaps the champagne slowed her down, but he had her unzipped in a flash. This excited him, she knew, as he wasted little time in exploring her bare sensitive skin.

"Denis, Mom will be home soon."

"I remember you said she'd be gone for a while."

"To tell the truth, I'm not sure how long she'll be gone."

"Okay, let's go to my place. I don't live too far from

here."

"If we go to your flat, you'll try to force me to have sex with you, and you know I'm still a virgin. Yes, a twenty-eight-year-old virgin, but you know I told you this many weeks ago, and you promised to be gentle and slow with me. I want to be sure you're the one who'll want to be my husband later. I don't want to be your trophy."

"I understand, and I'm trying." He paused for a second. "It's just that you're leaving soon, and I want so much to make sure we have something special before you leave." After he shifted away from her slightly she knew he had become upset, to say the least. While his attention had felt so good a few minutes ago it now felt like air had been let out of a balloon.

"Come here, I really enjoy you kissing me." She felt confused, but otherwise comfortable, thanks to the effects of the wine.

Slowly, he returned to her and kissed her again. With the kissing quickly intensifying, as well as the heat which returned to her body, his hand soon worked under her unzipped pants and found its way to the front. She wanted to stop him, but she also hoped that maybe a little something would satisfy him and keep him happy.

"You feel good." He whispered as his hand explored her lower stomach. When he slid his hand down to her panty line, and inched his fingers under the lacy front, she felt her body tighten as he worked his fingers through her pubic hair and then drifted even lower.

"You have great hands," she whispered as she felt him explore her.

"I want you." He intensified his kisses.

"I know. Perhaps one day when I return."

"Why not now?"

"You know. I'm not ready yet. I want the first night to

be special."

He removed his hand from inside her pants and sat still for a second. Reaching for the bottle, he poured another drink for them. "You know this is frustrating for me," he muttered slowly.

"I know it must be and I'm so sorry if I gave you the wrong impression. I do like you and I most definitely want you."

"I see." He handed her a glass and lifted his again. "To one long night ahead of us."

"What do you mean by that?" she asked.

"It means I'll keep trying until you give in, even if it takes all night." He lifted his glass and finished the whole drink in one swallow.

Sveta didn't know what to do or say. She didn't want to lose him, but was also so scared of what could happen as she lifted her glass and emptied the remaining champagne. Maybe her mom had assumed right; her destiny was to be an old maid. But then again . . . her destiny could be changed so easily tonight. She slowly glanced over at Denis and finalized her decision.

CHAPTER 21

The phone startled Sveta out of a deep sleep. Thankfully her mom moved fast to answer the incoming call. Since she knew she would receive very little sleep the next night she needed to get as much as she could now. As she slowly focused, she watched her mom listening to the person on the line with deep concentration, indicating just how important it must be. "Hold on a minute and I'll tell her."

"What is it?"

"Gleb is on the phone, and he insists that it's very important for you to come to the gallery this morning. He says the meeting won't take long, but it was very important."

"It will take me a few minutes to get ready." She hurried out of the bed. "Ask him what's going on."

"He said someone is at the gallery who needs to talk to you."

"Who is it?"

"Yuri wants to see you before you leave."

Fear quickly flooded her with a million thoughts of what this could be about, but she knew better than to ask her boss over the phone why he wanted her to come to the office. "Tell him I'll come as fast as I can, but I won't have time to prepare my hair or put on makeup."

Her mom turned to the phone and started explaining as Sveta rushed to the bathroom to get ready. She would work on her hair much later to have it look good for her party tonight, but this morning she would have to tie it in a knot behind her head.

Her mom waited for her when she came out of the room. "What do you think he wants with you?"

"I don't know. He's my largest client, and I've only met him one time before. I think he must have heard about my trip. You don't think he could cause me problems tomorrow, do you?"

"I hope not. If he were going to do that, I think he would have someone else do his dirty work for him. He's a powerful man, and for some reason he wants to meet you at the gallery. Do you want me to go with you?"

"No, I need to handle this on my own. I'll be back soon. We've a lot of work preparing things for the party tonight." She quickly left the flat and headed for the gallery.

###

Sveta soon discovered the door to the gallery unlocked when she arrived and with the lights on she could see the men walking around the far side of the gallery. "Hello," she yelled at them.

"Hello. We've been waiting for you. How are you?" Her boss flashed a smile which signaled to her that things wouldn't be bad.

"I'm fine and thank you for asking." After looking over at Yuri, she flashed a small, but inquisitive smile. "It's good to see you on such an early morning here at the gallery."

"You remember who I am?" he asked as he approached her.

"Yes, it's hard to forget my best client. I think it's a shame we haven't seen each other more often. We have many great articles in the gallery here."

"Yes, you have an impressive store you work in, and I have always appreciated the work you've put into obtaining the master paintings from Italy for me. Perhaps one day you can come to see them, and the special lighting that I've installed to highlight their remarkable quality."

"I would love to very much." She smiled, knowing a big blush registered on her face and neck.

"However, today I've come to talk to you about something I only heard about last night." Yuri's facials expressions turned serious. "I understand that you're going to America to enter a dance competition."

Since he already knew this much, she could only nod her head in acknowledgement, while her heart beat fast with all the anxiety. "I'm looking forward to the trip. It's something I wouldn't have guessed would ever happen to me. The situation presented itself to me, and is a once-in-a-lifetime trip."

He glanced around before he continued. "I did some fast checking last night, and after much thought . . . I have decided to tell you some things I think you'd like to know."

"I hoped you might have some answers to some questions I've had all my life, but I assumed it would be wrong to ask you."

"You're right in your assumptions, so remember that the things I'm going to tell you are strictly off the record, and you're not to repeat them to anyone. Is that understood?"

"Yes, I understand."

After looking over at her boss, he said, "I think we need to be alone for a minute. Perhaps she can show me something in the gallery as we walk and talk. I need you to be sure no one enters the gallery as we discuss this."

"Agreed." Gleb walked to the front door to lock it.

"First, let me say . . . it's intriguing that you're going to America to dance in a dance competition, like your father did."

"Well, he was dancing in a ballet competition, and I'm simply going to salsa dance. I don't think my chances of winning are that good since I've only been learning to dance salsa for less than half a year."

"Yes, but I've heard you're talented. Your father was also a great dancer. In fact, I was the one who helped recruit him and encourage him to enter that competition. He was to make Russia proud in the United States."

Sveta found it hard to even swallow. "Many people have told me he was good at dancing."

"If I'd known you were going to America to compete, I would have been glad to see you had proper lessons and training. You'll still be representing Russia, and I'd like to see you do well."

"That's kind of you. I started dancing because a friend of mine dragged me to a club one night. After dancing a few times I fell in love with salsa and have been going out to dance often ever since. I guess one thing led to another and the next thing I know—I'm going to America!"

"I did a fast background check on the guy you're going to see in New York and I didn't find a lot of information on him. He's traveled a lot and has never stayed in one place long. While he's a starving actor in New York City, he's known to be a great salsa dancer. This one fact will help you in the competition."

"I hope so."

"I think your father could have won when he went to New York. It's such a shame he somehow got involved in the theft of the major art collection from Russia."

"I've heard this all my life, but my father was a dancer, not a thief."

Yuri nodded. "I think you're right. He must have been in the wrong place at the wrong time and I think this mystery will never be solved. However, the reason for meeting with you this morning is to alert you to dangers which still exist. I've heard of renewed interest in your father. Many people have never accepted the fact that he died twenty-five years ago. Also, someone is leaking information on their operations, and landing many people in jail. "

"I think it's hard to imagine my father is alive after all this time. Why would he stay away from my mom and me?"

"I would tend to agree with you, and I think I may know why some people have all this interest in him now. I know rumors are also floating around, indicating the location of the lost paintings will soon be disclosed. I think someone is feeding information to the American CIA."

"What does all this have to do with me?"

"I'm afraid you may have been used as bait by the CIA to lure the guilty parties in the theft out into the open."

"That doesn't make sense." She began to shake. "I definitely had nothing to do with the theft. I was three years old when the paintings were stolen!"

"Here's something you didn't receive. A letter was intercepted about a week ago that I only learned about last night when I started digging into your trip." He handed her an envelope with a letter inside. The letter had been sent from America.

Her heart made flip-flops inside her chest as she reached for the letter. She saw a small receipt for payment of the registration fee for the international salsa competition she had planned to attend in New York. She read a note at the bottom, "Congratulations on your win in Russia. I know you will do great in New York."

She looked at him, as if she didn't know how to

understand exactly what it meant. "It's a receipt for the competition I'm going to enter. Why would my mail be intercepted for something like this?"

"Some people think your father is alive, and wanting to make contact with you. If he were alive, the Russian government, as well as the Lisin family, would love to talk to him. I personally think he's dead, and this is something being used by the CIA."

"But . . . why me?"

"They have little to go on, and are obviously using whatever they have available. Ivan Lisin has had to fight this cloud over his head for twenty-five years. While the intense scrutiny forced him to become more and more legitimate over the years, this is something he's actually enjoyed doing. He wants the future of Russia to be good for all Russians. He acted upset about the theft of something meaning so much to the Russian people. It's his brothers who have continued to operate in the shady area, and often without the older brother knowing what was going on."

"After all this time, it's hard to believe the paintings still exist . . . and why are the Americans are so interested in the paintings?"

"The Americans are interested in smuggling which has been going on for many years into the United States. Since the Lisin family controls much of that traffic, the CIA has been getting tips recently which have led to many arrests. The family thinks someone is feeding them information. If the lost art is recovered and the evidence proves the family is responsible, well . . . the revelation would have major ramifications."

"But I know nothing about this."

Yuri nodded again. "I know you're innocent. I could be wrong in all of this, and if I am, I will tell you I'm so sorry."

"Am I still free to go to America? I'm supposed to leave tomorrow and I have many friends coming to my flat tonight."

Yuri smiled broadly. "I think you already have your visa and trust me, I do wish you luck in the competition. If you need anything while you're in New York that you think I can help you with, please feel free to contact me."

"Thanks, I really appreciate your help." Wow! She could not believe she had such support now.

"Good luck." He smiled at her again before he walked toward the door.

After he left, Sveta decided to check her computer one last time. Danny wasn't in his chat room, but she did have a few messages in her e-mail. She strolled down them to read and came to a dead stop. The last one message came from an unknown sender. "Don't worry; you'll do great in the competition, my little lady."

CHAPTER 22

Sveta had soon discussed all the events with her mom and while some facts were too hard to understand, she knew something was taking place and she could trust no one. What am I getting involved in? The comments by Yuri had made her have many doubts about going, but it was too late to change things now.

"How are you doing with the salads?" her mom asked as she placed plates and glasses on the table. With such a large crowd expected, they had to make use of every piece they had available.

Olya arrived first, exactly what she would expect from her best friend. She wanted to help Sveta get her luggage in order. "I have some sketches you wanted, and some various photos of my work. If you can line me up a buyer in America, I'll be in your debt forever, Sveta."

"You never know since they buy a lot of art from us here. I'll be sure to find out what they think of your paintings."

"Can I help you with the salad?"

"Yes, you can help me cut some of these vegetables while I get some mayonnaise out of the refrigerator."

Olya glanced at the table setting. "Your flat looks good tonight. Do you have some candles to light for the table?"

Looking up from her work, Sveta answered, "I think we have some, but I knew I had one last errand I needed to do today." She quickly went to work searching for some, but only found a few short ones.

***

Olya suddenly felt useful as she offered. "Don't worry about it. I can go down to the corner store in a few minutes and buy some. Candles will make the table look good tonight."

"Are you sure? We can do without them."

"I'll be back in a second." On Olya's way out she recognized a friend of Mariya hurrying to the door. "You have more help coming, Sveta."

After rushing out of the building, Olya saw two men standing across the yard, and watching the building. While the food store was only a short distance away, it was long enough for the two men to disappear before she entered inside. As she located the candles and selected some extra chocolate, she heard a loud voice yelling at her. "Olya, wait up." Turning around, she felt surprised to see Andrew running over to see her. He was breathing hard. "I saw you going to the store. You had two men following you, and I became concerned about you. They are gone now, however."

Looking around, she saw no one. "Are you sure? I went for some candles."

"Yes, I'm sure they were after you. Sometimes you have to watch your back."

"I'll remember your advice. Are you coming to the party?" She hoped he would since she liked him being around.

"If you still want me to, I can visit for a little while. I know Sveta will be busy with all her friends and family, but I would like to tell her to have a good time, and congratulations on winning a trophy at the dance competition."

"She's trying hard to get all the food in order, but I'm sure she'd like to see you."

The two soon climbed the stairs as Olya turned and

watched the two men moving across the court in front of the building. Maybe Andrew was right about the two men who looked extremely shady. She would have to be safe when she left later during the night. Maybe she could talk him into taking her home.

Sveta was finishing the olivie as they entered the flat. "Look who I found outside."

"Andrew… it's so nice to see you! I'm so glad you came tonight," Sveta said.

"I can only stay for a minute. I'm sure you'll have many friends here soon. You're so lucky to be able to make a trip like this."

"Yes, I'm very thankful I've been given this opportunity. Have you heard from Denis today?"

"I was with him earlier. He hates not being here, but assumed it was best if he didn't come. Denis is a complicated guy, and has to decide what he wants out of life. The time you two spend apart will give him time to think and evaluate what he needs to do."

"When you see him, please tell him I'll miss him and I'll be in contact with him soon. I hope he understands this is the trip of a lifetime and he doesn't have to worry about me. I'm sure we will have a lot of time to talk later."

"I'll tell him. I really am not going to stay and I hope you have a great time in America."

Olya reached over and gave him a big hug. "Are we still going out on Friday?"

"Yes. I'll come and get you. We'll have a great time."

As soon as he left the door, Olya went to the balcony and looked out across the courtyard to scan all the area she could see, but she saw nothing of the two men.

"What are you doing?" Sveta asked.

"Andrew told me he saw two men watching the building who followed me to the store. I think I saw them as we headed up the stairs, but I'm not sure." Since Olya knew this might add more anxiety to Sveta's worries, she decided to not say too much.

"What did they look like?"

"I couldn't make out much about them. It was probably nothing at all." Olya smiled as she tried to down play the worry she had caused.

"I don't think it's too safe here anymore. You often hear about bad people. Perhaps you should spend the night here tonight. We have to leave early anyway. I see no reason for you to go home for such a short time."

"I might do that. It will be a long party tonight, and this way I can drink all I want." She whispered as she looked over the various drinks on the table containing a red wine, white wine, brandy, and several bottles of vodka. The champagne remained in the refrigerator to remain cool.

"Yes, this will be a great night." Sveta knew she was going to miss her best friend.

CHAPTER 23

With Sveta wearing a new suit she had purchased for this trip and her bags packed, she went over and over the list she had written to insure she would leave nothing she would need. All appeared to be in order. With the future ahead of her, she knew she could not turn back now. While she still had no answers to many of her questions, she knew that somehow all of this would make sense soon.

When she heard a loud knock on the door, she knew it had to be her boss, Mr. Sergeevich, who had insisted on coming by to personally take her to the airport. His car would be much more comfortable than taking the metro and since he resembled the closest thing she had ever had to a father, she would miss him.

"Hello, how are you this morning?" She asked as she watched him enter and walk immediately over to lift the luggage.

"I'm trying to wake up. As you know, I usually never wake this early and this is the second day in a row. However, I wouldn't have missed seeing you to the airport for anything in the world." A big smile flashed across his face. "Before I forget, I want you to have this to take with you." He handed her a tiny package.

"Why? What is it?"

"It's a surprise, which means you can't open it until you're on your way to America. I promise the package has nothing in it that will get you in trouble, but it's something belonging to your father that I've been holding onto. I think he'd love for you to have it right now."

"Thank you so much." Her eyes watered slightly as she thought of her papa. "I hope I can make my father proud of my dancing."

The four soon headed for the stairway since she knew they faced a great deal of traffic and needed to get in front of it.

"Which airline are you leaving on?"

"I'll be leaving on Delta which is a direct flight. They said to allow three hours to clear all the customs and baggage checks. Since I've never done this before, I want to arrive at the airport early to make sure I do things correctly. I would love to have someone going with me, but such a dream isn't possible. I just hope Danny is waiting for me at the airport in New York. Without him, I'll going to be totally lost."

"When did you talk to him last?" Gleb asked.

"I called him about an hour ago. He told me to call him any chance I had and that he didn't mind me calling collect any time to his cell phone. He's really a nice guy."

"I hope you're right, but in case you have any problems, I want you to call me. I have friends who can help you. Just remember that this ticket is for a roundtrip fare and it will return you safely back home. If you need extra money, contact us any way you can."

"Don't worry. I know I'll be fine."

As they all settled in the car, and started to pull out of the parking place, she saw two men headed for a car behind them. Were they planning on following her to the airport?

CHAPTER 24

Sveta didn't see any men following them as they rushed to the airport. Maybe she was imagining things earlier. While she felt glad to have the support of the most important people in her life, it would have been nice to have Denis join them, but since he recently had acted so jealous, maybe it was for the best that he didn't come. However, she knew that his emotions were understandable to some degree; after all, she was going to see another guy in a foreign country.

While standing in front of the gate leading to check-in, Sveta knew that she wouldn't see everyone again for several weeks. The excitement quickly became overwhelming with her nerves playing havoc with her stomach as she tried hard to stay in control.

Her mom gave her a large hug. "I am going to miss you so much while you're gone. You're the most important thing in the world to me. Please promise me you'll be safe." She said, as small tears formed in her eyes.

"You know I will be. This is like a dream for me. Don't worry about me. You know I'll call you as much as I can."

Olya smiled at Sveta's mom and added, "I guess I'll have to be your stand-in daughter for a while."

"I'll be glad to have you over anytime you want to come. I would love to have the company."

Next, her boss gave her a big hug. "Have a great time on your trip. You've never had a real vacation like this and I'm so glad for you. I know your father would love to see you make this trip."

If her boss knew the whole story, he would be shocked. She hoped that one day she would be able to tell him. She knew she would miss him. "Thank you for all you've done for me and my mom. I hope my trip doesn't cause too many problems for you at work."

"Don't worry about anything. Perhaps you can make some fantastic connections in New York and make this trip pay off nicely for you and for me. Don't forget to open the present I gave you once you get in the air. Perhaps I should have given this to you earlier, but I know your Papa would have wanted me to give this to you when it would be . . . good time."

"I'll open the present soon and I can't wait to see what it is." With one last big smile, Sveta turned and entered the gate to the check-in point.

She hurried to the line. They completely examined her luggage, and all proceeded normally until they saw the unopened present. "What is this?" The examiner asked as he studied the package.

"It's a going-away present one of my friends presented me with."

"I'm sorry, but the package will have to be examined."

"I understand. Is it possible to open the present and not show me? They made me promise not to open it until after I left."

"That may be possible. Let me open it, and I'll let you know if I have any questions for you."

Sveta turned her head as he started to open the wrappings. She hoped the gift wasn't something which would get her in trouble.

"It isn't a problem," he soon stated after he had opened and resealed the present. "I think you'll enjoy your present. That will be all. Have a good flight."

The next line moved faster as she stepped in front of a

lady in an official uniform. "May I see your papers?" she asked.

Not knowing exactly what she required, Sveta handed her all the documents she assumed would be needed. Her heart raced. She hoped she had remembered everything. "Is there anything else you need?"

"I see you're going to the United States of America. What is the purpose of your trip?"

"I'm going to visit a friend and enter a dance contest."

"The visa lasts for ninety days and I assume you're aware you have to leave the country by then. Also, if you decide to marry, you'll still have to return home and apply for a different visa."

"I have no plans to marry anyone. This is a trip to visit New York City and to enter a dance competition."

The officer continued to ask questions until she had satisfied herself. "Have a good trip."

"I will and thanks." Sveta laughed, hoping to hide her nervousness.

After passing all the checkpoints, she walked toward her plane while her breathing returned to normal and her stomach started feeling much better. Before she arrived at her gate to enter the plane, she saw a telephone on the wall. She walked over to it and searched for her phone book, thinking it would be good to give Danny a quick call before she went on the plane.

After she dialed his number, he answered on the first ring and as if he had been expecting her call. "Hello."

"Hello." she laughed. "Since I've cleared customs and I'm about to walk on the plane, I wanted to give you a call. This will be the last time I can reach you before I arrive in New York."

"I understand. So all is okay?"

"Yes, all is good. You're going to be waiting for me

when I arrive at the airport, I hope? If not, I'll be so lost."

"Don't worry. I'll be at the airport."

"I hope so. I'll see you soon."

"Good. I'll see you as soon as you pass through customs. I cannot wait to see you. Thank you so much for coming."

"Thank you for inviting me. Goodbye for now."

As Sveta returned the phone and leaned into the wall, she noticed a tall man standing close to her—so close that he could have heard her conversation. While he acted as if he was studying his travel papers, his presence made her feel very apprehensive.

Nervously, she quickly walked over to the check-in desk and handed the lady her boarding pass. "Is all in order on the flight?"

The lady looked over her paperwork before staring at her. "Yes, the flight will be on time and we will start boarding in about thirty minutes."

"Thank you. I'll have a seat and wait."

"You have time to visit the duty-free shop, if you want." She pointed to one side.

"I might do that. Thank you."

The thirty minutes passed slowly as she maintained a close eye on the man who had come too close to her earlier. While he acted as if he was paying no attention to her, he made her feel uneasy the entire time. Her thoughts eventually drifted back to Denis as she wondered if she should have called him before she left, but since he had acted so strange the last few days, it was perhaps best that she didn't. She now wondered if she had made a mistake the last night they were together at her flat. While she had made her choice and wasn't upset about her decision, she did have the events of the evening on her mind. Hopefully, Denis would be waiting for her when she returned. If not, she might have made a bad mistake.

She heard the call announced on the overhead speaker indicating it was time to board. It would be so good to get on the plane, stretch back, and relax. It would be a long flight and she could just imagine how the jet lag would be bad for her. Although many of the passengers looked Russian, they didn't say much while acting anxious, much like her.

Sveta located her seat on the aisle and glanced at the two girls in the seats next to her. They looked Russian and to be in their early twenties. Sveta greeted one of them as she moved into a seat beside them.

As her stare turned into a small smile, the girl next to her returned the greeting, but continued the conversation in Russian. "This will be a long trip and it would be nice to have someone to talk to. Do you speak any English?"

"I speak a little English, if you need me to help you with anything."

The girl words gave no indication of how good her English was. "My English isn't too good, but I hope to receive some lessons when we get to America."

"I see. Have you been to America before?"

"No, this is our first trip." She motioned to the girl beside her, as if they were together. "My sister speaks no English at all."

"This is also my first trip. Do you plan on staying in New York?"

"Yes, we do. We've been offered jobs doing modeling." Her eyes had a twinkle of excitement in them.

"That's great. I only know one guy who lives in America, and he speaks no Russian."

"Why are you going to America?" the girl asked.

"I'm going to see my friend and to enter a dance competition."

"Great! Are you going to get married?"

"I don't think so. We've never met before, except on the internet." Marriage would be interesting, but it would mean leaving her Mom, something she wasn't sure she could do.

"I hope your plans works out for you. I've heard many bad things about the internet."

"Yes, I've heard many stories of bad things happening to girls meeting guys online, but for some reason, this guy seems reliable. I'll see when I arrive."

"You're lucky if you speak English. Not understanding the language has been our biggest fear about going. I've learned of a place close to New York City called Brighton Beach. Have you heard of the area?"

"Yes, I have. There's supposed to be a large Russian community there and a place where you also can find Russian food and other necessities."

"The company bringing us to New York has arranged for us to stay in the Brighton neighborhood. You'll have to come visit us when we get all set up. Do you have a way we can stay in touch with you later?"

"I can give you my friend's number since I don't think he'll mind too much. We'll be working a lot together to prepare for the salsa competition."

"Having your number will be great."

As the stewardesses stayed busy checking with the passengers, the plane jolted slightly from the transporter pushing the aircraft away from the gate. Everything appeared to be happening as it should and she finally was on her way to America. She enjoyed the bright young smiles coming from her newfound friends.

As the plane climbed into the air, she leaned over to look out the side window where she soon watched the city below disappear when they passed through several clouds.

When the plane leveled off and the "buckle seat" sign vanished, she had an immediate need to go to the restroom. However, less than ten meters down the aisle, she froze—the man standing close to her earlier had boarded the same plane. While he had a familiar look about him, she couldn't place who he was. He again pretended not to notice her, but she could feel his presence.

After passing him, she hurried to the restroom. Was she being followed, or was she being paranoid? She knew she had to be careful since there were so many signs of other people having a big interest in her. Perhaps one day she would have answers as to why.

When she passed the stranger on the way back to her seat he had leaned back in his seat, and appeared to already be asleep. She would have to do her best to lose him as soon as she landed in America.

Her new friend studied an English language book she had brought with her. "It's so hard to learn. I'll never be able to speak English properly." The girl's face appeared tight and stressed, as she apparently had been working on this for some time.

"Don't worry. English will become easy for you as you practice. How long do you plan on staying in America?"

"We hope to stay permanently. Life in Russia is hard and we have no real future. It's been a dream of my sister and mine to go to America forever and I'm having a hard time believing that our dream is coming true."

Looking over at the other girl, who had a headset on listening to music, Sveta could see they looked alike in many ways. They were both tall and slender and their eyes sparkled like dark green emeralds. Sveta understood how they could do well as models. They also had the one thing Sveta wished she had more of—larger breasts. "You and your sister will do great in America. You both have great features."

"Thank you. Modeling is something we've never done before, but we're willing to learn. We're lucky to have been chosen by the talent scout who came to our village."

"If I understand correctly, you've never modeled before, and this is your first time?"

"Yes, we were shocked when they asked us to join their modeling agency. Our parents had many reservations and they have tried to persuade us not to go, but what choice do we have? We want more out of life than what we could ever have in Russia."

"I understand fully. Are you sure the agency is honest?"

"I think so. They have a lot of money and they gave our parents many presents. I think they wanted our parents not to worry about us not having money. They still don't believe in the agency, but they finally realized that we were determined to go."

"I think I understand how they must be suspicious. I'm sure they have heard the many stories about Americans, and how they think they're better than everyone else."

"It's my sister I'm worried about. She hasn't been the same since they asked us to join them in New York. It's like she's in another world. She now feels like she's special, and better than others."

"I noticed she's quiet and reserved. Do you think she'll be all right?"

"I think so. She stayed in the photo shoot for a long time the first time they came to the village. She won't admit this, but I think they talked her into doing some . . . personal and . . . perhaps very intimate shots of her." Her facial expression turned to one of worry.

"That doesn't sound good. She could get herself in

trouble in a foreign country."

"I've told her the same. The main reason I'm going is to protect her, but I think all will be good."

The stewardesses started moving along the aisle and taking orders. Thinking about the long flight, and since the beverages cost nothing, Sveta decided to order some wine. A long nap would be great. After receiving her wine, she stood for a minute and reached into the overhead to retrieve a pillow. While standing, she quickly glanced over her shoulder and noticed that the stranger was still stretched out and apparently asleep.

With the girl next to her reading a book, Sveta suddenly wondered about the present Gleb had given her. She decided to retrieve the package which felt extremely light from her purse. Because the gift came from her father, she was very anxious to find out what it was and why she had to wait until she rode on the plane to open it.

While the package was sealed with tape and had to have been beautifully wrapped at one time, the inspector had torn the wrapping several times in opening it. Nevertheless, she felt happy someone thought enough of her to go through all that trouble.

"Ohmigod," Sveta whispered as she looked at the tiny canvas someone had painted. It was a beautiful but still simple painting of a lady standing to help a little girl walk, or maybe even dance. The words below the painting caused her heart start to flutter: "A Mother and a Little Lady." Tears swelled in her eyes since this had to be painted by her papa. The painting looked like her mom teaching her to dance when she had turned three years old. The work looked simple, but it was detailed enough to leave little doubt that the drawing depicted her mom teaching her to dance.

The reference to her being the "Little Lady" drew her

attention, freezing the words in her memory for a long time. How remarkable, she thought. She hadn't heard that her papa could paint, or that he even had an interest in it. Why had her boss never shown this to her before and why did he decided to give this painting to her at this point in time? Was the painting yet another signal that her papa was still alive?

The painting, on a piece of canvas of about eight by ten inches, had been folded for a long time, with permanent creases in the canvas. The quality of her mom's face looked remarkable, and the feeling in the painting reflected a warmth and tenderness. She wondered how long her boss had hid this painting, and how he had initially received it. She would love to hear the story.

The stewardess soon walked back along the aisle, handing out magazines and papers. "Would you like something to read?" she asked.

"I think it would be good to read a paper, if you have one."

"Yes, we have the morning paper from St. Petersburg. Here it is." She handed Sveta the paper.

"Thanks."

Sveta clicked on the light above, and placed the painting in her purse again. She would have to look at the details closer later when she had time. At the bottom of the front page of the paper, an article immediately caught her attention. The Lisin family was being investigated for various crimes in America, and their assets they owned in America had being frozen.

Ivan Lisin had denied all wrongdoing, and had agreed to meet with the American authorities to clear up all charges. The FBI and the CIA were also investigating further charges against his company. The source of their information wasn't disclosed or full details given as to what they knew. Ivan stated that he had always stayed in full compliance with all laws and regulations. He insisted that no laws had been broken and that he would cooperate fully with all law agencies to prove it. Specifically he stated, "It's time to stop thinking of all Russian businessmen as crooks and felons. The 'New Russians' are businessmen and aggressive, but law-abiding, honorable men." The news article continued to quote him as she studied the picture at the bottom of the article. Sveta stopped breathing when she recognized the man in the photo. He was sitting several seats behind her on the plane.

CHAPTER 25

As soon as the plane landed, Sveta rushed to the front of the plane. She didn't want to be recognized by Ivan Lisin. He was a powerful man and while he had many problems to handle in America, members of his family might also have killed her father. While she wished she had answers to the events happening around her, she also knew that she might never know.

The girls who rode next to her in the plane hurried to keep up with her. "Wait up," they yelled as they moved fast to catch her. She pretended not to hear them and continued as fast as she could, but the crowds became heavier and quickly slowed her down. They were all going in the right direction, she thought, as she saw several bends in the hallway, but no way to exit.

When she could finally see booths ahead and single file lines forming, she hoped she could move even further ahead of the crowd behind her. She quickly joined a line and hoped she had made a good choice.

Luckily, the two girls joined her as they flashed signs of anxiety. Going halfway around the world can be scary, since it's hard to know exactly what to expect. "Do you know what they'll be asking us here?" the girl asked.

"I'm not sure, but I assume they'll be checking our paperwork and our visas here."

Sveta didn't want to turn around and give Ivan Lisin a chance to identify her. Why was he on her plane?

When she approached the girl at the counter, Sveta offered her all the paperwork she assumed might be needed.

An older lady smiled and started reading the visa before she spoke in English while glancing at the photo. "Are you here for business or pleasure?"

Sveta paused as she became fully aware that she might have to speak in English the rest of the trip. "I am here for pleasure."

"I see. Let me check things and—"

Sveta didn't like the way she stopped in mid-sentence. "Is something wrong?"

"No . . . all is in order, but you'll have to go to an interrogation room for an interview. Please step over to the side and have a seat and someone will be with you shortly."

It felt like her heart stuck in her throat. What could they want now? Having no choice in the matter, she strolled over to the chairs the agent pointed to and had a seat.

Within minutes, the two girls joined her. They looked as apprehensive as she felt. "What do you think they want to ask us now? I assumed we had everything in order."

The wait soon became long and tiring as others joined the holding area and were called into a small room for questioning. Surprisingly, they called the two girls in before her. When both returned from the room they looked tired and scared. What had they been told? They didn't say a word to Sveta, but hurried on down the hall to go through customs, leaving Sveta alone with her thoughts.

When she felt the presence of a man moving into the seat beside her, she glanced over to see Ivan Lisin smiling at her. "Hello," he said amiably in English while leaning closer to her.

"Hello," she weakly replied. In fact, she must have looked scared as he turned his head to look straight ahead.

Turning back around to face her he continued, "Don't

worry about the interview. It's a common problem. I've been through here many times, and I can almost tell you the questions they'll ask."

"This is my first time to America, and all this is new to me." She tried to hide her shaking hands, hoping he wouldn't recognize her.

"I understand. Would you like some chocolate? I saved some from the plane and the quality isn't too bad—really."

She glanced at him and noticed a friendly smile reflecting in what would otherwise be considered a hard and rough face. He looked nothing like she would have pictured him. "Thanks, but I'm not hungry right now."

"Are you here by yourself?"

"Yes, I'm traveling alone, but I'm meeting someone here who lives in New York City. I just hope he doesn't give up on me with the interviews taking so long today."

"I'm sure he'll wait for you." He flashed a big smile.

"If he doesn't, I'll be totally lost." She couldn't believe that she continued to have this conversation with this guy.

"I'm sure you'll have a great time here. New York is a large and diversified city. Are you getting married in America?"

"No, just visiting."

"I'm glad to hear you're only visiting since so many girls going to America to marry an American later learn that life there isn't all it's made out to be."

As a woman exited one of the rooms, she called for Ivan Lisin. He stood as he offered Sveta a warm smile. "Your turn will be soon, I'm sure."

"Thanks." As she watched him leave and wondered more about how he behaved when he ran his family organization, she felt thankful he hadn't recognized her.

He was still in the room when they finally called her to

another one. She hurried inside and waited for the interviewer who appeared to be a young man in his early thirties to close the door. He was dressed as a professional wearing a dark suit and polished black shoes

"Please have a seat, Ms. Panova."

Sveta did as he instructed. "Is everything in order?"

"Yes, your visa is in proper order. I'm with the State Department, and I want to be the first to welcome you to America. And at the same time, I want to ask you a few questions."

"Sure, I will be glad to answer them."

"We have many women entering the United States who are never seen again. We see a lot of organized crime, and trafficking in women for immoral purposes. Our job is to make sure that doesn't happen to you. Let me start by asking how you decided to come here?"

"I met a guy on the internet who loves to salsa dance. Salsa is a dance I love also. Over a period of time, we became good friends, and he invited me here to compete in a dance competition." Sveta handed him the invitation she had completed and faxed to Danny several months ago. It had information about the competition and places where the eliminations would be held.

He looked over the information and removed his glasses. "Have you been offered any money or other incentives to come here?"

"My friend paid for my way here since I don't have the kind of money required for such a trip. He seems to be a nice guy and I'm looking forward to seeing him in person."

"How long do you plan on staying here?"

"The competition is the last week of the year and I plan to leave soon after the competition. I have a return ticket already paid for by him."

"Do you have a job to return to in Russia?"

"Yes, my boss is a nice man who I have worked for many years. I have a good job I enjoy and I live with my mom in a flat we own in St. Petersburg."

"I see. Just the same, I'm going to give you a card with my number. This is for your protection. If for any reason you feel threatened at all, please feel free to call me."

"Thank you. I will."

"Have a good time in America. You are free to go."

CHAPTER 26

With her luggage firmly in hand, she headed for the final checkpoint to enter the main part of the airport and where she hoped Danny would be waiting for her on the other side. If not, she didn't know what she would do. While she had seen his picture on the internet, she was scared that she wouldn't recognize him in person. That would be so embarrassing.

She was in a small crowd, as she pushed her way through. She glanced around with her head spinning. While she saw so many people looking for someone, she silently walked through them, and found a quiet place to stand.

From out of nowhere, she saw him standing in front of her about ten meters away. He had the most gorgeous smile with sparkling white teeth. She forced herself to blink to make sure. Yes, he stood still—patiently standing in front of her. She wanted to rush to him and wrap her arms around him, but she decided to wait for him to come to her. He walked slowly, but deliberately in her direction, as if stunned by her presence. When he neared a few meters from her, he rushed forward and wrapped his arms around her before lifting her off the ground. "You made it!" Danny's voice sounded exactly as she remembered on the phone. "I've been waiting for you. Your plane landed several hours ago."

"I know. They made me go to an interrogation room for questioning. I thought they would never be through with me."

"I love your accent. It sounds so good to hear you in person."

"I don't speak English too well. I hope you'll be patient with me and speak slowly." She smiled at him and reached down to squeeze his hand. This felt like a dream come true and she couldn't believe this was really happening to her.

Danny moved over to her luggage and reached for the long handles. "We need to move out of the traffic here. Let me move this over to the side for a minute." As he moved the luggage, he continued to talk. "How was the trip?"

"It was a long trip, but I don't mind."

"Are you tired? I know the time is late for you, and it will take a while for you to get your days and nights straight."

"I am not tired now, but know I will be soon. Do not worry about me—I will be fine."

Moving over to the far side of the traffic, Danny stopped again to hold her close. "It is so good to have you over here." Sveta felt so happy to be with him, and couldn't quite stop looking him over. He looked gorgeous!

She moved closer to him and focused directly into his eyes. She waited for him to kiss her, but instead he hugged her and reached for the luggage. "We need to get going. I need to get you out of here before you collapse."

As he hauled the luggage toward the exit of the airport, she walked beside him. Once outside, they found a waiting taxi where he quickly placed the luggage in the trunk before they made their way to the back seat. As soon as Danny told the driver the address they quickly entered the traffic.

They soon drove into the city itself, where the size of the buildings and the crowds were enough to scare anybody. In Sveta's case, the narrow streets between the buildings dominated her thoughts. This place looked so fascinating and in a way she knew she could never explain to her friends back home. "Do you live close to here?"

"Yes, not too far. I hope you like my place. While the apartment is small but comfortable, the main thing I like about my place is that it's close to everything." He paused. "I hope you're not expecting the Ritz Hotel."

"I'm sure your place will be all we need. It is so great to have you invite me to come here. You are great."

"We'll see. I'm just me." He pointed to many landmarks as they rushed through traffic narrowly avoiding collisions on every turn.

She felt lost and knew she had to depend completely on Danny. It would take a long time for her to learn her way around. "I'm looking forward to seeing everything. This city is so large and exciting." As her eyes tried to take in all of the sights, she felt sleepy, but for right now it would be impossible to fall asleep.

"Are you hungry? I wasn't sure what you might like, so I bought several things from the local grocery. We'll have to go shopping soon." He explained as she continued to study each attraction on every turn.

"I am a little hungry, but not too much. We ate on the plane and the food wasn't too bad."

The taxi eventually made a hard right and stopped in front of a building. "This is the place," he said as he opened the door and reached for her hand to help her out. As the trunk opened, he retrieved the luggage and reached into his pocket to find money that he handed to the driver for the fare. "Keep the change." He turned to Sveta. "I hope you're in good shape since the apartment is on the fifth floor and the elevator doesn't always work."

"Here, let me help you with some of the luggage," she said as she wanted to help.

"It's okay. I think I can handle the load, but if you can, please help me with the smaller one."

After they slowly climbed the stairs with the luggage, she waited for him to unlock the door, where she could only imagine what his place would look like. She was actually moving in with a guy from New York—a very gorgeous guy from New York.

Once inside, she felt amazed at how neat he kept his place. If he had prepared the inside for her benefit, she definitely felt impressed. He had decorated his place with many art items which included bright and bold colors. While the apartment was small, he had a large room serving as a kitchen and living room, a tiny bathroom and a separate bedroom.

"I told you my apartment was small, but for New York, I'm lucky to have the separate bedroom. The rent is outrages here."

She laughed. "Your apartment is much larger than my place back in Russia."

He carried her luggage to the bedroom. "I have a closet you can use and I have moved my clothes to one side to make room for you. I hope you like the bed. It's a little old."

"I'm sure the bed will be fine." She smiled at him as she walked over and sit on it. She had often wondered about the sleeping arrangements and what would happen when she arrived. He had promised to be a good guy and not bother her, but she didn't really believe him or even expect him to honor the noble gesture he had made when he first asked her to America.

As if he was reading her mind, he continued, "I know you're thinking about the sleeping arrangements. I made you a promise and intend to keep my word. I'll never force you to do something you don't wish to do. I have a couch in the living room which turns into a bed." He walked to the couch and showed her how it folded out into a bed.

"I do not want you to be uncomfortable. I will be glad to sleep on the couch and let you have the larger bed."

"No. I want you to have it. I keep my promises. The restroom is small, but clean. Since you've had a long trip, I'm sure you'd like to have a shower and freshen up. I'll let you sleep as long as you wish, since I know that jet lag is a problem that might take you several days to recover from."

"You're so kind to me." Sveta smiled. "I don't know how I'll ever make this up to you."

"I think you do." A big smile passed over his face. "Help us win the salsa competition. The trophy would be the best present anyone could ever give me."

"I will do my best, but we'll have to work hard." She was looking forward to dancing with him.

"Yes, we will, but for now you need to rest."

Sveta walked over to the bed and opened her suitcase. "I could not bring much because of the weight limits. Perhaps we can buy a few things here I will need."

"I'm sure you have many items you might need. You can give me a list later, or we can go shopping when you're better rested."

"I'm looking forward to seeing the city. Do you know New York well?" She looked for a window, but saw none in his apartment.

"I know some of it and I'm sure you'll find the city much different than Russia. I have some towels and wash cloths in the restroom, but please let me know if you need anything else. I'm going to read a little while and prepare for a part I want to try out for."

"I think a good shower would be nice, and I will try not

to bother you. Thank you again for inviting me here." She wanted to offer him a kiss, but hesitated.

"You're welcome. It feels great to finally have you here."

Sveta entered the bathroom and closed the door as she thought about how Danny acted so nice and gentle. She wasn't sure how this time would go when she met him. She enjoyed the way he acted like a perfect gentleman and made her feel completely safe in getting ready to take a shower.

She removed her clothes and folded them, since she didn't have much with her, and wanted them to stay as presentable as long as she could. As she removed her bra and panties, becoming totally naked, she looked around and felt somewhat uneasy, but all remained quiet. She stepped into the shower, and soon had the hot water working miracles for her. The water felt great.

After she dried off and put on her nightclothes, she went into the small room to check on Danny, where he was stretched out on the couch asleep. Apparently he was also tired, much like she was. She slowly approached him, leaned over, and kissed him on the forehead.

CHAPTER 27

After Sveta slept for most of the next two days, she was slowly adjusting to the time change. With the city noises constantly echoing off of the tall buildings she wanted to start exploring and forced herself to realize that she had actually traveled to New York City. Danny apparently knew she was ready to see parts of the city as he prepared to spend the day sightseeing with her. She assumed he had seen much of the city, but she hoped he still had an interest in seeing more.

"I hope your shoes are comfortable since we'll be doing a lot of walking," Danny said as he prepared to leave his flat.

"They are good shoes. In St. Petersburg we do a lot of walking also. Where are we going today?"

"I thought we would go downtown today and see the financial district and the site where the World Trade Center stood. I would love to see how the area looks now with the new construction. Then we can go to SoHo, Little China and then Little Italy while we are in the area. Today will be a great day and if we have time we'll go to a point where you can see the Statue of Liberty."

"That would be great. I look forward to seeing it."

"After we return, I want to take you to a studio that a friend of mine will let us use. He knows I'm getting ready for a competition and he lets me use his studio for free. In return, I have agreed to help with giving lessons when his student load gets large."

"You give lessons also. So . . . you are good."

"I just help out. Since he has many more women taking lessons than men, he appreciates the help."

Thanks to the money Danny had sent her, Sveta wore a stylish all white outfit that fit her body perfectly. "I have my camera, and I hope you do not mind if I take a lot of pictures today."

"Not at all—I know you want to remember everything here."

"Yes, this is the trip of a lifetime."

"When we finish in the studio tonight, I want to take you to a few places where they dance salsa. It's time for you to see how they dance here, and to see how you like it."

"Wow, I'm so excited. I hope you're not disappointed in my dancing ability, since I'm still learning to dance the salsa."

"I think you'll be great. I really want to know how you dance different from what we do here."

The trip downtown raised many questions for Sveta while she heard several languages being spoken. As the people rushed around her, they all acted cold and unfriendly, but it wasn't that much different from people in St. Petersburg.

"We have to catch the subway here." He pointed to some stairs heading down. The complex looked large and had people moving fast in all directions. Stopping at a gate, Danny produced some coins, and they walked toward the subway. "We'll be there soon."

Sveta felt nervous about seeing all the people. Feeling uneasy, she had to make sure she didn't become lost. Danny was her only contact here. "Don't move far from me. It would be scary to be here all by myself." She glanced at Danny and held his hand.

The day quickly passed as they went from one place to

another where she realized the sheer size of New York offered her with many unique places to explore. The food in the windows often caught her attention since she had never seen food like this before. "Is all of the food here spicy?"

"I don't think so, but it might be something different for you. Would you like to try something?"

"I'm hungry a little. I've heard the food is spicy, and I'm scared about trying some of your food."

"Perhaps we should try a salad. I know you like salads. What do you think?"

"Yes, a salad sounds good."

Danny eventually pulled her through a door leading to a basement restaurant. The inside looked plain and simple, but clean. As they found a seat, a waitress came over and placed a menu in front of them. After Sveta opened the menu and started looking at the items offered, she didn't understand most of the food choices. Since she didn't want to appear ignorant, she decided to look over at Danny and ask, "What are you going to have?"

"They have many items to consider." His eyes went down the menu several times. With a big frown, he looked at her and said, "I think that maybe this is the wrong place for you. I keep forgetting how you're not used to the spices here yet. Perhaps you can try a chef's salad."

"I like salads. I know it will be tasty." Eating out was special for her as she glanced around.

Danny seemed to recognize a lot of difference existed between Russian salads and American salads. "I think we need to take you shopping for food you might like."

"Do you know of some places where we can buy Russian foods?"

"Yes, there's a place where many Russian people live. It's called Brighton Beach."

"I have heard of this place. Do you know much about the area?" Sveta felt a small growl in the pit of her stomach, reminding her that she needed to eat something.

"Not too much, but from Manhattan we can take the Q line. It isn't too far. Perhaps we can go to Brighton tomorrow."

"I think I would like to visit Brighton very much. Tell me more about Brighton."

"I know some, but I think you'll understand the place better when you see it. It's an area where you see Russian words on the buildings and many items for sale, like electronics, books and music, and of course some Russian foods."

"Brighton sounds great!" Sveta studied Danny and how he looked almost exactly as she had pictured him.

"Brighton Beach has a lot of restaurants, stores and banks and it's next to the Coney Island area and the Boardwalk. To get there we will walk right under the Brighton Beach Avenue subway station. You will see that it's an area where many people from the city go to visit."

"I know I will enjoy it. Thank you again for bringing me to America."

"You're welcome."

After the food arrived, they both ate as if they were starved. It would not be long until they had to hurry back to the studio.

CHAPTER 28

Exiting from the subway, they hurried down the street to the building housing the studio. It was on the third floor, and Danny indicated that the fastest way to the studio was by the stairs. They raced to the top almost like kids to see which one was in the best shape. It was close to a tie.

After stopping in front of a fogged glass door, making it impossible to see through, Danny paused. "My friend who owns this place may be working with someone, so we have to make sure we don't disturb him. This is how he makes his best money, and his private lessons are expensive."

"I understand. Are you sure he does not mind us using his studio to practice?"

"Don't worry about it. All of the details have been worked out. He's getting a teacher he needs and this isn't costing him anything other than a little bit of electricity. He also knows if we win, it will provide him with some greatly needed publicity."

"And if we do badly, it will not be good publicity." She forced a small laugh.

"We'll do well, but we need to work hard since we have very little time to get ready. Are you sure you're ready for this?"

"Yes, the competition is why I came here. I really want to learn how to be a good dancer."

"In order to win we have to be fantastic. We have to be able to dazzle the audience with every movement and leave nothing to chance."

"Do you think winning is possible? I mean, after all, many of these dancers have danced all their lives and learned this dance since they started walking."

"Yes, they have a natural rhythm which will be hard to duplicate, but the difference is that most of them have never had formal training. Their movements aren't elegant and they've only learned one style of dance. To win, we'll have to show them a style they're not used to and one which will be hard for them to duplicate. We have the element of surprise on our side."

"I hope you're not disappointed in my ability."

"All I ask is that you put all your energy into the dancing. We have a lot of hours ahead of us."

"I will do as much as you want me to do for you."

After Danny pushed the door open and looked around, he soon waved for Sveta to follow him into the studio that looked quiet and abandoned. "Is anyone here?" Danny yelled as he crossed the floor.

"Back here." Carlos replied as he moved around a door leading to a small office. "I thought you would be here soon."

Danny reached over and slapped his shoulder. "I really appreciate this."

"Don't mention it. So this is the girl I've been hearing so much about." He looked Sveta over from top to bottom, while his face remained emotionless. "She has the features of a dancer. Her posture is good and she's slim. She even has the legs of a dancer."

"I'm glad you agree." Danny offered a big grin.

"However, "Carlos continued, "she'll need to look sexy to win a competition like salsa. It's something we can work on."

Sveta didn't know how to take the comment, but

decided to smile. She knew she had tiny breasts, but since there was nothing she could do about their size, she blushed internally as she felt the rush of heat. "Do you teach salsa most of the time?" she decided to ask.

"Yes, salsa is the dance that's most popular. Have you been to the clubs in the city yet?"

"No, I have not been here long, but we're going to see some later tonight." She walked closer to Danny.

"Good. It will be nice to hear what you think." Carlos winked at Danny, sending a message she couldn't understand.

"I'm looking forward to dancing. Danny has told me much about the clubs, but I know seeing it in person will be much different."

Carlos turned toward Danny "You know how to lock up when you leave, and feel free to stay as long as you want. I enjoyed meeting you Sveta, and I'm looking forward to seeing you dance later."

"Thank you for everything. You're so kind to us."

Carlos quickly contorted his smile as he left. "Thanks, but don't tell anyone—it might ruin my reputation."

Danny walked over to the stereo system and selected some music. After the music started, he adjusted the volume to a medium level before he smiled at Sveta. "I guess we need to start with the basic step."

"That is a good place to start." She waited for him to present a frame, knowing they had a lot of work to do.

Three hours later, they were still working on the basic moves. They had learned totally different styles. She learned to start on one and Danny always starting on two. While she acted rigid and formal, he danced more loose and freestyle. While this was simply a first attempt, they enjoyed each other's company and laughed at the missteps they often made.

"Are you ready to go to some clubs and see what salsa looks like here?"

"Yes, it will be exciting watching the dancers and I want to see you dance with some other girls. I need to see what style they dance here." She said as she glanced around the studio.

"It will be good for you to dance with some other guys also. Just be sure to let all of them know you're with me. I don't need to have someone think you're a free woman and try to hit on you tonight."

"Do not worry. I'll not wander too far from you. I'm totally lost here. Please don't leave me alone too long since this is still new to me and a little scary."

"I can understand so don't worry. You'll be safe with me and I'll introduce you to some friends I've made who will help to keep an eye out for you also."

"I appreciate it. I'm ready when you are."

After locking the door, they walked down the flight of stairs to the street below. The active sights and sounds of the city confused her. She felt lost. "Is the club far from here?"

"No. It's about two blocks. We'll be getting to the club about the right time. I've several places I like to go, and this one usually isn't too crowded. You'll see some people I dance with, and they know I've been waiting for you to arrive and want to meet you."

A thought crossed Sveta's mind. She wished she'd had time to work on her hair since it had to look bad by now. She wanted to make a good impression, but she had no time to take care of her hair and face now. She also worried about her English. While she knew English fairly well, she was concerned about how good her pronunciation would be when she met many people, especially when the music played loud. "I wish I had time to prepare myself better for your friends."

"You look fine, and this is a small group. We'll help you look much better soon. I know we need to go shopping and buy you many things tomorrow, but tonight is just for us to have a quick look at what we have facing us. Don't worry, I won't embarrass you tonight."

"I'd like to quietly sit and watch tonight." Sveta offered a small, but desperate look of despondency. "Please let me take it slowly at first."

"Don't worry. We'll do as you wish." He held her hand, as he escorted her toward the club. She knew he wanted to make her feel safe.

Stopping in front of a building with no name on the outside, he led her down a flight of steps and through a door. The other side was dark, and had no signs of advertising or indications of where they were going. Entering another door, she saw a door attendant standing in front of them.

"Can I see your ID please?" He remained firmly in front of the door.

Sveta turned to Danny. "Do I need my passport?"

"Yes, it will do. He wants to make sure you're of age to enter."

After locating her passport, she handed it to the door attendant who glanced at it and then again at her. "I guess the ID will do."

"The passport is all she has." Danny said as he smiled at the door attendant.

After he perched his lips and relented by moving to one side, they passed him and walked to the bar. In the center of the room she saw a large, square bar with a center area for the bartenders. They could serve patrons on all four sides which stretched about ten meters at the most. They had to walk around it to enter the backside of the club. On the right side of the club she saw many tables and chairs for people to rest and drink while on the left side she noticed the dance floor.

"Let's walk over to the right and find a seat." Danny pointed.

Sveta nodded her head and followed his lead. The place looked dull, and lacked any real charm. The people all had a way of being in their own little world, but the mixture of different nationalities fascinated her. Many of them looked strange to her. With the sounds coming from all over the club, she had a hard time understanding any one particular person talking. The various conversations sounded like a loud murmuring.

Finding a vacant table, Danny pulled one chair on one side over to the table to match another one. He held it for Sveta to have a seat before sliding around to his seat. "What do you think?"

She didn't know how to answer, but decided to try, "Interesting . . . do you come here much?"

"Not too much since it isn't the best place, but I thought you might like to see a few different clubs and this was the closest one. The dancing gets better in here on Wednesday night when they cater to salsa dancing. The other nights they do a mixture of dances."

"I see. Do you have friends here?"

"I know some people here, but I don't see any of them right now."

When the band played another rock song, Danny leaned closer to ask, "What would you like to drink?"

"I do not care. Whatever you are having will be fine with me."

"I'll buy us some beers. Stay here and I'll be right back."

As Danny strolled over to the bar to place his order, she

looked around the place and started wondering what she had gotten herself into. Since this place didn't look too safe, she hoped the other places they went to would be much nicer. This wasn't the image she had of nightlife in New York.

As Danny returned to the table, the band changed songs again. This time they played a Latin sound, and a big smile came over Danny's face. They had started a cha cha rhythm, which she recognized from the dance class in St. Petersburg. "Do you know how to do the cha cha?" he quickly asked.

"I know some. Would you like to try?" she asked, as she held out her hand to be escorted her to the dance floor. While it wasn't salsa, the music would give them another chance to become used to each other, and learn how to discover the feel of their different dance movements. On the floor, surprisingly, they danced smoothly together.

When a few other couples joined them on the floor, she noticed the band members enjoying the fact they had dancers on the floor. As if taking the small crowd as a cue, the band followed with a festive salsa number to get the night moving.

Sveta presented her arms held high for Danny, but just like Denis had done back in Russia, he lowered them and looked at her intensely. After moving in a Latin motion, going back and forward, he soon had her doing the same by matching his movements which were much more rapid then what she had learned in Russia. He mesmerized her with his intense look. "You have to feel the music. It has to become one with you. You'll see."

Sveta didn't say anything, but attempted to move with him. She wanted to learn. With the music playing loud and the place hauntingly dark, the rhythm of the music dominated her every thought.

The intense stares coming from Danny reminded her that she needed to concentrate on her movements. As she became used to his presence, his gestures indicated how much he loved to dance. Why he went to this place, she didn't know. When the floor became more and more crowded until she had little room to move, Danny would pivot her around to other locations. His movements felt amazing and she loved how he managed to dominate a little place on the floor.

Finally, he stopped and smiled at her. "Let's go to our seats for a minute and rest."

"Rest sounds good. My feet are getting a little tired."

At the table, he held out her chair for her before walking around to his side. He looked like he wanted another beer, but asked for his check instead. Apparently he had another place he wanted to go to next.

Once they left the club, they again entered the hectic street scene. The city had lights everywhere capturing Sveta's attention. Again, people were in a hurry, going in many directions at once and paying no attention to others around them.

"Stay close to me. We have several blocks to walk to arrive at the next place." As Danny moved in a hurry, Sveta did her best to stay with him. People constantly bumped into her, and the various languages she overheard made her even more nervous of her surroundings. New York was a strange place, and she felt so glad to have Danny with her.

"How much further is it to the next club?" she asked, as they waited for a light to change to green.

"It's one more block. You'll like the next one much more than the last place. It's almost ready to start, and I'll introduce you to some people I met a few weeks ago."

"Thanks. Are they good dancers?" She looked forward,

trying to guess where it was.

"Yes, I think they're good. They go dancing every night, and I've located many of these places with their help."

At the end of the next block Danny turned to his left before he proceeded down the street. He soon glanced upward to study some signs before walking over to a door and opening it for Sveta. "Follow me." He held her hand and led her up a short flight of stairs to a large door at the end of a hallway that had a massive sign above the archway. It read "Latin Quarters." As he opened the door for her, she studied the elegant details of the furnishings where she loved the fine wood and subtle lighting. The stonework added an expensive touch.

As a man approached and offered to take them to a table Danny pointed to the far side of the bar, where the dance floor waited for him. "We're here just to dance tonight."

The man quickly lost interest in them. "I see. Please feel free to go to the bar and wait; the band will be starting soon."

"Thank you."

After making their way over to the bar, she saw two men raise their beer bottles toward Danny. He quickly waved back at them. "Those are some of the regulars who come here."

"Is this where you dance often?" She felt cool air blowing on her from above.

"Yes, it's one of the best places. Tonight we'll watch others dance and try to learn from them. Many of the dancers who come here love to compete, and we need to watch and study them. They will also be our competition in a few weeks."

After walking around the ornate and flashy bar, they

found some tables in front of the dance floor that were close enough to give them a good view of the dancers later. Danny removed his jacket and wrapped it over the chair, indicating that he obviously planned to establish a permanent location at the table. "How do you like this place?"

"I think we have a great spot. I hope the good dancers you mentioned will show tonight. It will be fun to watch them." With so many sights to take in, she felt dizzy.

"I'm sure they'll be here soon. Would you like some more beer, or maybe a glass of wine?"

"I'll have whatever you're having."

"In such a case, we'll be drinking margaritas tonight."

"Thanks, I've had one before and I would love to have another one." Her mind floated back to Russia where she was introduced to them.

While Danny went over to the bar to order the drinks, Sveta looked around the partially vacant room. The band had already arranged their instruments on the stage, but no one remained by them. Since she saw many drums and horns, she assumed that they must a large band playing tonight.

Danny hurried back over with the drinks. "I hope you like these. It's one of my favorite drinks." He handed her one of the glasses, and raised his. "To salsa . . . and to great music."

"I agree. To a great evening." She tapped her glass to his.

"I have to go to the restroom. I'll be back in a minute, but you'll be fine."

"Yes. I'll hold our table. This is a fascinating place."

Danny quickly vanished walking across the floor, as the two guys she had seen earlier floated around the bar to greet some girls who had recently entered. The bar looked unlike anything else she had seen. She couldn't believe she had flown halfway around the world to learn salsa dancing.

On the other side of the dance floor, she saw a new couple wearing all black and looking specifically dressed for the occasion move to a table. While standing tall and slender, his extremely good posture radiated an irresistible composure. His full head of shiny jet-black hair that was combed straight back along with his high cheekbones made him look like a perfect candidate for a modeling career. Perhaps she had arrived in New York after all.

As this new guy surveyed the room and analyzed the people around the dance floor, he eventually turned in Sveta's direction, where he stopped and stared at her hard. Obviously he was trying to decide if he had seen her before. When he leaned over and whispered something to his partner, she, in turn, glanced over at Sveta and smiled. Sveta returned the smile, but then looked away.

She felt glad to see Danny returning, since she hated to be left alone for long. He had a big smile on his face. "I saw some of the band members a few minutes ago. They're all talking about the competition which will be here in a little over a month. We have so little time to make our dance look great. This is the first place we can qualify and it's also the most highly sought after. We'll come here often, but the Latin Quartets won't be the only place we'll go."

The girl across the dance floor soon stood and danced around her man. She floated in an elegant, but sexy manner. She wore a black and red gown with a slit on one side to almost her hip. By leaving her long leg exposed, it was obviously designed for flashy dancing. With legs like hers, Sveta thought, she would want to show them off also.

Danny must have seen her analyzing their clothes. "Don't worry. I know we need to take you shopping, and we'll start tomorrow. Tonight we're simply going to watch."

"I am good at sewing, and will be glad to make some if you want me to." She felt her face flush slightly, since she didn't want to be too much of a burden on him.

"Don't be silly. I'm looking forward to taking you shopping tomorrow. It will be fun." Danny motioned over to other couples coming in as they began to fill the room. Apparently everyone knew what time the band started.

The band members soon entered the room and started welcoming various people. It looked like a big family where they knew the regulars. As the sounds became louder, she couldn't hear the individual conversations around her. "Do you know other people here?"

"I know some of the people a little, but none of them too well. I haven't been in New York long. I came here to try my luck at acting. So far, it hasn't been too productive, but it's the dancing which has held me here this long."

When the band members arrived on the stage, they started preparing their instruments to play. The leader was a black man with a rugged face and shaggy beard, and from the sound of the crowd he was extremely popular. "Hello, everyone! Tonight is going to be a great night. We'd like to thank you for coming and hope the night will be as great as usual. We have some great music and look forward to seeing you on the dance floor. Tonight, as I'm sure you already know, is salsa night which is my favorite night."

He turned and pointed to the band, and the bongo player hit the first rhythm in stride. He generated the key beat, as the rest of the group added layer after layer to his notes.

The couple across from them entered the floor first. They looked like they were used to having the floor, and it was easy to see they loved to show off their impressive moves as they wasted little time in moving into some complicated turns and twists. They executed every movement and step in perfect harmony with each other. Sveta could not take her eyes off them while the moves unfolded in such rapid succession it would be hard to remember them. The woman was limber and had a way of coming across very sexy when she wanted to. However, the heat and the passion of their dance was soon answered by others entering the dance floor. They quickly had major competition from others who were determined to keep them from stealing the show.

Sveta noticed Danny, who appeared to be in a trance, as he watched each movement of the dancers. He looked like he had transformed into a machine, recording every move. He obviously came to study and not be a silent observer as his intent on his observation never faded.

The margarita disappeared soon, and had a soothing effect on Sveta. The drink made her light hearted, and feeling a little free and uninhibited. She soon wished Danny would ask her to dance, but he maintained his intense gaze on the dance floor.

Eventually, he leaned nearer to her to be heard. "We have to learn all the moves they're making and add some of our own. Our presentation will have to be something they aren't expecting. We have to work on a movement that is both unique and different."

Sveta wasn't sure what he meant, but he obviously had something on his mind, and she would have to ask him more about his thoughts later. For now, she was happy watching the dancers. "Danny, do you think we can dance good enough to compete?"

He spoke close to her ear. "I think we can dance much better. To win, we'll have to be better and more exciting than not just these, but all the others around town."

The night of dancing lasted until early in the morning. While Danny purchased several more drinks, he never lost focus on the floor, which he studied the entire time they were there. He constantly pointed out various steps.

A large hand slapped Danny on the back. Danny jerked around to see his friend Carlos from the dance studio. "How are you?" he asked. "For some reason, I thought I'd find you here."

"Yes, I'm watching the dancing, and I see some great dancers here. What do you think?"

"I think you need to be on the dance floor. You will never learn on the sidelines."

"Perhaps, but it's not always true. Sometimes the best way to prepare for a competition is to study your competition. I've seen many moves we'll need help with." Danny pointed to several of the dancers.

"I'm glad you're taking this competition so seriously, and dedication is a good thing. We'll see if you have the real heat in a few weeks." He reached over to Sveta, and extended his hand to her. "I hope you know what kind of crazy salsa dancer you have on your hands here. If he becomes too much for you, please let me know." With a quick smile, he turned and crossed the floor to where a young girl had recognized him.

"This will be fun night for Carlos since he comes here to dance with some of his students occasionally. But . . . he's right about there being no substitute for dancing on the floor."

"He's a good dancer." Sveta said as she watched him lead the girl through some difficult moves while making them look rather simple to execute.

"It's his job to make the ladies look good and this is why he makes a good living teaching dance. He's extremely well liked. He makes the rounds to many clubs every night, hunting for new students."

Sveta yawned and quickly covered her mouth, as the time had turned late for her and she still hadn't fully recovered from her jet lag. "I'm sorry."

"Don't be sorry. The time is late and we do need to being going home. We have a big day tomorrow."

CHAPTER 29

Sveta had slept heavily during the night, but was still sleepy the next morning when Danny attempted to wake her. She would have loved to sleep longer, but she knew they had to go shopping this morning. While she hated having to ask Danny to buy her clothes and food, she knew she needed some items. Additionally, she was looking forward to being around people who spoke Russian today.

She got out of bed and headed for the bathroom, where a cold splash of water in her face was what she needed. The sparse gown she wore revealed her body in many places, but she was getting used to having Danny around, and after all, he had never made a single pass at her. This confused her at times.

He smiled at her as she left the bathroom. "I'll have everything ready to go in a minute." He waved his hands to indicate that he wanted her to move fast.

"I'll try to hurry."

"I understand. We've many shops in Brighton Beach to visit and we have to return home by late afternoon. Tonight I'll work at the restaurant and I need to make some money. The tips will be good on the weekend, and I will also need to work for the next three days."

"I understand—you have to work."

"You'll be fine here tonight, and it'll give you some more time to rest." They soon headed for Brighton Beach. "I have something else I want to show you when we are near Brighton. I remember the story you told me about your father, and I thought you would like to see the place he was tossed from the bridge. The bridge is more like a pier, but it's not far from the shops we're going to."

Sveta stopped walking. She had always wanted to see this spot, but now that the time had arrived, she felt uneasy. "How did you find the spot?"

"I decided to do some research after you told me about what happened to your father. It wasn't hard to find the information on the internet."

"I understand. The internet can make research easy. I would like to go, but not today. I need to prepare myself for it, and I want to be able to toss some flowers off the bridge to say goodbye to him in respect. Do you understand?"

"Yes, I can." He leaned closer to her to give her a brotherly hug, instead of a more intimate hug she would have loved to receive. Perhaps American guys were much more shy than Russian men.

They soon arrived on Brighton Beach Ave., where they went shop to shop. Sveta quickly felt right at home and found many people who spoke Russian. She smiled and showed the various items to Danny that she recognized from back home, as the sacks of purchases he carried became larger and larger.

"I think we'll need a truck to deliver all this." He quickly laughed as he followed behind her.

She studied his arms loaded down with merchandise they had purchased. "I'm sorry. Perhaps we've purchased too many things today."

"No, we're fine, but I do think this is all we can carry for now. We can come back again soon. I know you'll like Russian food and it'll be nice to see how you prepare it."

"Yes, I'll prepare a tasty meal for you tonight." She hoped he would love it.

"Don't worry about tonight since I'll be working until late. We'll have a good lunch tomorrow."

As they worked their way along the street, two girls caught Sveta's attention—the two girls she had met on the airplane coming to America. "I know those girls." Sveta pointed them out to Danny.

"How is it you know them?"

"They were on the plane with me." She strained to focus on them better.

Danny studied them also, but said, "It looks like they're working the street. You'll see many hookers in New York City. I think you must have made a mistake."

As she watched the two girls walk into a store, she felt almost certain it was them, but then again, they were all of the way across the street. "I may be wrong. They told me they had jobs in modeling or entertainment, I think." Sveta looked at Danny who was struggling with the packages and tried to help him by carrying more of them. "I hope you do not hate me for all of this."

"Don't worry. I need the exercise." He offered a big grin.

Not long after they arrived at Danny's apartment he had to leave. "Sveta, please stay inside while I'm gone, and call me if you have any problems. I hate to go, but it's necessary."

"I'll be fine. If you do not mind, I will do some house cleaning for you while you are gone." She waited on a goodbye kiss. Would he offer her one?

"You don't have to. Please . . . relax and watch TV." He quickly hugged her, and walked out the door—no kiss.

While she was still unable to understand him, she walked to the door and locked it behind him. She had no idea what to do in the apartment, but would make a good effort in trying to clean and organize it to some extent.

She soon learned how to operate the TV controls and found many stations to flip through. While looking for anything to occupy her time, she really hoped for a Russian station, but found none. Eventually, she went to the refrigerator and starting putting the food away. Since he only had a few carry outs from restaurants inside, it appeared that he didn't cook his own food very often.

She decided to drink one of his beers, since she knew the night would be long. As she sat in front of the TV, she stopped flipping the stations when she saw information on a news station that stopped her cold. Someone was interviewing Ivan Lisin. He looked to be on some steps leading out of a government building of some kind. She saw many people around him pushing microphones in his face.

She increased the volume so she could hear a news reporter standing in front of him. "I know this is a mixed day for you. How do you plan on handling the next round of hearings?"

"I'm glad to finally have a day in court where I can answer charges against me. The judge agreed with our case and had all charges against me personally dropped. This, of course, is a great feeling." Ivan smiled directly at one reporter.

The reporter's image reappeared. "I'm sure it is. I assumed you were confident of the outcome, or you wouldn't have been so willing to come to New York."

Ivan appeared to be relaxed. "In the import and export business, we have to maintain good relationships, or our business will not grow and prosper."

"With regard to the company you own and the ones affiliated with you, the outcomes were not so good today. Would you like to comment on these outcomes?" the reporter asked.

Ivan continued, as his knowledge of English amazed her. "Under advice of counsel . . . I'm sure you understand, I can't say too much at this time other than we'll rigorously defend ourselves and work to make sure that any problems which do exist will be handled properly."

"So . . . are you admitting you have problems?"

"No, we're not responsible for any problems, but we have agreed to do our part as responsible international citizens to end problems that may have been caused by others." A large group yelled to get in the next question, but he raised his hands to be able to speak to all of them. "I'm sure you all have questions, but for now, however, I need to wait until after the hearings tomorrow to answer any more of them. I hope you understand." He turned and followed several men who were protecting him from the crowds. A few seconds later, he hustled inside a large, black car, which quickly sped off.

The station switched back to a girl at a desk. "It has been a very unusual day with the head of a major Russian company coming to America to defend himself. Obviously, he has obtained the support of many politicians and businessmen in his straightforward way of dealing with questions."

New photos of Ivan were posted as she talked. "The courts today have agreed to arguments that not enough evidence existed to hold him personally responsible for smuggling and racketeering charges. The fates of others in his organization aren't so fortunate, however, since information the government has been obtaining lately is rumored to be coming from inside the organization. It has been very damaging."

The camera switched to another man. "The problem with an organized crime family is proving what is happening, and then somehow tying the evidence back to the boss. In this case, I think it is widely believed that Ivan is honestly trying to make his company into a legitimate operation. However, his company is large and run by others who may not be so in tune with his philosophy."

The first girl returned to the screen. "In addition to smuggling, they're also facing charges of drugs and prostitution. You would think that in our modern age like we are in now, white slavery and forced prostitution would be things of the past. The information released in the hearings was very shocking. Stay with us as we bring you more information in a special report later tonight."

Sveta watched the TV for the rest of the night as she continued to flip the stations, hoping for more information. She never heard any more concerning the case. Perhaps she could buy a paper tomorrow morning with more details of what was going on.

Eventually, she had fallen asleep by the time Danny returned from work. The couch felt comfortable. She had so many thoughts about the two girls she had seen on the street and thought that they might be in trouble, especially after Danny mentioned that they looked like hookers.

Somehow, she would have to see if she could help them.

CHAPTER 30

After Sveta heard the sounds of the city echoing around the streets below, she opened her eyes. With Danny making some noise in the kitchen, she thought about staying in her bed for a while. Since she didn't remember making it to bed, Danny must have carried her into the bedroom last night when he returned.

While knowing that she had to face the day, Sveta slowly strolled into the kitchen. "Good morning."

"Good morning," he returned her greeting. While he was still unshaved, he looked great. "How did you sleep?"

"I fell asleep waiting for you last night. What time did you get in?"

"It was about midnight. Some of the waiters and bartenders went for a quick drink after we closed. We had many people eating at the restaurant last night. It was a good night for tips."

"I'm glad you had a good night. I saw a special on TV last night. The program had to do with a Russian who is here being investigated for smuggling. Have you heard anything about this trial?"

"I've seen it in the news some, but don't worry about what you see. It won't have any effect on you here."

"I understand, but they talked about white slavery and prostitution rings. Do you know of many of them existing here?"

"This is a large city with many known mafia families. I'm sure it does, but, like I said, don't worry. You'll be fine with me."

"I am not worried, and you have been nothing but kind to me." She thought maybe too nice. He never made sexual advances toward her at all. "I was thinking about the two girls we saw yesterday on the street. I still think they rode on the plane with me from Russia. You said yourself they looked like hookers. They have been here less than a week. Do you think it's possible?"

"I don't think so, but we'll be going back to Brighton soon. We can look around some, if you wish."

She felt relieved that he would work with her to determine the truth, but still this was a big city. "Where are we going today?"

"Today we're going shopping for clothes you will need to dance in. I want you to look fantastic. I hope to make this a fun morning, but you need to hurry since we have a lot of shops to go to."

She studied the nightgown she was wearing. "I'll be ready in a few minutes, but I would like one more thing, if possible."

Danny smiled at the request. "What do you need?"

"I want a newspaper. If we could find a Russian paper for me to read I would love it even better."

"I'll see what we can do." Danny glanced at the door briefly.

"I would appreciate it."

He offered her a quick kiss on the cheek, but then quickly turned away. "I'm going down to the corner to buy a bagel and I know of a news shop close by. You have a yogurt in the refrigerator we purchased yesterday. It will take me a while."

Since she never saw him staring at her body, she felt no need to cover up better. Okay, she knew she had small breasts, but really. "I'll be ready when you return. Go on, I know you want something to eat."

An hour later they left the building and headed for the shops as the crowds made their own way to unknown destinations. Even with so many people on the street, she soon felt like someone was following her movements. After stopping abruptly in front of an electronics storefront, she turned to look inside, giving her time to memorize the people passing her.

After they all continued on their way and soon walked by her, she glanced at Danny. "Is it all right if we look at this portable stereo for a second?"

"Sure, if you want to." He looked slightly confused, but smiled as he opened the door and they strolled in. As a store clerk approached them, he asked, "How much is it?"

"It's about three hundred dollars, but produces a very high quality sound."

"I understand. It's too expensive for us, but thank you for letting me look at it."

When they exited the door and continued their walk, Sveta studied everyone as they passed them. She had to walk another block down the street before she saw him. While he quickly lowered his head and began reading a paper, she guessed that he had been waiting for them. She tried hard not to notice him, but she knew.

Minutes later, they entered the shops Danny had promised her. The Latin style clothes looked exciting. As they left one shop and entered another, she almost always saw the guy standing around somewhere. He had to be someone from the Russian family who was following her.

Danny interrupted her thoughts as he pointed to some more dresses. "I think these will be good to practice in, but we'll decide on one for the competition later since that dress has to be special. I think for us to win we'll have to dazzle the crowd and the judges."

She glanced at the dresses. "I'm not used to such

outfits. It will take a while for me to adjust to them."

Danny appeared to be very pleased with her. "We have one more place to go. The most important item we need to find is good dancing shoes. You'll need to have some for practice, and some for competition. The competition ones also have to be broken in since we don't need to have blisters on your feet."

"I have one good pair I brought with me that I received as a gift, and I still don't know who purchased them for me. No one ever admitted to it."

Danny smiled, but didn't say a word. He didn't have to. His grin gave away a secret.

CHAPTER 31

The weekend flew by. With the dance studio vacant on Monday morning, Danny quickly opened the door before they went inside. The dark studio soon came to life as Danny starting preparing the room. "It will be good to warm up some before we start working."

Sveta had already taking off her shoes to massage her feet. Since she knew the new shoes would be stiff and uncomfortable for a while, she had wrapped her feet with band-aids earlier. "I think you really take dancing seriously," she said as she watched him begin to stretch.

"Yes, I want to win, and I want to win for you. I know the competition is important to you. We'll work hard." Danny soon moved over to the stereo, and placed a CD in the player. As the music started playing, he flashed a big smile before he crossed the room.

"What are you smiling about?" Sveta asked, as he approached her.

"It's so good to have you here, and working with me for this competition. I've been thinking of this moment for a long time." He reached around and hugged her. It felt so good to have him hug her. He treated her so nice. "Are you ready?" he finally asked as he prepared to go to work.

"Yes, I'm ready."

Several hours later, Carlos walked into the room. "I see you're already working hard. I'm so glad."

"We know we need to put in some serious time." Danny laughed loudly. "We know we have to find some moves which are different and extraordinary if we're going to win, but first we need to have the basic moves down perfectly and this will take a lot of practice. I hope you can help us later with these special steps that will add the much-needed sizzle that we'll need."

Carlos pointed to a cabinet. "I have many tapes you need to watch. Some of the best competition in the world is right here." He opened a door and pointed toward the tapes he must have been collecting for a long time.

"It will be good to watch them. Do you mind if we take some home with us?"

"Not at all—I think they'll do you some good." Carlos turned toward Sveta. "Do you mind if I dance with your girl?"

"Be my guest. I think she might be better than me. I know the moves, but she has so much more natural ability than I do."

While they danced for several songs, Carlos forced her to spin and bend, as he pushed her harder and harder to follow his lead. "You're good at following." He paused for a second, as if in deep thought before he added, "Tonight we need to go dancing. I've been invited to a special party, and I want you two to go to it with me. A client of mine is having this social, and I'm sure bringing you with me will be all right with them. You need to practice in front of people and convince them to like your style. Here, I'll write down the address for you." He left to find a piece of paper in his office.

"We have to leave soon since he'll have students coming in," Danny leaned over and whispered as he left the room.

"I understand. If you don't mind, I think I would like to go back to Brighton Beach. I cannot get those girls out of my head."

"We can go there, if you really want to. We can also

purchase some flowers to pay respects to your father, if you wish."

"I would like that. Thank you."

As Carlos returned to the dance hall and handed Danny the paper with the address on it, two men entered the studio wearing dark suits. "Sorry for breaking in on you during your dance practice, but we need to talk to Miss Panova for a minute."

Sveta felt shocked that they knew her name. "Who are you?"

"We're with the CIA here in New York." The first man pulled a badge out of his suit to show her.

"Have I done something wrong?" Sveta began to breathe hard.

"No, it is nothing like that, but your name is on our list of people to watch. As you may have seen in the news, we're holding some hearings with some Russian businessmen who are being investigated for smuggling and racketeering."

"I have seen some of the news, but what does that have to do with me?"

"We're not sure at this point, but we have reason to believe, based on some recent information which I can't fully disclose, that they appear to have a large interest in you. For some reason they think your father is still alive, and they've hired people to watch you."

"My papa . . . ."

"Yes. As you know, a large collection of paintings was stolen about the time your father vanished. Some people think the paintings are still here in New York and if your father is still alive he will be the key to finding them."

"That's impossible to believe."

"We think so also, but these people are dangerous and unpredictable. You need to be careful, and if you're threatened in any way, please contact us. Their world is crashing around them and they may do some crazy things. Just in case, if you hear of anything from your father and we're wrong, it would be wise to contact us immediately." He paused to smile. "It's great to have you come here to dance and we wish you well."

She felt confused. What did he really know? "Thank you very much. Can I ask you something?"

"Sure. I'm not sure we can answer, but we will if we can."

"My father's body was supposedly never recovered. Is it actually possible that he might still be alive?"

A long paused indicated how much he had to select his words with care. "Since your father's file is heavily sealed, the truth may never be determined. I guess some questions will go unanswered forever and always remain a mystery."

The other agent spoke without looking directly at her. "I'm sure you've heard of the hearings being conducted on the Lisin family business in America. The main piece of evidence against them is a secret witness who will be revealed later. No one knows who this witness is, and this is what has the Lisins worried."

Oh shit! That must be as close as he can tell me that my papa is alive? "I understand that I will never know all the truth, but I will never believe that my father had anything to do with a theft either. Yes, I wanted to come to New York and see the place where my father was murdered. While it would be great to obtain some answers, I don't think anyone is ever going to help me."

Danny stepped forward and spoke rapidly. "Is she in any danger right now? Do we need to hire a bodyguard or something? Can you offer us any protection?"

"There's nothing we can do and I'm sorry to have to

talk to both of you at the same time, but we thought we should. Trust me, we have completed background checks on both of you and have no reason to suspect either of you of anything."

"Why would you be checking my background?" Danny asked.

"We checked on you because of your connection with Sveta. I hope you understand it is our job" He offered his first full smile. "I think you'll make a great dance couple and we wish you the best." They glanced at each other and left the room as quickly as they had appeared.

"What was that all about?" Danny asked as they left. He had a shocked look on his face.

"Danny, I am so sorry for getting you involved in this. I should have told you everything." Damn! What is he going to think of me now?

"I think we need to have a long conversation tonight." After turning toward Carlos, he continued, "I'm sorry for all this. If you want, we can go somewhere else to practice."

"Don't worry about it. This is the kind of harassment my family is used to. We've had to live with this all of my life and it is nothing new."

Sveta glanced around. "I thought I was the only one having to live with this."

"Trust me; the whole world is like this when you're an outsider. However, you're part of our family here now, and we'll take care of you."

Danny reached over and hugged her much tighter than any previous time. "You need to tell me what's going on. I'm lost and I want to help in any way I can. We can hire a lawyer if we need to."

"No, we do not need a lawyer. This is nothing new. I have had this sort of thing happen all the time. After twenty-five years, you would think they would drop it."

What has my papa gotten involved in, and where is he?

CHAPTER 32

After Danny stopped and helped her pick out a small bouquet of flowers, he soon fulfilled his promise by taking her to the spot where her father was reportedly thrown to the water below. She was unable to speak as they made their way to the spot. While she now felt like her father was alive, she knew she had no way to know for certain. "Thank you for doing this for me," Sveta said as she fought the tears forming in her eyes.

"You're so welcome. I know this must be hard on you."

While looking into the waters below, she tried to imagine the events that had happened almost twenty-five years ago. How did my papa get involved with something like this? Why, oh why did I have to lose my papa like this?

"I have had dreams of this place all of my life and it now feels so funny to actually be here. It isn't like my dreams at all. This place is so different. I still do not completely believe my father was murdered as reported by the Americans. You know the Russian police and the mafia still think that he was involved and later defected to America."

"Yes, I've read the stories. I'm so sorry."

A man glancing over at them from the top of a building broke her attention. While he acted as if he was taking pictures of the city, he often readjusted the aim of his lens at them. Perhaps she acted paranoid, but the words of the CIA agents still scared her as she whispered to Danny,

"Do you see the man on top of the building over there?"

Danny turned as the man vanished. "I don't see anyone. Who was it?"

"I'm not sure, but I think we were having our picture taken by him."

"Many people bring cameras to New York to take pictures. You'll get used to it."

"I'm sure you're right." Her thoughts returned to the two girls she rode the plane with. "I still want to return to where we saw the two girls in Brighton Beach the other day. I want to make sure they're safe." She could fully imagine them being abducted now.

"We'll go there next just in case, but we'll need to be careful. If they are under the control of the mafia, it will not be safe to interfere openly and it will be best not to make too much direct contact with them there."

"They seemed like such nice girls. I hate to have them abused here."

They soon arrived on Neptune Avenue and walked over to Brighton Beach Avenue where the streets looked as she remembered them. While walking, she saw other shops she wanted to explore, and it did feel so good to hear Russian voices everywhere.

She suddenly felt hungry and stopped in front of one café. When she saw pelmini on the menu, she asked, "Are you hungry?"

"Yes, I would love to eat. Did you see something you wanted?"

She pointed to several things on the menu which were written in Russian. "Yes, these are good."

Danny flashed Sveta a big smile before he added, "I think you'll have to decide for us." As soon as they ordered and received their food, they moved to a table by a large window. Danny explored the food and produced some inquisitive faces.

"Come on, try it, you'll like it."

Danny started to eat, but stopped to say, "Hey, this isn't too bad."

Sveta was enjoying the meal as she glanced out the window. She suddenly stopped—the two girls she was looking for were strolling down the street. She pointed so that Danny would see them. "There they are. Do you see them?"

"I think I see the ones you're talking about. Are you sure it's them?"

"I think it might be them, but they are dressed differently."

As they walked along the street, both had on short dresses and long boots. When a car passed by, both girls waved at it, but it didn't slow down. When they reached the corner they stopped and looked around before returning down the street.

"I think they must be hookers. Perhaps you're wrong."

Could it be possible they were forced into this so quickly? "I need to go talk to them."

"If they're working for a pimp, it could be dangerous. Let's watch them for a minute."

While it was hard for Sveta to remain sitting for so long, she did as he asked, knowing it might be right. They watched the girls walking up and down the street for most of an hour until a large dark-blue Chrysler slowed down to talk to them. She studied the flashy car, which had lots of chrome and ornaments, but dark tinted windows which didn't allow her to see the driver or occupants. "That must be the pimp they're working for," Danny whispered. She thought Danny might be right. They might be hookers. If these were the girls she had met on the plane, they had been turned into prostitutes in a short period of time.

As the car speed off Danny leaned even closer to keep his voice from being overheard. "Now may be the best time to talk to them. Even if the pimp will be gone for a while, we don't need to make a scene. If they've been abducted, we need to provide an address where they are staying so that we can have the authorities come in to help them. You have to promise me that we'll leave soon since we don't need to create problems for ourselves either."

"I feel sorry for them. I want to check on them."

As they walked to the street corner, the older sister turned and glanced at Danny, where she spoke in broken English. "Would you want date?"

Sveta moved closer to her and spoke quickly in Russian. "I saw you on the plane coming from Russia the other day."

The girls' faces flashed a coded horror as they glanced around. "It isn't safe here. You have to help us."

"I understand. Don't worry. We'll have someone come here soon."

"You can't do anything. They'll kill us! Run away as fast as you can. We also have our family back in Russia to think about."

"Where are you staying?"

"It's not far from here and maybe about two blocks that way. You can't help us. Get away from us as fast as you can!" The girl tossed her head and headed down the street with her sister following her.

Sveta spoke softly while looking away from her. "We'll be back later. We won't leave you like this."

Danny pulled Sveta's hand hard. "We have to get out of here."

Sveta hated to leave, but knew she had to trust Danny. These two girls were in a bad situation, but she didn't need to get herself or Danny in trouble.

As they approached the subway and could relax a little, Sveta remembered the card she had been given by the interviewer at the airport. "I need to make a call." She handed him the card and smiled.

"Agreed, but we need to make the call from a phone where we won't be traced." He headed for a phone on the wall at the station. "This will do fine."

After he grabbed the phone and deposited money an operator soon answered. "Yes. I think there's something you need to know. Some girls are being worked as prostitutes in Brighton Beach. They're Russian girls who arrived in America a few days ago. They're on the street now and they should be easy to spot."

Danny replaced the phone and hurried over to the subway. "That's the best we can do for now. Don't worry; I'll follow up on the call more at a later date."

"I want to know they're safe. We need to go back and see if the police respond. Please."

Apparently, Danny knew she was right. "We have to be careful, bad men run these operations." He turned to go back.

All looked the same as when they had left, but she saw no signs of the two girls. They decided to go back to the café they had lunch and watch. After Danny ordered some drinks, they went to the same table where she knew they could do nothing but sit and wait.

About an hour later she heard a female voice whispering in Russian that was coming from behind them. Sveta turned to see the younger sister standing there and motioning for her to come to the back of the store. Sveta and Danny hurried as requested. In Russian, she talked to Sveta. "My sister said she talked to you. The men we came to see for work lied to us. They say we owe them a lot of money and our parents will be hurt if we go to the police. They have beaten and raped us from the first day we arrived here, and our passports have been taken from us. We don't know what to do. They are scary men."

"Where is your sister?"

"She's in the hotel with a man now. He wants beer and they sent me here to buy some. I can only stay a minute."

"We've called the authorities. They'll be here soon."

"The police won't do any good. They have been called many times already. These men will get mad at us and hurt us more tonight." She began to weep.

Danny stared at the girl before looking around. "Both of you stay here. I'll be back in a minute." He left the café and had his phone to his ear where apparently he had to make a call he didn't want anyone to hear. He remained on the phone for almost five minutes.

He rushed into the café and spoke to Sveta. "Tell them that help is on the way, and to stay here." His eyes focused deeply on her. "However, we have to leave. They will be taken care of now, so don't worry." He grabbed Sveta's arm. "You have to trust me. We have to leave now."

As he headed out the back door, he made several quick turns before waving down a taxi. After they made it inside, he told the driver to take them back to his apartment. "Don't worry, she'll be fine now."

"Who did you call?"

"Friends—you'll know soon enough."

CHAPTER 33

After entering his apartment, Danny closed the door and gave Sveta a large hug. "It's so good to have you here. I don't want anything to happen to you."

She enjoyed receiving such a hug from Danny since he acted truly concerned about her. Perhaps he knew better. She had traveled to a foreign country, and she didn't know the way things operated there. However, she had heard many stories and wondered if they were true.

After separating from her slightly he said, "We have to prepare for the party. We can learn a lot about salsa dancing tonight since these people are wealthy and can afford the very best lessons."

"I do not know. My English is not so good. They will ask me questions and I will not understand."

"Don't worry. I'll be with you, and we won't stay too long."

After he selected some clothes, he went to the bathroom to change. She smiled, realizing how shy he acted. In the time she had been with him, she had never seen him naked, and it felt highly unusual. However, she went to her room to decide what she would wear tonight since she wanted to look as good as she could.

After she dressed, she heard the TV and noticed that Danny had the news on and was watching a reporter intensely. "Come here, they have news about the girls from Russia."

A reporter stood on the street with many policemen around her. She talked as if the story had recently been reported. "The hotel behind me is where most of the girls were located. As many as fifteen girls were reported as being held against their will. The Russian mafia is said to be involved, but it will be a while before we know the full story. The girls are too scared and afraid to talk at the moment."

"I understand exactly how they must feel." Sveta glanced around nervously.

The reporter continued reporting, "The reputed Lisin family is being accused, but none of the girls are talking. The word from sources is that solid proof will be given shortly from a guarded informant. With the current hearings on the Lisin operations, this new development will be extremely important to follow. The court will resume hearing testimony regarding the case tomorrow. This could not have happened at a worse time for the Lisin organization."

Danny looked over at Sveta. "Don't worry. Your friends will be taken care of now."

"I know of the Lisin family. They are a powerful family in Russia. Can we go to the court to hear the hearings?"

His smile disappeared. "Yes, they're open to the general public, but it may be crowded and I'm sure they have limited spaces."

"I'd like to go and see. Will you take me to see if we can watch it?"

While he looked apprehensive, he soon relented. "Okay, we can go, but I'm not sure if we can enter the courtroom or not. So, I make no promises."

She wondered what he had really asked. Should she really do this? It was best to change the subject for now. "I understand. Are you ready to go to the party?

"Yes. And you look great in your new dress." He gave

her the most sincere smile she could ever remember receiving.

"Do you really like the dress?" She swirled slightly in it.

"Yes—very much."

Sveta enjoyed his compliment as she started to like Danny more every day, even if he still remained a little weird.

Soon, the elevator stopped on the floor where the party was being held. Danny winked at Sveta and held her arm as they looked for the right apartment. A man soon opened the door as they started to explain who they were. Fortunately, Carlos stood close to the door and rushed over.

"I'm so glad you decided to join us." Carlos turned his attention to the man at the door. "These are friends of mine from the dance studio that I told you about. This is Danny Martinez and his friend from Russia, Sveta."

"It's good to meet you. He's told us about you. We love to dance salsa, and we welcome anyone who can teach us something different. Please make yourself at home. We'll have some music playing soon and want to see you dancing on the floor."

"Thank you for allowing us to join you tonight. We also love salsa," Danny said.

The room contained maybe fifteen people who all looked like they had come to dance. Many already had on their dancing shoes. As she studied the large apartment decorated so expensively, she realized that the owner must be very wealthy to afford so much space in New York City.

Several people walked over to them as they made their way across the room while Carlos stayed with them and introduced them one at a time. Sveta heard many names and became lost in trying to memorize them. They all acted friendly and asked her questions. With many of them interested in her accent, she often blushed and kept asking them to excuse her for her poor English.

They finally met each of the guests before ending up at the table of food. They decided to have a glass of wine from a bottle already open on the table—a pinot noir. As Carlos poured a glass for them and one for himself, he lifted his glass to them. "I think we need to toast to new friends tonight. These are the people who can help you very much. They also want to learn. It's a two-way street. But remember, these are also some of the people you'll be competing with."

After finishing the glass of wine, Carlos headed for the stereo and selected some music from a CD holder he had with him. As the music started, he lowered the volume for a minute so he could talk. "I'd like to thank our host tonight for this great party and refreshments. His lovely wife has been working hard to learn the salsa, and I think you'll agree she is a fantastic dancer. With her husband's permission, we'd like to show you what she's been learning."

The crowd quickly made a circle around the dance floor, which was large and accommodating. From several large windows on the far side of the room that overlooked Central Park she saw lights from below that sparkled and added a special charm to the room.

As Carlos walked to the center of the room, a woman crossed to meet him. She looked stunning in her mannerisms and charm, and the jewelry she wore . . . completely dazzling. If money could truly talk, it shouted right now. Sveta studied her dress which looked impressive and cut in a sexy design to highlight not only her large breasts but her shapely legs. Carlos' back stood straight and professional while his black hair gleamed from the overhead lights. As he rigidly waited for the start of the music his eyes focused intently on his student. This quiet moment heightened the anticipation as all waited.

When the music finally erupted in typical Latin style, they maintained their pose for several beats to make their movements in perfect rhythm with the beat. As he moved her through several initial moves with ease, the crowd applauded loudly. The start looked fantastic, and the timing superb.

As the dance progressed, Carlos added more and more complicated turns and dips. She danced like a professional, and followed his every move. He also offered her space to freestyle several times. The hours they had prepared for this semi-private exhibition showed well for their effort.

Sveta constantly watched for some new movement she had never seen before. She needed something special to add to their dance, and since she knew this might be such a point of inspiration she concentrated on every move. However, this girl looked so beautiful that Sveta had a hard time concentrating on her dancing ability.

At near the end of the dance when they finished, Sveta saw what she was looking for. When the girl stretched out wide before curling back into Carlos's arms, he dipped her impressively. Sveta had another idea as she wondered how the step would look if they added a carry on the lady's return. The movement would be hard to perform and she wasn't sure it could be possible. The step would be more of a ballet-style move, but choreographed for salsa.

She could not wait to discuss her idea with Danny since this step would be the kind of excitement he had been talking about, and she wanted to make him happy. As the dance ended everyone clapped again, and the other girls in the room rushed to the student to congratulate her. She beamed with pride, as she should—the dance looked professional. Carlos had worked his magic to perfection.

Over the next hour, Carlos danced with all the girls, and also helped the men with their dance. The party turned out to be much like a group dance lesson. Sveta danced with several of the men at the party, but had a hard time following most of them. While they made her feel uneasy, she tried as hard as she could to follow their leads.

Sveta felt glad when Danny finally asked her to dance with him. He started with a basic move before adding one layer after another to the steps. He made her feel great with his ability to control and lead her. While studying Danny's dancing ability she suddenly wondered how he had learned to dance salsa so great. Danny soon stopped, however, and raised her hand to kiss before speaking. "I think the time for us to leave has come." He winked. "I've several more places I want us to check out tonight."

"Okay! This party has been fun here tonight. We need to thank them for letting us come to their party."

"We will." He reached for her hand. "They were nice to let us come and practice with them."

CHAPTER 34

As Sveta rested on the couch she reflected on the last several weeks where they had worked constantly on their salsa dancing. They had practiced every day and went to clubs late at night, where they had obtained many friends who had also taught them many new steps. The dancers at most clubs often talked about the upcoming competitions. They had also obviously started to put in a lot of time in perfecting their dancing.

She squealed with excitement as she thought about the first club which would host a preliminary in just two more days. This is where everyone would start sizing up the competition for the finals. She knew that everyone expected the bar to be crowded, and with no limit on the number of entries she anticipated it to last most of the night. It would soon be time to find out if all of their hard work would pay off.

Danny had gone to work for a while tonight, but she expected him soon. She soon decided to watch the news on TV as she waited. News of the Lisin trial started after a few minutes. She remembered going to several hearings until the judge finally allowed for a rescheduling for a week to allow time for the defense to present more information.

The trial would begin again tomorrow, and Ivan Lisin had apparently talked his brothers, Boris and Michael, into attending the hearings. If the state could not prove its case, they wouldn't be able to retry them later. The major bust resulting from the tip Danny and Sveta had secretly sent to the police had hurt the Lisins' case, but with the two brothers in the court to defend the charges, the state's case didn't seem to be looking good. While they had promised more information would be forthcoming which would prove all allegations, they acted as if they were also stalling.

After she heard a knock on the door, she assumed that Danny must be home. She ran to the door to let him in. However, she quickly jerked backward in shock as she recognized the caller in the hallway. She watched Denis Molev studying her as he moved forward.

"What are you doing here?" Sveta squealed. This was the last person in the world she had expected to see. She felt excited about seeing him, but the cold look on his face made her realize something was wrong.

He spoke Russian in a deep rough tone, as she quickly wondered if he knew any English. "I've been brought here to talk to you. Things are not as you think. The Lisin family thought you would lead them to your father."

She had never seen such a menacing look on his face before. "My father?"

"Yes, we strongly believed he's still alive. The Lisin family has obtained word the paintings exist and whoever has them has insisted in dealing only with Boris and Michael directly. This trial gives them the perfect cover to come to America to handle this."

"Do you mean you work for the Lisin family?" Had she been so taken in by him? Oh God—no!

"Yes. I'm sorry you had to find out this way, but with the trial coming to an end soon they need to make contact with him soon. Have you seen your father since you've been here? We need to know!" He reached for her arm and squeezed it tightly.

She tried to pull from him. "I have not. And if I had, do

you think I'd tell you?"

He grabbed her arm and jerked her closer to him. "There's only one reason you're alive right now. We don't want to scare him off. You are being watched constantly and if you try to warn him or don't cooperate with us, we'll have to deal with you."

"I don't know what you're talking about." She quivered as she studied his vicious hands squeezing her arm.

He offered another sinister smirk. "Do you really think I was interested in you back in Russia? I was hired to watch you and see when you made contact with your father. We know he's tried to contact you many times."

"So, you admit you only went dancing with me to try to find my father." Her hands went to her eyes to cover the tears flooding them.

He increased his hold on her. "So that you know. The girls you thought you were helping in Brighton are under our control again. They'll be reassigned to other cities. You'll be added to their ranks if you don't cooperate with us, but if you do help us you will be rewarded. The decision is up to you."

"You want me to turn my own father in?" She started to scream.

She smelled vodka on his breath. "He's a dead man. He either died twenty five years ago, or he will die soon."

"I hate you! You lied to me." She leaned forward to glare in his face. "How could you have done this?"

"I think you'll show more respect soon." He released her arm. "We'll be watching you so you need to think about what I said. By the way, you have a nice new boyfriend. It's funny how he knows nothing about what's going on. You need to think about his safety. It would be a shame to have him pay for all of your mischief." He turned and disappeared—like a ghost appearing at one moment and vanishing in the night the next.

What do I do now?

Sveta continuously shook on the floor until she heard a knock on the door again. She eased toward it, but looked out the peephole this time. Danny was standing on the other side, waiting for her. She quickly swung open the door and rushed into his arms. "I missed you!" She yelled as he looked surprised to see her flying into his arms.

"Wow, you make me feel good to be missed." He put his arms around her to hold her, but he soon appeared to know that something was wrong. "What is it?"

"I had a visitor. I need to talk to you." This was going to be hard, she thought.

"Who was it?"

"He's a guy from back in Russia that I dated. I know I told you about him. His name is Denis."

With a strong flash of concern, Danny rushed into the apartment. "Denis is here in New York?"

"Yes. He's not who I thought he was. He's working for the Lisin family."

"That isn't good. What did he want with you?"

"He's convinced that my father is alive and wanting to see me."

"What's wrong with your father wanting to see you? And I thought your father was dead?"

"Some people think he's still alive, and I would like to believe he's alive myself, but it has been twenty-five years now."

Danny glanced around. "I don't think I'll be able to leave you alone anymore. It isn't safe."

"I saw on the TV where the trials will begin again tomorrow. Will you take me to see them? I need to see what is going on."

"Are you sure you want to watch them? Doing so

might not be safe."

"Since the police are everywhere, the courtroom might be the safest place for me. It will not be unusual for me to be in the courtroom, since I am Russian and interested in this case."

"We can go if you wish. The trial might give you some closure to this, if you know the answer to some things. All this will be over soon."

"One more thing, he also told me the girls who we rescued the other day are back under their control and will be reassigned to other locations. Is that possible?"

"I don't think so since the American authorities have them. I would think what he said is impossible, but I'll check on his comments tomorrow morning."

"I hate getting you involved in all this. It is not fair to you. You've been a perfect gentleman to me the entire time I've been here."

"I promised you that you could trust me, and I plan on keeping my promise. We only have a few more days to prepare for the competition. We need to concentrate on wining. From what I know so far from you, I think your father would have been proud of you."

Approaching the sofa, Sveta retrieved her shawl and slipped on her shoes. "Tonight I think I need a drink."

"Don't worry. I know a place where they have margaritas at half-price and the music isn't bad either. In fact, the band is extremely good."He paused to give her a hug. "It will be good to watch some of the dancers tonight and it will be good to try some new moves of our own also."

CHAPTER 35

The night had lasted until the early morning. In fact, Sveta now remembered so little of it. She had had too much to drink and even Danny drank much more than usual. Something was bothering him, and she had a hard time pinpoint his thoughts. Perhaps he was regretting inviting her to America.

"What time is it?" she asked in a surprisingly hoarse tone when she entered the main room.

Danny offered a soft moan from the blanket where he slept under. "Give me ten more minutes. I have a bad headache."

"I understand. I do also." She leaned toward him and started rubbing his head. Minutes later Sveta started to rub and massage his back. He felt warm—masculine.

At first, he acted as if he enjoyed it, but then he suddenly sat and looked at her. "All right. I'm up."

Sveta wasn't used to this and it started to bother her. Why did he remain so distant in his affections for her? Was she too bad or ugly for him? She knew she had small breasts, but the rest of her looked nice enough, she thought. What was it about him?

He dashed to the bathroom as he said, "I need to take a shower. I won't take long."

Sveta thought about surprising him in the shower and seeing what his reaction would be, but decided against it. She would make her move later. "I'm going to buy something to eat. Do you want anything?"

Since she didn't hear an answer, she assumed that he

had already entered the shower.

CHAPTER 36

The courthouse was packed with people as Sveta and Danny arrived. The media covering the story was obviously looking for all angles as the first day of the trial resumed. She had heard how the prosecution hadn't proven its case too convincingly as of yet. They still hadn't produced their star witness, and apparently the Lisin family thought they had none. She thought, like many people were that they would soon be back in business as usual.

As Sveta and Danny approached the door entering the courthouse, a policeman stepped forward and asked, "Do you have any weapons, knives or cameras on you? If so, they have to be left outside. You will also need to show some identification."

She remembered the same routine as before, but when Sveta showed her Russian passport, the policeman stopped her this time and asked, "Are you a witness for the defense?"

"No, I'm just interested in the hearings."

"Please wait here for a minute."

A few minutes later a man in a dark suit approached her and flashed an FBI badge as he asked, "May I see your passport, please." After she handed it to him he read the name and added, "I've heard of you being here and of your father. I can understand that you would be interested in this case, but I do have to ask you some questions which will only take a minute. Will you please follow me?"

As Danny started to follow them the agent turned and faced him. "Are you related to Miss Panova?"

"I'm her friend in the States. She's staying with me."

"I see, but I need to talk to her in private for a minute." He pointed ahead. "You can go on into the courtroom. She'll join you shortly."

Since Danny appeared to have no choice, he entered the courtroom ahead of Sveta. She really owed him more explanation, and hoped to do so soon.

Sveta turned and followed the FBI agent into a separate room. "Please have a seat." After she complied, she waited for him to proceed. "I need to know if you plan on taking any part in this trial, as a witness or other source. The stakes are high here, and we don't need any surprises."

"I do not, but it's important for me to see what is going on."

"The report I have is that one of the Lisin brothers is responsible for the death of your father, but that he was also recently murdered in Russia. I have to warn you that these other brothers can be much more vicious than he was and it may not be safe for you to be here. If they think you're going to testify against them, they'll find a way to get to you."

"I have nothing which can be used against them. I'm simply a single Russian girl making a trip to America to dance in a salsa competition."

"That's the story I've heard, but I have a hard time buying it. I can't stop you from watching the proceedings, and I would advise you against being here, but it's your choice." He stood and waited for Sveta. "You're free to go."

She left the room and headed for the courtroom where the hearing would be held and Danny was waiting for her.

"Is everything all right?"

"Yes, they wanted to make sure I wasn't here to testify or bring new evidence to the trial. They are suspicious of everyone and especially anyone of Russian nationality."

"I can't say I blame them since this is a high profile case. It's peculiar that it's being heard while you're here." He acted concerned, but still willing to be there for her.

As Sveta looked around the room, she saw many people studying her, and especially those sitting at the defense table. For some reason, she definitely had their attention. A tall man with deep-set eyes and a heavy brow soon pushed away from them and headed up the stairs to the balcony where she was. He had a calm but professional smile on his face as he approached her and spoke in Russian. "I am Semion Knoff, one of the attorneys representing the Lisin companies. Is it all right if I ask you a couple of questions?"

"What do you want to know?" she asked.

"I've heard you were seen going into a closed room with the FBI. Are you here to testify?"

"No, we're here simply out of interest and curiosity." she glanced around.

"I'm glad to hear you say that, and I hope your interest stays that way. The Lisin family would like to end the proceedings as fast as possible."

"I'm sure they would." While she felt intimidated, she also had a surge of confidence she had never felt before. "Is there anything else?"

Continuing in Russian, Semion told her he had heard about the misfortune of her father and felt sincerely sorry about what had happened.

Sveta told him thank you as he left.

Danny, who apparently didn't understand a word of the Russian quickly asked, "Is everything all right?"

"Yes, but I didn't know I would be spotted so fast, but perhaps I should have known since I'm apparently being watched by everyone."

"Are you sure you want to stay and follow this?"

"Yes. I have always had an interest in the workings of the Lisins. For the trouble they have caused my mom and I, it would be good to see justice being served, even if it is in the United States." After she studied the various other people at the table with the attorney she was finally able to identify the three Lisin brothers. Ivan sat in the center and had the others around him. She could also recognize Boris and Michael on one side. She remembered the time they had come to her work and asked her questions.

"I think I need to go to the bathroom, but I will not be gone long." She glanced around as she left.

"I'll stay and watch to see if anything happens while you're gone."

"Thank you. I will hurry." She wanted to offer him a kiss, maybe one day.

The restroom was down a long hallway, and she had to navigate around many people trying to enter the courtroom. She heard many conversations in English discussing the possible outcomes, but most of the comments were too hard to understand fully. She felt glad to blend in with the crowd.

On the way out of the restroom she entered the main hallway, but only to run directly into the path of Ivan Lisin who stopped for a second to speak in Russian as she recognized her. "You're Nickolay Panov's daughter, Svetlana Panova, aren't you? I'm sorry that I didn't recognize you the other day at the airport and it's remarkable to see you here."

Her muscles in her entire body tightened. "Yes, it's fascinating. I'm here to dance in a dance competition and heard about the hearing while I was here. I didn't know about the trial until I saw it on TV."

"I just heard that you're here dancing in a competition, and much like your father did before you. However . . . I understand you're dancing in a Spanish ballroom competition and not the ballet that your father excelled in."

Damn . . . what have I got myself into? "I'm not the great dancer that I heard my father was. I have only recently discovered salsa dancing, one thing led to another, and now I'm here in a competition. I'm still not a great dancer."

"I know how bad it is to not have your father with you as you grew up. His death has also caused major changes in my life." Ivan paused. "The investigations around his death and the extreme scrutiny the theft has caused forced my family to turn to legitimate business. Because of our long history, the truth is hard for many people to believe. Yes, we still have many problems, and we will for a long time."

While he sounded sincere, she still had doubts. "I wish I could believe what you're saying, but remember that I live in Russia and have to live with reality. We both know that your brother was heard saying that he was the one who killed my father."

Ivan lowered his voice. "Yes . . . he had a loud mouth, but one which also cost him his life."

"I know he was your brother and because of that I will say . . . I'm sorry, but . . . ."

"Don't worry. I understand how you must feel. While Russia has been through a lot of problems for a long time, it's time to progress forward and despite what you may think of me, I'm extremely dedicated to Russia and its future."

For some strange reason, she felt like he was sincere in his statement. "I guess time will tell for sure."

As if deep in thought, he paused for a minute before he asked, "Are you sure you're not here to testify or provide any information to the prosecution?" His sudden conversion to things at hand surprised Sveta.

"No, I'm here as an observer, and that is all."

"I hope so since this is something I don't think you want to become involved with. I expect to have these hearings over soon. Good luck on your competition." He turned and walked away.

She quickly hurried to her seat next to Danny. "Did anything happen while I was gone?"

"Nothing really—all the conversation is at the tables. I think we're getting another motion for a continuance from the prosecution. It appears that they still don't have some information they're waiting for."

"Let's go, if this is the case." As Sveta stood, she obtained one last, long look at the defendants' table. One row behind them, a tall blonde guy stood and stared directly at her—Denis.

CHAPTER 37

Danny yelled through the bathroom door, "Hurry—we don't want to be late! The crowds at the competition will be large, and we need to find a good table to watch the other dancers. It'll be a long night and we'll become very tired of standing all night if we don't get a good seat."

"I am hurrying, I promise."

As she emerged, she saw Danny in a stunning new dance outfit he had purchased. The almost all black suit had some fancy white highlighting. With a new haircut and his flashy white smile adding to his charm, he looked more than professional—he looked totally irresistible tonight. "I'm ready. Can I get you anything to drink before we go?" he asked.

She watched him study the new bright-red and eye-catching dress he had purchased for her. It offered a sexy style which fit her perfectly. While the low-cut top revealed her shoulders and upper chest, it was also perfect for her small breasts. With a long, revealing slit running along her right side inhibiting her some, she, at least, loved the way her makeup had transformed her into more of a professional-looking dancer. Now, what did he really think?

"You look beautiful!" He shouted.

"I'm still not so sure about all of this and I think I look like a clown with this much makeup on. You should have not spent so much money on a makeup artist for me. The cost is too much."

"I think the professional makeup will help us a lot, and

your hair really looks great. The girl did a great job on styling, even if she had you in the shop for a long time." His smile beamed as he leaned in closer to her.

She decided to shift the attention back to him. "Look at you. You look so handsome tonight."

"I have one more surprise for you. Don't get excited. They aren't real, but no one will know the truth except us." He opened a cabinet door and retrieved a tiny package. "Tell me what you think?"

Sveta accepted the package and immediately opened it to study the earrings and a necklace inside. They sparkled like real diamonds, but Danny had already told her the truth. In any case, they looked flashy and they would do great. "Thank you so much. You're great." She hurried back to the bathroom to try them on. When she returned, she knew that they would make a good couple tonight.

As they arrived at the club, she noticed how busy it was in spite of still being several hours before the contest started. After she glanced around, she realized that Danny was right in that the club would only have standing room later. He quickly obtained a choice table and placed his carrying bag containing their dancing shoes and towels, which they might need later, on one chair.

When they received a pat on their backs, they both quickly turned around to face Carlos. "I see you arrived here early. Your decision can be good and bad since nerves can work on you in many ways. Are you two ready?"

"I hope so, Carlos. You've been a big help. We could have never gotten ready without your help."

"Danny, my boy, you're a great dancer and your partner is everything one could ever ask for." He offered Sveta a quick kiss on the cheek. "This first few will be the hardest competitions to win. However, as the best dancers win and over the next week the others become discouraged and quit you will have a much better chance in winning. Those competitions will be your best time to qualify, but you have a limited number of times to qualify and need to do so as quickly as you can. It will be important to pick the best places to attempt to win." He glanced at both of them. "Do you think you have your special steps and movements perfected? They will make a difference."

Sveta's smiles covered her face. "I think we have the steps much under control. Everything depends on the other dancers and the room we're given. The movements work best when we have a lot of room to do a carry, like the one we worked on so hard."

"I'll be pulling for you tonight. We'll talk after the competition and win or lose; I'll buy the drinks tonight when the competition is over."

As the night progressed the club grew more and more crowded until the time finally arrived to start. They allowed five couples at a time on the floor, but even at that rate, it would take hours to give everyone a chance to dance. Each couple would be allowed to dance to three songs. While the club management would determine the winner, they constantly played the crowds by asking for them to applaud. With the competition in such a festive mood, it felt hard to believe this was also such a serious time.

During the second dance they finally had a chance to demonstrate their signature move when the other couples had moved to one side and allowed them the room they needed. Danny set it up perfectly as he grabbed both of Sveta's hands and finished a basic step. After he raised his left hand, allowing Sveta to pass under, he never let go of her hand, and pulled her close to him instead. As he let her unwind away from him, he held on to her with his right hand until she was fully extended. She raised her right hand in true Latino style at this point.

This represented nothing complicated so far, but now was the time—their time. He pulled her back to him as she executed a double spin. When she came face to face with him, he didn't freeze, and he didn't dip her, as so many others did. Instead, he bent his legs slightly as she stretched onto her toes, setting up a lift with little effort.

After Danny supported her weight on his right leg momentarily, he shifted all the weight to his left foot which he swiveled around on. The movement was executed fluidly, making the step a perfect mixture of classical ballet and salsa. The crowds appeared to love the move as they applauded, and quickly grabbed the interest of the other dancers who wondered what had just happened.

As the music prepared to end they had to hurry to prepare for the finish. They had planned a classic spin and dip which they executed perfectly. They could not have asked for any better timing. The decision now rested with the club management, and the judges. When they left the floor and crossed over to their table, many patrons came over to congratulate them. While it had been an exhausting dance, they still had one more time to show what they could do. The competition had to know they had scored points on their last move, and would be turning it up on the last one.

"You danced great!" Danny yelled as he laughed loudly.

"You made an excellent carry. I'm so glad we didn't fall."

With a big laugh, they both yelled at each other. "We did it!"

The other dancers soon waited on the floor to start the final dance. With the passion of the dance heating up, all dancers knew this would be their last chance to influence the judges. Two of the couples in this group appeared to be among the best and flashed smiles indicating that they knew each other.

Before the music started, the couples let it be known this dance would be different. They had already proven they had style; now, the time had come to display how sultry and sexy the salsa could be. They waited provocatively, awaiting the start, as the first girl teased her hand around her partner's face.

Feeling the beat with each pounding of the drums, the animalistic movements of the two couples heightened continuously, as each couple tried to outdo the other. Mouths dropped open and dry as the dance finished. This represented about as close as you could get to the origins of the salsa. Their movements displayed pure, basic and raw sexual excitement. The Cuban form of salsa is addictive and seductive beyond any other dance and these two couples had perfected this style.

Sveta looked at Danny. He had no smile on his face—just deep concentration. This style they hadn't worked on. Their technique remained more professional ballroom. He looked around and saw the crowds. They loved the dance, but all he could do was lower his eyes. She could not understand why he resisted dancing like the others. They would have to talk.

CHAPTER 38

For most of the next day they didn't talk much as Danny appeared to have something on his mind. She had never seen him be so quiet. The competition the night before had been fierce, as they assumed. Something needed to change, but they had no time to adjust anything since they had another competition lined up for tonight.

"Are you all right?" Sveta focused on his eyes since she knew they couldn't lie to her.

"Yes. I'm doing a lot of thinking. Perhaps we should have practiced more styles. If the final decisions rest with the crowds, we need to be exciting when we finish. We're going to need more help, and fast."

"Does being sexy with me on the floor bother you? I feel like you do not want to touch me, but I promise you I don't mind." She leaned closer to him.

"You're a beautiful girl, and I think it's me. I'm sorry, but somehow we'll work it out." Before she could respond he added, "I need to go somewhere for a little while, but I won't take long." Without another word he walked out the door.

As she remained on the sofa, she started to think about her trip and how exciting it was to be in New York City. The dancing was so much fun, and it was something that she would never forget. However, she had so many thoughts going on which still puzzled her. Why did everyone have such an interest in her? She knew nothing about what really happened when she was three years old.

She eventually felt tired of staying inside and thought a

little air outside would be good for her. Since she had no way of knowing how long Danny would be gone, she decided to go to the corner store and buy some sparkling water that she liked. After walking out the door, she glanced around at the clear but cold day on her way to the corner store. The coat Danny had purchased for her felt warm and was greatly appreciated. He had spent a lot of money on her, and while she wasn't exactly sure how much, it felt strange that he would do that for someone he hardly knew.

She had almost arrived at the store when someone yelled to her from behind. "Sveta—stop." She turned around to see a man in a dark suit who she thought had to be a government employee of some kind even before she saw any kind of identification. She waited as he caught up with her. "I'm glad I ran into you. I have something I need to discuss with you."

"What is it?"

"We've just received word that the Lisin family thinks you may be here to testify against them. I just found out that your life may be in danger."

"What?" She started to tremble.

"It may be good if you accept some protection. We're going to post some men around here until after the hearings are over. How much longer do you plan on staying in New York?"

"I'll not be here much longer. Everything depends on if we can win a preliminary or not. We didn't do so well last night." Maybe coming here was a bad idea after all.

"My superiors are asking me to provide protection for you, but we'll try to stay out of the way as much as we can. One of our state senators has also called. He was the one who helped to get you here. I think Danny must have made a direct plea to him. Anyway, he's asked us to provide help and said to tell you if you need anything, he would be glad to if he can."

"I appreciate your interest very much. Perhaps I can call him later to thank him. Danny has said nothing about this to me."

***

When Danny returned later, she decided not to tell him about the police protection. She didn't want to alarm him, or have him involved any more than he had already become. He didn't say where he had disappeared to, but he did seem much happier when he returned.

***

They soon arrived early at the next club hosting a competition and this one looked much smaller than the one from the night before, but with the same expectant crowd. While it wasn't near as easy to find good seats tonight, they managed to obtain some chairs from where they could see the dance floor. He soon smiled and maintained the same confidence as the night before. "Tonight we'll do much better. I feel it."

"I hope so. We still need to talk. We have to add more sparkle to our dance."

"I understand, and we'll work on the sparkle tonight, especially since I think we have nothing to lose. What do you think?"

She felt shocked to some extent, but just perhaps, at least she hoped so, she might get to see a different side of Danny tonight. "I think you're up to something." She winked at him and wondered what he had planned since they had no time to make a change in their dance this late.

The dancing soon started much like the previous night, until Danny suddenly unleashed a passion for the salsa she hadn't noticed before. He hovered close to her, as if on a mission tonight and when he twirled her into a close position, he lingered tightly against her. When he prepared for the close, he changed the steps. While he set up the signature step early and executed the movement precisely for the normal finish, he continued to spin on one foot. OHMIGOD! He completed a double spin while carrying her.

When he stopped, the crowd exploded with applause. No one had ever seen such a move before and even the other dancers applauded in awe. Danny bowed before rushing back to Sveta to hug her.

While the night consisted of many passionate dancers, he had set the tone early. In fact, he had upped the ante at the very beginning. "Why did you decide to do that?" She licked her lips to moisten them as they waited for the next dance.

"I want to win. The reason is much more important than you realize."

The second dance started much as the second, but he added new styles Carlos must have taught him. While their variety kept the other couples off balance, she knew the third dance had to be absolutely mind blowing. He glanced over toward her as they headed for the floor. "Do you want to win?"

"Yes, of course. Winning would be great."

Danny offered a devilish smile. "Good! Please follow my lead. We have to pick it up even more."

Sveta followed Danny to the floor. Whatever he had planned, she felt willing to follow as she simply closed her eyes and put her faith in his hands.

***

Even several hours since the announcement, Sveta couldn't believe it—they had won! Danny had revealed a side of himself that she couldn't explain. He became full of passion and excitement, and those few moments on the floor made her realize just how strong her urge had become to have sex with him. He kissed her in front of everyone. Not just a kiss, but wow, what a kiss. Apparently the crowd loved it as much as she did. She couldn't understand what had caused him to change like this. Her heart never slowed down.

As they stood around a table and celebrated with Carlos, an older man approached their table and held out his hand to Danny. "I don't think we've ever met. I'm Senator Knighton. You called me a while back for help arranging for your friend here to come to America to enter this dance contest."

Danny quickly jumped to his feet. "Yes, I remember talking to your office. You don't know how much I appreciate your help. The people in your office were outstanding in helping me."

Knighton surveyed the bar as he waved at several people. "I've heard a lot about your partner, and had to come see for myself how things were working out. America can be a great place and sometimes we forget the appeal to people in other countries. America is still open to all who meet our requirements for citizenship and I think this is so important to demonstrate to the world."

Sveta spoke fast. "I want to thank you also. It has been great dancing here and meeting so many fantastic people."

"If you think of anything I can do for you at all, please let me know." He started to turn away, but hesitated. "I know your father would have loved to see you dance. You are the kind of daughter that can make one proud. I will never forget the research that was presented to me when I received the request. It was very impressive---very eye-opening . . . I would have to say."

"Thank you for saying that, but I think my mom is the

one who would be shocked to see me dancing like this and I'm not sure she would understand this world."

"Is she still back in Russia?"

"Yes. I need to call her and let her know we won tonight."

With a big smile, the senator raised a hand like a timid little schoolboy. "I'll have to do some checking, but if I could make some arrangements for her to come see you dance in the finals, do you think she would come?"

Sveta stopped breathing for a few moments. Was he serious? Could he accomplish such a feat? "I don't know."

"It's just a thought I had. When you talk to her the next time, ask her and let me know."

"Sure, I'll ask her tonight, but I'm not sure what she'll say."

CHAPTER 39

Sveta woke early the next morning, despite not sleeping much the night before. She felt so excited about winning the competition, but after having a lot to drink the night before she now had a headache. The heaviest thought on her mind this morning, however, was the fact that she might be able to bring her mom to America. She hadn't expected this at all!

She got out of bed and stalked over to the door. When she opened it, she saw Danny still asleep on the sofa, but he had already told her she could rise early and call her mom. She quickly returned to the bed and retrieved the phone. While she had called several times before and knew the routine, her heart beat fast. She still didn't know exactly how to approach her mom on this.

When her mom answered the phone, Sveta told her how much she had missed her before giving the details of winning the dance competition the night before. She felt excited and talked so fast she hoped her mom could follow her.

She could hear her mom crying with happiness. "I am so proud of you," Mariya started sobbing as she talked.

"I want you to be here, mom. You wouldn't believe how it is in New York City."

"I'd love to, but I have no way at all."

"Mom—I think you can come. Last night I met a Senator at the club. He's the one who helped me obtain my visa so easily. He's taken a liking to Danny and me, and he thinks it's great we're doing so well. He told me last night if I wanted to bring you here, he would help."

Sveta waited on a long silence on the phone. She knew her mom would be in shock. "I can't believe it."

An hour later she had her mom calmed down and talking sensibly. Sveta knew her mom thought this was a trick to bring her to America. She didn't trust Americans since they had taken her husband and her life, but since her daughter had advanced to the finals and wanted her to come; she finally conceded and agreed to come.

Sveta knew the final details had to be worked out, but believed they would be. "Mom, you'll love it here. New York has so many sites to see."

"Yes, I'm sure there are, but I'll be so lost. You know I don't speak English like you do."

"Don't worry about it. I can speak a little English and will be with you all the time." Sveta glanced around the room and wondered where she would sleep.

"I'll do as you ask. You'll have to tell me what I have to do."

"I'll send you the information as I receive it. I think you'll be here soon." She wanted to scream with joy, but knew Danny was still sleeping. "I'll call you back later."

An hour later, Danny slowly woke and started to make noises, as he started to make some coffee. Eventually she heard him knock on the door. "You wanted to call your mother this morning." His voice boomed through the door.

"I have already talked to her on the phone. I managed to talk her into coming."

"That's good news. I'll have to call the Senator's office since he did promise to help bring her here soon. She'll be here before you know it."

"I know it. She's aware she will have to leave soon."

"Tell her we'll be wiring her some money today, and I'm looking forward to meeting her."

"Thanks, I will tell her when I talk to her next time."

As she left her bedroom, she saw Danny stretched out on the sofa. "I don't know how I will ever thank you for all of this. This is a dream come true for me."

"I'm so glad you're happy." His hair was a mess, but he still looked fantastic.

"I want to go back to the court hearing next week. Do you mind?"

"Sure, but we need to practice as much as we can until your mother gets here." He rubbed his chin, indicating he needed to shave.

She knew she really needed to visit the bathroom first since she would require more time. "I will not take long to get ready for practice. Please give me a few minutes." She reached over to give him a kiss as he turned his face and only allowed one on the cheek. While she still could not understand him, she shrugged her shoulders and headed for the bathroom.

She knew she would have to eventually force him to talk to her and tell her what was going on. This was not natural.

CHAPTER 40

A week later, the courthouse shifted into a heightened frenzy with the anxiety in the air penetrating the crowd which now completely surrounded the building. The media had continued to cover this major event by covering it every day on the news stations and in the papers.

Sveta and Danny knew the routine as they found their way to the courtroom where only a few seats remained, and for which they felt extremely lucky in finding. As the frenzy scattered across the court she studied the various groups forming, and from their body language she could tell the emotions were running high.

When the judge entered from the corner of the room, everyone in the courtroom quit talking and quickly settled in their seats. He lost little time in addressing everyone. "I have been approached by the defense with a motion for an immediate dismissal. Do you have any new evidence the prosecution would like to present at this time?"

The lead attorney stood. "Yes, your honor. We've just received some significant information and we have men attempting to retrieve it as we speak. This evidence will directly link members of the Lisin family to all the crimes we've been working on, plus others. Some of these crimes go back over twenty-five years. We need to recover these items and log them in as evidence."

The defense attorney stood. "Your honor, this is the same delaying tactic we've had for weeks now."

The prosecution continued to make his case. "We have newly discovered shipping documents listing items stolen out of Russia over twenty-five years ago." He approached the judge and handed him the document. "A few minutes ago, we were granted a search warrant to go to the warehouse."

The judge looked over the document. "What do you expect to find in the warehouse?"

"We've been told by an informant that many documents in the warehouse will shed light on many other crimes as well."

The judge looked over at the defense. "I'm going to delay this for one more day, and based on the above I'll also ask you to stay in town. I want to see everyone again tomorrow at the same time." As he stood and left the room, the defense table gathered in a large huddle. This definitely presented something new for them to consider.

Danny intensified his stared at Sveta. "I think we need to leave here as fast as we can. I'm sure they're trying to find out who the informant is and they will be suspicious of everyone."

"I agree. It might not be such a good thing to be here today." They headed for the exit. While the media stood in the entrance, looking for anyone who could help make their story, they fortunately didn't recognize Sveta or her connection.

Danny tried to be as protective as possible by pulling her quickly behind him. "We need to be careful. It wasn't a good idea to come today."

After making their way out of the building, they never slowed down since they needed to leave as fast as they could. Sveta's mother would be arriving later in the afternoon and just in time for the final competition which was tomorrow night.

***

The trip to the airport was simple enough, but the

waiting was tiring since Mariya Panova's plane had landed several hours ago. While she had still not cleared through customs, Sveta remembered the long wait she had when she went through the process and she knew English. She could only imagine what her mom must be going through.

While waiting in the lobby outside the customs exit, she felt like someone was constantly watching her. She saw one man in particular; a guy who stayed off to the side, but never left them.

"This guy makes me feel extremely uncomfortable." Sveta motioned to the man again.

"I understand. Maybe he's waiting for someone also." With a TV playing in a waiting area down from where they waited, Danny walked toward it and started to watch. When a special feature played, Danny yelled over to Sveta, "You need to come over here and see this."

At the bottom of the screen, a message flashed giving an update to the Lisin trial. Danny and Sveta moved closer so they could hear. "There are new reports of events evolving today. The FBI has uncovered records from the Lisin family dating back for many years and apparently they had arrived just in time as members of the Lisin family were attempting to destroy the records. A gun battle developed ending in several deaths. It is now being reported that two of the brothers in the Lisin family, Boris and Michael Lisin, had escaped and were now on the loose and are to be considered extremely dangerous."

"Can you believe all this? After all these years, the truth is coming out." Sveta concentrated on the TV.

"Yes. Things are happening fast now. I hope they catch them soon, and they don't manage to escape back to Russia."

While they were concentrating so intensely on the

developments, they didn't notice Mariya walking through the gate. As she wandered over to them a man yelled toward her, "Mariya Panova?"

They both turned around to see her as the man rushed toward them. Sveta answered with a fighting rage. "I'm her daughter. What do you want?"

He flashed a badge. "I'm with the FBI. It's important you come with me."

"All right. Is something wrong?" Danny asked.

"It's for your safety. I saw you watching the news. I know you want to say hello to your mother, but let us move her somewhere secure first."

Two other men motioned for them to follow. Sveta knew she had little choice, but rushed to hug her mom anyway and spoke to her in Russian. "We have to go with them for a minute, but it will be all right."

They followed the men down a hallway and into a small room. "I'm so sorry for the intrusion on your family getting together, but I just received a call on the Lisin situation. For now the two brothers have eluded us and we're taking all possible precautions."

"Are we in any danger?" Danny asked.

"I don't think so, but the Lisin brothers are mad right now. Someone has set them up, and done a damn good job of it also. From what we know the brothers were enticed to come to America to collect paintings stolen twenty-five years ago, but when they went to collect them they entered a room full of documents detailing their illegal operations in America."

Another man spoke. "The FBI was tipped off also, but our tip came shortly after their tip. It was as if someone wanted them to be available when we arrived. For your own good, we need to provide you with some better protection. We know a senator has made this trip for Mrs.

Panova to come to America possible. For what it is worth, someone has much more information on what is going on than me, but for now I'm taking orders."

Sveta looked at him and asked, "I heard talks of the paintings being discovered which were stolen twenty-five years ago. Can you tell me anything about the news report?"

"I heard the paintings have not been found, but rumors are flying everywhere about them. Like I said, my orders are to keep you safe."

They all looked at each other and wondered what was going on until Danny looked over and asked, "Are we going to be able to dance tomorrow night?"

"Yes. In fact . . . the senator has insisted that you dance, even if we have to guard the entire place. You don't have to worry since you'll be well protected at all times and I also fully suspect the two brothers will be captured soon." He paused. "I do need to ask you one question. Can you think of anything you know that you think I need to know?"

Sveta felt an internal rage overtaking her, but fought to control it. "We're not connected to any Lisin family. If anything, we are the ones who have been living in fear of them for years!"

"I think you're right. We have thoroughly investigated you and know your history, but we still don't know much about Danny." He glanced at him closer. "A large part of your history is missing. Living on the streets doesn't provide us with much information on you, and we know you've had a hard life. I know you're thinking how you became involved in all of this. I guess that's what happens when you play on the internet."

"I didn't know you were still investigating me." Danny stared back with a sudden look of interest.

"This case is important to us and we can leave nothing to chance."

"I think I can understand." Danny reached for her hand.

"We need to see about getting you all home or to a hotel room for the night. A guard will stay with you while you are here."

Danny looked at them. "We have to practice tonight. A friend wants to video us one last time, just to make sure we dance perfectly."

The two men in the room looked at each other until one grunted before answering. "We'll have to go with you."

"All right and we do need to stop somewhere to buy something to eat."

"Don't worry. You'll be the guest of the state tonight." A grin followed the agent's comments.

They all stood and headed for the door, where a third man had remained outside. After a short walk they hurried into a waiting car outside. Once inside, Sveta finally managed to hug her mom. "I'm so sorry for getting you into this." Her mom looked scared and it was obvious that she didn't know what was going on. After Sveta told her the story in Russian she finally added. "We're going to the dance studio now and someone will bring us food later."

They soon arrived at the studio where all remained quiet inside. Danny checked the lighting and sound system, as Sveta's mom walked around the room and admired the large dancing space. Sveta had told her they needed one more night to prepare for the final competition.

Carlos had a wild look on his face as one of the FBI agents escorted him to the door. "What's going on here?"

Danny talked fast. "I think the Lisin family has been nailed and a lot of information on their operations has been discovered. The FBI is providing protection for everyone remotely connected to the case. There was a shootout today, but two of the Lisin brothers escaped."

Sveta decided to ask one question to the FBI agent that she hadn't thought of. "What about the older brother, Ivan. Is he under arrest?"

"It seems that he's cooperating with the authorities and with all the information pointing to the other brothers it will be interesting to see how this develops later."

Danny looked over at Carlos. "I know this is bad timing, but we still plan on dancing tomorrow night. Can you still help us with a video tonight?"

"Sure, helping with the video is why I came, but it will take a minute to have the equipment ready."

Danny and Sveta changed into their dancing clothes and for the next two hours they repeated the dance many times to perfect each movement. Finally, Danny stopped and breathed in deeply. "I think this is the last dance we'll do for now."

The FBI agent smiled and said, "Understood. We'll wait for you outside."

"Thanks, we'll change before we leave."

The agent nodded his head and headed for the door. "Take your time."

***

After looking over at Sveta, Danny knew that he had to work fast. "Tell your mother to help you change."

After Sveta and her mom went to the changing room, Danny found a secret panel where he retrieved a tape he had hidden inside. He quickly placed it on the chair with a note which read, "I am a man of my word and the location of the stolen paintings is detailed on this tape. I appreciate the offer of protection in the witness protection program, but I do not trust it and I think you understand why." Danny looked at the signature of Nickolay Panov before turning his head.

Danny knocked on Sveta and her mom's door. "Hurry, we have to leave now."

"What do you mean?" Sveta asked.

"You have to trust me." He quickly rushed Sveta and her mother through a hidden door and down a hallway. It looked dark, but he knew the way.

"Where are we going?" Sveta yelled. "Danny, what are you doing?"

Danny turned for a brief second and spoke in perfect Russian, "We have to hurry . . . our papa is waiting for us."

The words our papa stunned her as she switched to Russian. "What do you mean … our papa?"

He continued in Russian. "I'll explain soon, but we have to hurry now." They reached the end of the hallway and Danny opened a door to where a car was waiting for them. As they rounded one side a door opened and they saw one man waiting in the back seat. Before they could see well in the darkness the door shut behind them and the car rushed into the traffic.

CHAPTER 41

What do you say to someone you thought had been dead for twenty-five years? The silence turned intense. Who would talk first? Could this be true and really happening? Suddenly the man on the far side of the limo whimpered in Russian, "My family, my family. I finally have my family with me."

Danny interrupted for a second as the car continued to speed and navigate curves rapidly while they made their escape. "We'll be out of the city soon. Don't worry, all has been prearranged and is proceeding as planned."

"Kolya, is this really you? We thought you were dead." Mariya asked as she openly sobbed.

"Yes, it's me. I know you have many questions for me and it's time you had answers. Let's drive out of the city first and you'll have them. We have a long trip ahead of us." He held her tight and sobbed with her as Sveta rushed over to him to join her mom. He was alive! Their dream of a lifetime was coming true.

As Danny reached over and placed his hand on Sveta's shoulder, she blinked her eyes and raised her head. "You said OUR PAPA. What do you mean—our papa?"

He answered in Russian. "I think you'll understand soon. Many things have happened over the last twenty-five years, but we're all together now and we'll make sure of it from now on."

Nickolay rose. "I need to make one more phone call. Please give me a minute." He opened his jacket and retrieved a cell phone where he punched in some numbers.

"Senator. Thank you for keeping your word. The Lisin brothers are heading for a small airstrip in upstate New York near the town of Lisbon. You should have no trouble finding the location. With your help, their operation will be closed for good. Remember that Ivan Lisin has helped a great deal in this investigation and I expect you to help clear him. It isn't his fault he had brothers like he had. This can be a time when Russian-American relations can grow and be fully appreciated." He offered a long pause. "Yes, I remember my promise concerning the stolen paintings and icons. In the hearings tomorrow, Ivan will receive a letter saying where they are. I hope you understand that this will be the last time you'll hear from us and I can count on your word."

After he ended the phone call they drove in silence for a while. "I've been thinking about this day for a long time and I have produced a tape for you. You'll see that it answers many of your questions, but now we'll have a long life, and have a lot of time to discuss what has happened to us."

Nickolay opened the CD player and placed it inside. The video started with him sitting at a desk. "I guess the best way is to start from the beginning. I loved you Mariya, and our baby girl, more than you could ever imagine. I went to New York to prove the Russians had the best dancers in the world, but if I had known what was going to happen, I never would have gone.

The angle shifted slightly. "On the night I vanished I was in the wrong place at the wrong time. In the hotel where I was staying, the Lisin family had a room next to mine. They were having a large party and celebrating heavily. I had a hard time sleeping and went outside to obtain some fresh air. On the way back to my room, I heard loud noises coming from their room. A girl was being thrown out of their room. She was totally naked."

He shifted in his seat. "She was a young girl from Russia who they had smuggled to America for prostitution. They had abused her all night. When I helped her stand, one of the men came out the door and hauled her back into the room. He yelled at me to leave and mind my own business, which is what I did by going back to my room. I could hear this girl and others being raped by the men in the room next door for most of the night."

"When the party stopped, I heard a knock on my door. She had part of her shredded clothes on, begging for help. Since the men were now sleeping, I helped her to the front of the hotel and gave her money for a taxi.

"The next morning, when the men awoke, they heard from one of the doormen that I had helped her escape and they became very upset. This girl had taken something of theirs they wanted. It was documents describing a shipment. I would find out later that they had stolen paintings and icons from the gallery in Russia and had shipped them to America. While I had no knowledge of this at the time, they didn't believe me. They drove me all over New York looking for this girl. They knew she was in the Brighton Beach area somewhere, but not sure exactly where.

There was another shift in the angle he was being videoed from. "It was on the bridge, the one where Pavel Lisin was trying to scare me into telling them what I knew, that he managed to push me too hard and I went over the top of the side rail. It was a long fall and I still remember how much it hurt when I hit the water, but somehow I survived. The girl I helped earlier had been following us and saw me go over the side where she managed to rescue and hide me. We lived like dogs on the street for several days, not knowing what to do."

There was a long pause. "Knowing we could not survive on the street for long, she did what she had to do to make money. Prostitution, regrettably, raised enough money for us to plan our escape. She had the one thing they wanted—the shipping documents to the smuggled art. Eventually we managed to have the paintings moved to another location and have since then moved them several more times. We had no idea what to do. I knew the Lisin family would never rest until they found us and killed us. If they knew my family had any knowledge of us, you would be killed. When we tried to reach the Americans with our story, we were told we would be prosecuted for being in possession of stolen goods."

While their speeding car blurred the outside world he continued. "This girl who helped me died after we moved to New Orleans. She died giving birth to Danny. I was left to raise him on my own. Danny and I have been through much in the last twenty-five years. He's very special.

Danny patted his dad on the shoulder as the tape continued. "To support us, I turned to one interesting skill I learned. I discovered I was good at painting. In New Orleans I managed to paint and make very good money. Since this was a way for me hide I painted in this refuge for a long time. It looked like I was destined to live out my life alone until one day I had a chance to go to Italy and paint. In Italy I finally discovered a way to make things work out."

A big smile reflected the next secret. "By the way, Sveta, I want to thank you for selling my paintings in Russia. I'm sorry I had to remain a recluse in the mountains of Italy for so long, and I had a reason for the paintings being the size they were. You will soon learn that the stolen paintings from the museum are behind my paintings. It required almost seven years to have the paintings all returned, but the last one was finally sent. I think Yuri will be happy to know they're safely returned to Russia, and where they should be."

He leaned closer to the camera. "It was a lot of work breaking into the Lisins' business and learning about them. For years, I've accumulated information on them and now the evidence will be more than enough to take care of them forever. This tape was made in case I didn't make it. I knew that you would have many questions and I wanted this just in case."

Nickolay leaned forward and stopped the tape. "I think it's best that we destroy the tape now." He hit the erase button on the player.

After taking all this in Sveta turned to Danny. "Does this mean that you're my . . . brother?"

"Yes. I guess it does."

"I thought you had some reason you didn't make a pass at me," Sveta offered in a teasing voice.

Nickolay turned to his wife. "I love you and I have always loved you."

"I love you too." They kissed passionately.

Sveta glanced around "What do we do now?"

"Very simple—we start a new life. We've been offered one in the witness protection program of the United States; however, I don't trust them. I know they still have many questions as well as the Russian government. I also fear that many inside the Lisin family will always be hunting us."

"Will we be living as fugitives for the rest of our lives?" Sveta asked nervously.

"No, we'll have a good life and I've made good plans for us."

Sveta snuggled closer to her papa. "Do you think Ivan Lisin will keep hunting us?"

"I don't and if anything he'll actually be glad concerning the news of the paintings. The evidence will clear him once and for all since it was his brothers who ran the illegal part of the business. It was when they killed his brother Pavel that he decided to move against them. He was the one who set them up for the trip to America."

Danny spoke. "It would be nice to see what happens tomorrow. I wish we could see the look on everyone's faces tomorrow when the tape is played and the news is released on the painting." He had a big smile on his face.

Nickolay continued to hug his wife and daughter. "We have a long trip ahead of us, and we all need to get some sleep. I'm sorry, but we won't be able to stop anywhere. We have a safe house where we will stay for a while, and then leave the country when the time is right."

CHAPTER 42

While almost no one had slept, the long drive eventually ended at a house in the backwaters of Louisiana that was so far in the swamp the alligators were the only neighbors. Sveta thought the home site didn't look too bad at all, but it was so isolated.

"This is where I lived for many years." Nickolay glanced around. "I used this location as my studio and home. I'm going to hate to destroy this place, but we will have to make sure nothing exists when we leave. Just in case they decide to backtrack on some earlier paintings this place has to be destroyed."

"Destroying this place will be a shame," Sveta said as she walked around the house, admiring some of his work. "I can see your style in the paintings. I have always loved your work."

The driver of the limo helped to carry all they had with them into the house before Nickolay motioned for him to come over. "I want you to meet one more person. This is Amos. He's been with me for a long time and I never could have made it without him."

Amos laughed and clapped his hands before speaking in a deep south dialect. "It's good to finally see the family together. Kolya has talked about you forever."

"I think it's time to see how things are in New York." Nickolay walked over to his computer and turned it on. "The news will be out of the ordinary, I'm sure."

They saw articles all over the internet as it continued to be a major story. The Lisin brothers had been intercepted trying to leave the country where a gun battle had erupted leaving both of them dead. "I guess they knew they would be tried and found guilty, and I'm sure they would rather die fighting."

They listened to various discussions on how the information was discovered and who the mysterious man was who had led the police to it. A tape had been discovered which included more critical information. The FBI wasn't commenting on the tape other than to say the information was being investigated jointly with the CIA. They stressed how they were limited to discuss everything as many issues of a national security nature existed. In another article, they saw Nicolay's name mentioned as they read, "A source has disclosed how a Russian ballet dancer, a guy thought to be killed twenty-five years ago, may have played a key role in the latest developments. He is believed to be in a witness protection plan, but of course there is no confirmation of it."

Soon other articles materialized from various news reporting services as he continued to search. "I still don't see the one item I wanted, but I'm sure we will see it soon. Today was the day in court where the prosecution had to present its case."

Sveta watched her papa work the computer as she tried to imagine what her future would be like. She had a father now to take care of her, and hopefully soon to give her all the answers she had wanted all her life. She quickly gave him another hug. "I'm so glad you're alive."

"I'm glad we're together again. We won't be separated again since everything is going as planned." He stopped on one news service and read slowly where his name was at the top of the article. Ivan had interrupted the hearing and had an announcement. He had received a letter Nickolay had sent to him.

He was quoted as saying, "It is a great day for Russia. I have received proof where Nickolay Panov is alive and where he has completed an almost impossible mission, taking most of his life to complete. He has found a way to return stolen paintings and icons to Russia over the last seven years. In my opinion, he's a national hero."

"Can you believe this? I'm now a national hero?" Nicolay stepped back from the screen, mocking the very possibility of such.

"Does this mean we can go home now?" Sveta wanted to know.

"I'm sorry, but it doesn't. I see too many uncertainties in the world, and I'm sure some are those inside the Lisin family don't like what happened. Ivan has already showed us how he can't fully control his family business. The American government and the Russian government both have issues, but we should know soon if they agree to keep their side of a deal I made."

"What kind of deal did you make?" his wife asked him.

"In exchange for getting both of you here and full amnesty for all crimes, I would give them hard evidence on the Lisin crimes and tell them where the stolen paintings were hidden."

"This you accomplished. We are proud of you." Sveta hugged her papa tightly.

Danny moved over and placed his hand on Sveta's shoulder. "We've been working on this for a long time."

Sveta looked around. "I still can't believe I have a brother."

Looking further at the article, it read, "All personal charges against Ivan have been dropped due to his cooperation in bringing his brothers to justice."

Ivan was quoted as saying, "Today will be a new day for Russia and our relationship with the West. A treasure taken from us has been returned, and we have seen a new direction in leadership which I will maintain to the best of my ability. I do not know if I'll ever have the chance to thank Nickolay Panov for all he has done, but I think all of Russia owes him a big thank you. If I can find a way to ever repay him, I will."

The family remained quiet and thankful, but it had been a long day and a long ride to New Orleans and they all acted tired, but not too sleepy. Danny walked over to a TV and turned it on. "We have one more thing to watch and this will be the highlight of the evening."

Sveta had no idea what he was talking about as they watched him flip channels until he finally found the station and glanced at his watch. "It's still a little early, but perhaps I need to find some champagne and have it ready."

"Why champagne?" Sveta wanted to know.

"I had a reason for making the tape of us dancing in the competition. As part of the deal, the senator from New York said he would try to have it played at the finals in the competition tonight. I know we can't win, but it will be great to know we competed all the way to the end." Danny reached over and hugged Sveta. "You worked so hard and I'm proud of you."

Sveta leaned forward. "I still can't believe I was falling in love with my own brother."

Danny laughed. "It was hard for me to keep quiet during all this. I hope you understand."

***

Nickolay heard the conversation, but didn't say a word. He had a deep, serious decision to make. He knew they had developed a serious relationship. It was going to be one of the hardest things he had ever done, but somehow, he knew that one day he might have to reveal another deep secret.

The time moved slowly until they started watching the various dancers at the final competition in New York. They frequently interrupted the presentation with commercials. A man appeared on the screen and finally announced, "Tonight we have something special for you. Two of our dancers are not able to be with us tonight. Sveta is the daughter of Nickolay Panov who I'm sure you've heard his name mentioned on the news tonight. He's the one who presented the government with information on the Lisin organization. He's also responsible for returning stolen paintings to Russia. While he's being hailed as a special hero by his fellow countrymen tonight, he has gone back into hiding and the government admits they'll have a hard time ever finding him again. However, Sveta and her partner have left us a video of their last dance which they taped last night. With the permission of the judges, we're able to show you at home their last dance."

Sveta and Danny looked at each other at this amazing development and while only the future knew what new twist would be added to their lives, they were happy to be together now.

CHAPTER 43

The next morning everyone slept late since it had been a long night. While the house was large and comfortable, it was decorated sparsely and even Sveta suspected that many items had recently been moved from it. As she rose and looked around, she studied the odd surroundings and heard many sounds coming from outside she didn't recognize. The birds and other creatures in the swamp sounded strange for her.

When she heard doors shutting and someone clambering around, she made her bed and put her clothes on. She had to see what was going on. After passing through the front door, she could see her father loading items into a black van. "Hello, papa." Sveta smiled as she headed in his direction.

"Hello," he yelled back as he flashed a big smile. He was much as she thought he would look, but older. The years must have been hard on him living like he did.

"I heard all the noise and thought I'd see what you were doing."

"We'll only be here for a little while since it's almost impossible to imagine the manhunt going on for us now." He gave his daughter a large hug. "You've grown to be a beautiful lady. It's like I thought for a long time."

"Where are we going when we leave here?" She glanced at the house again.

"We have to destroy everything in this place before we leave. It's going to take all day. We need to travel at night and make only a few stops, if any."

"Is this where you lived for a long time?"

He waved at the surroundings. "Yes, I had to have a place isolated like this. It became a perfect place to paint."

"I can see that. How did you learn to paint?"

"I'm truly a self-taught painter. It was one of the only things I knew to do where I could stay unknown and make money to live."

She felt a pride rising inside her. "You've become great. I've always thought you were a master painter."

"Your opinion means a lot. You don't know how much I wanted to tell you earlier, but I had to be careful. The years of preparation are about to pay off for us."

Sveta looked at the stuff being loaded. "What can I do to help?"

"You need to let your momma sleep for a little while since I know she's tired. To have the events of the last day hit her all at one time has to be a tremendous strain on her, and I'm sure the jet lag of the flight will take a few days to adjust to. It's so good to see her again."

She continued to study his expressions. "Mom never quit loving you, and we never believed you were dead. We still have so many questions about the last twenty-five years, but I'm going to love hearing all the stories that I know you have."

Amos came around the corner of the house, carrying several large boxes. "I'm sure you'll want these later. It's going to be such a shame to tear all this down today." Amos had a look of regret on his face.

Sveta turned to her father. "What is he talking about?"

"We have no choice but to totally erase all evidence of ever being here so we won't leave a trace of anything. Deep in the swamp as we are, it will be easy to make it all disappear."

"I think I understand."

Amos looked over at Nickolay. "I think it's time for me to go rent the bulldozer. It might take all day to push this into the swamp. I'll be back in about an hour."

"I'll have it all packed soon. Let me know if you have any problems."

"I don't anticipate any, but I'll call you if I have to. You enjoy your family."

Nickolay placed his arm around his daughter's shoulders and escorted her back into the house. "I think it might be great to have one last breakfast here before we destroy it."

***

The smell of fresh bacon drifting through the house had an immediate effect on Danny and Mariya as they walked in the kitchen, waiting for the food Nickolay had prepared. The feelings of family togetherness grew stronger as they constantly exchanged hugs and kisses. Mariya stayed quiet and almost fearful, however, as this was very stressful for her.

Danny seemed cheerful and happy. He had the family he had always wanted. His father meant the world to him and he felt so glad he could help to make it a reality. "I slept well last night. It's great to be back in my old bed."

"Have you packed all your things? Amos will be back soon."

"Yes, papa, I have it all in the room and ready to go in the van. I know we have to leave soon. It's going to be hard to see all this pushed into the swamp, but I know it has to be done."

From outside the house, they could hear the sound of a large truck coming down the dirt road. It had to be Amos.

"We all need to decide what we want to take with us into the van. It won't take too long to do what we have to do."

CHAPTER 44

By the end of the day all evidence of anyone ever having lived at this location disappeared. They pushed everything into the swamp behind the house, knowing that the fresh dirt would soon be covered by the swamp and it would take a few days for the stained water to return to normal. The swamp would grow over the rest in a short time and this part of history would vanish forever.

After they loaded everything into the large van they only had one last thing to do as they pushed the limo into the swamp where it quickly vanished like the house. Hopefully, the dark waters would hold this secret forever.

Nickolay yelled over to Amos, "We'll follow you to the equipment rental place and pick you up about a block away."

"Okay, I'll see you soon."

***

The trip to Tampa, Florida lasted all night, but it allowed the family time to talk and ask more questions. While everyone tried to sleep, no one could. Soon, Amos pulled into a rest stop and surveyed the area. Yes, they had to make a few stops, but would do so as quietly as possible. The quick stop would only take a few minutes. Nevertheless, everyone knew how to dress and not to look at anyone. Nicolay had told them to go inside and make use of the facilities and leave.

All went as planned as they walked inside, leaving Amos to stay with the van as a lone Florida state police officer started making his rounds. Eventually, he walked in Amos's direction. From the corner of his eyes, he could see the family starting to return so he slowly moved over to the officer to make conversation and provide a diversion. "How are you?" he asked, as he tried hard to stay calm.

"I'm fine—just making my rounds. It's kind of quiet tonight. Where are you headed?"

"We're going to Orlando. How's the traffic today?"

"It will be fine this early in the morning and you should have no problems at all."

"Do you have any maps?"

"I think I can find you one. It's on the wall inside."

"A map will be great." Amos headed for the inside lobby and walked slowly so the officer would follow him. He didn't want him to see the rest of the family getting back into the van. Inside the lobby Amos pointed to a large map and asked a few questions to continuously divert the officer's attention. Luckily, he appeared helpful and looked bored with his job. "I really appreciate you showing me this. This will save me some time." He smiled as he headed back toward the van.

As he entered the van, Sveta asked him, "Are we okay?"

"Yes, but we'll have to be careful. I'm sure all officers are giving reports of certain people to be on the lookout for. Fortunately for us they're not expecting a black man to be involved with this."

"How much longer is it?"

"It's about another four or five hours. We'll try not to make any more stops except for gas. All this will be behind us soon and it will be good if you go to sleep for a while."

"Aren't you sleepy? You've been driving all night."

"I'm fine. When we get safely on the boat and into

international waters, I'll rest."

***

Danny whispered to Sveta, "We're in Tampa."

"What do we do now?" She rubbed her eyes.

"The boxes have to be loaded first and we'll have clearance soon. After the boat is checked, we'll all rush on board before it leaves. Every detail has been planned out months ago."

A long time later Danny and her father returned. "All is clear. We need to hurry aboard."

The boat looked much larger than she could have imagined and while she would have loved to explore it more they ushered her to the lower chambers with her mom. She thought it looked absolutely beautiful inside. It felt like a dream unfolding in front of her since she knew that would soon be out to sea and on their way to a new life in Italy. Amos had told her that this boat was how Nickolay had made the trip so many times before. Life was going to be great.

CHAPTER 45

The long boat trip to Italy allowed Sveta and her mom more time to become reacquainted with Nickolay and learn more about Danny. The sights along the way looked incredible as she expected, but it was nothing in comparison to the Mediterranean and the Italian coastline.

Nickolay smiled at his family. "We'll be in Rimini soon where I have someone who wants to buy this boat. He plans on repainting and changing the name. It's one of the items needing to be taken care of so that no one will ever be able to track us here."

"We have the old van from the gallery waiting for us also." Amos laughed. "It won't take us long to drive to the hillsides of Tuscany." Looking around with a mischievous look on his face, Amos continued to talk. "This place was selected as the legal location of the Italian painter Antonio."

"I would love to see the studio. It has to be fascinating." Sveta glanced around.

"It may not be too much so. This place is staged to look like the studio I used. It would be proper to assume the people wanting to find us may want to track down the painter who sent the stolen art back to Russia. Since this is all for their benefit we have a few last touches to make it right for them." Nickolay had a big smile on his face.

"Okay, where is your studio?"

"It isn't too far, but we'll actually be living close to Umbria. We'll be home tomorrow and then you can see the real studio. However, it's been going through some renovations since my days of being a painter are over."

"Why? You're extremely good."

"I think my new interest will be just as rewarding." He offered an even larger smile to everyone.

Sveta looked over at Danny, who had the same large smile on his face. The grins became contagious as Sveta's sparkling smile joined theirs. "What is it you're going to be doing?"

Danny smiled at Sveta, and said, "It's another secret I think you and Mom will enjoy."

"Tell me, I can't stand any more secrets. You two are going to drive me and Mom crazy for a while, I can see." Sveta glanced around, as she laughed.

"As soon as we get to the old Antonio's studio and plant the necessary items to lead to many false ends, we'll go to Bellagio for the night. I know a restaurant I think we'll really enjoy."

***

As Danny reached over and gave Sveta a large hug, Nickolay tried hard to keep a straight face. He still hadn't told Danny the truth. This revelation needed to be done soon, but it was going to be hard.

As soon as the boat docked, they began removing the luggage and boxes they had with them and carried them to the old van. The keys to the boat were hidden exactly where they had told Nicolay. He knew that this boat would soon become extinct, much like the rest of his life. He and his family would soon totally vanish into the air.

As Amos drove the van to Tuscany, Nickolay opened one box and handed papers to everyone. "This will be our new identity. I hope you like it."

"Do we have to learn Italian?" Mariya asked.

"It will be helpful if we do, but not totally necessary. We'll stay on our estate most of the time, but at times we'll want to go to a few places." Nickolay could see the joy in his wife's eyes as she looked over the rows and rows of grapevines. While the countryside of Tuscany looked beautiful, the wine country remained quiet and peaceful in the wintertime. "You'll really enjoy these hills in the spring and summer." He held her close to him.

"This has been a dream of mine for as long as I can remember. I never thought it would come true." Her eyes looked moist, as he knew the emotions were building inside of her.

"We'll soon be there. It's important for us to get in and out as fast as possible. Amos, do you think we have enough to convince everyone?"

"Yes, I think this will add the right touch to make all tracks end here."

***

The old farmhouse soon appeared in front of them, with the look and feel reflecting much as Sveta had imagined. After they entered the house, she saw many large rooms and one perfect for a studio where he could create massive paintings. The colors scattered around the room from a lot of previous work indicated how much he had worked in the past.

"I love it." Sveta whispered as she explored around the house. "Why don't you want to stay here, papa?"

"I think there is too much of a chance that this location might be traced and after all the work we've done preparing for this we must leave nothing to chance. It's been completely thought out."

"But then why are we staying in Italy?"

"I think it's the last place they would assume that we'll stay. They'll assume we'll want to get as far away from here as we can. The papers we'll leave for them will lead them to many false ends."

Danny made several trips around the house. He apparently knew it well. "I hope we have everything removed we need to."

"Don't worry, all is well."

They left and drove on to Bellagio, where the scenery mesmerized her and made her feel like she was living inside a dream. This had to be one of the most beautiful places on earth. The Lake Como area had so much romantic charm to it Sveta could see why her Papa had so much inspiration to paint.

"Amos, please stop here for a minute. I want to show Sveta a scene and see if she recognizes it." He pointed to a side road leading to a point on a miniature hill. The river on the other side curved around the lovely countryside.

As they all explored around the point, a smile came to her face. "Yes, I remember it. It's the location of the first painting you sent to us." Her heart raced as she glanced over at her mom. "This gives me memories of a dream I have had for a long time."

Danny stood and studied the scene. "I know of no place in the world like this."

"This was the place where I realized how to send the paintings back to Russia. I missed my family very much and I felt lucky to have my old friend hire you at the gallery. Since I knew the paintings would sell in Russia this became the one way I could secretly send money to you and your mom." Nickolay's voice sounded full of passion and conviction.

Amos stood off to one side before he added. "I know this is good for your soul, but my stomach says it's time to visit Tony."

"What's he talking about?" Sveta asked.

"He's referring to his favorite place to eat. The owner is known as Tony by the regulars. We'll be eating soon."

***

The restaurant looked unspectacular from the outside, and was probably an old residence which had been converted to a restaurant at some time. Her father had told everyone not to be overheard talking loudly in Russian, and that he and Danny would handle ordering the meal.

The heavy door to the entrance was easy to open in spite of its massive size. A man stood on the other side greeted Danny immediately in Italian. While they spoke in Italian, Sveta had no idea what they were discussing. She knew it would take a while to learn this new language. "Danny, it sounds like you speak Italian fluently. I'm impressed." Sveta felt proud of him.

He returned her smile. "You'll speak Italian great in a few years also. It isn't too hard."

Nickolay next shook hands, smiled and received a short kiss on the cheek from this jolly little man. He hastened his family to follow him to a back room as Danny whispered to Sveta in Russian, "I think you'll like this place. It's private and has a great atmosphere. I'll also tell you the history of this place later."

After everyone found their place around the table, Nickolay raised his hand to order some wine. The waiter knew instantly what he wanted, and without asking left to retrieve a bottle. With no one close to the table, he reverted back to Russian for Sveta and Mariya. "I really want your honest opinion on the wine I ordered. This Chianti is produced not far from here and I think it is . . . shall I say . . . unique."

The waiter quickly returned and handed the bottle of wine to Nickolay for his approval. He raised the bottle higher to allow his wife and daughter study the bottle. Sveta quickly noticed a painting of a woman and a little girl dancing ballet together on the front of the bottle, the same one she had received as a gift when she had left Russia.

"Ohmigod." Sveta's voice became soft, but deliberate. "I recognize this painting. You painted one like it for me and presented it to my boss. He gifted it to me on the way to America."

"Then I assume you approve." He handed the bottle back to the waiter who opened and poured it. When everyone had a glass he raised his glass and waited for the waiter to leave. As the others lifted their glass and waited, Nickolay stared intensely at his glass. "How do you like the color?"

Everyone looked at their glass and studied the deep red, almost purple color as Danny raised his glass and added, "Notice how the velvet color looks so intense and powerful. Not bad."

Looking pleased, Nickolay leaned over and smelled the fruity scent of the rich grapes. He motioned for everyone to do the same as his eyes sparkled. "I don't think any wine I can remember could carry a bouquet as great as this."

Mariya whispered, "I love the smell. The aroma makes me think of great times and celebrations."

Nickolay smiled at her comment. "Yes, we'll celebrate life every day we're here." He raised his glass higher. "To the sweet life in Italy where we'll be a family forever more." They tapped the glasses together and all enjoyed the excellent wine.

Sveta looked over to her papa and asked, "Is this wine expensive?"

"I hope so." Her papa suddenly laughed loudly. While Sveta and Mariya had a puzzled look on their faces, Danny simply let out a slight laugh that he could not control. "The wine you're drinking is our future. It's from a small winery Danny and I have been restoring for the last several years. The paintings I've sold have provided us with the money to acquire the old vineyards. It has also served as the perfect place to hide my studio for so long."

Sveta and Mariya looked at each other. "We're going to be in the wine business?" Sveta asked.

"Yes, but it's a tiny operation and won't be promoted much. The only contact with the public will be through Amos. It's the perfect way to do something I think we'll love and to keep our privacy. So what do you think?"

Danny smiled. "It's much more involved than you can imagine, but it has some great rewards."

CHAPTER 46

Life on the winery exceeded Sveta's imagination. She had so much to learn, and on the estate they had no problem talking in Russian. With the internet remained their main source of communication with the outside world, the news stories of their disappearance constantly amazed everyone.

"Good morning." Nickolay smiled as he caught Sveta on the computer again. "Do you see anything of interest this morning?"

"Good morning, Papa. It's the same stories. It's so good to have a good connection here. I'm trying to find out how life is back in Russia." While she wondered, she knew she would never go back.

"I'm sure it will be as it always is."

"I think you're right."

"When you finish playing, we have some work to do today." He pointed to winery.

"I won't be too long." Sveta waved at the screen as her Papa left and headed out the door toward the large barn they used to work on the vineyard. Sveta continue to play on the computer until she finally decided to go to her old e-mail site, just out of curiosity. It had only been established to have contact with Danny, and she felt surprised to see that she had several messages in it.

She looked at it hard for a long time before she decided to open it. She thought she would perhaps see some last-minute e-mails from Danny, but she froze when she saw the e-mails—they came from her old friend, Olya. She could not believe it.

After looking around the room as if she was being watched she eventually clicked on the computer, opening the e-mail letters. "Sveta, I hope you receive this message. On your computer at work, I found this site. Don't worry. It has been erased now from the computer. I've been watching the news on you and your family and I really want to know if you're okay. Not knowing how you are doing is driving me crazy. I have set up a new e-mail, and I hope you'll contact me sometime, if you can. All you have to do is hit the reply button."

Sveta missed her friend since she was the one person she could share things with. She would ask her father and see what he thought. Tears came to her eyes at the thought of never seeing her again.

As she went to the large barn, looking for her father, she found him busy working on some farm tools. He glanced at her instantly. "I see you're ready to get busy this morning."

"Papa, I saw something on the computer I think you should see. You remember my friend, Olya. She found my old e-mail address and has sent me an e-mail. She's worried sick about me. I know it."

Sveta knew her father felt touched by this. They had talked about her friend many times. "I know you miss your friend. I've been thinking about it and I may have a way for you to see her. The operation will be difficult, but I think we will make it work."

"What are you thinking about?" she asked as she tried hard not to raise her hopes up too much.

"I think a study on the painter who returned the museum paintings back to Russia could be a worthwhile endeavor. In fact, I know the way to see that someone has an interest in this. A struggling young artist might be chosen for the research. My old friend, your previous boss, might be able to pull this off."

"Do you think she could come here to study the painter known only as Antonio?"

"We left the previous place as it was. I think she would be a good choice to examine it."

Sveta felt a heat glowing inside her as she tried hard not to go crazy with the thoughts of having her old friend with her. "Having her here would be so fantastic." She rushed over to her Papa and gave him a large hug.

Danny entered as they talked. He looked dirty from working in the vineyards, but she knew that he loved the work which often reflected in his smiles. As he looked over at Sveta, he smiled larger. The two had so many things in common and their way at looking at life was identical. "What are you two talking about this morning?" Danny asked.

"Papa may know a way to let Olya come here to visit me."

A troubled look entered Danny's face. "How can we do that?"

"I have an idea. We'll discuss it soon, but we won't do anything to compromise our new life here."

Danny decided to join in with her happiness. "I hope we can work it out."

CHAPTER 47

The last several months had passed slowly as Sveta became anxious about her friend coming to Italy. While all the details had been worked out the visit wouldn't be long, and she wouldn't be allowed in the winery. In fact, she wouldn't be given any details at all since it was in the best interests of everyone.

Sveta remembered the last e-mail she had received from Olya before she left Russia. "I cannot thank you enough for letting me know you're doing well. It's going to be so great to see you again."

While Sveta knew her friend well and the messages had to be short and sweet, she recognized something different about her friend. Olya wanted to know how things were with her after she left, but the words she used sounded a little different. It was as if she was under a lot of stress in her life.

She had heard how Yuri Zotov had listened with interest to the request to go and do some research on the painter known as Antonio. He had to relinquish the paintings he had purchased, since they were associated with the theft, but he still had the right to market the copies produced from them, and he would make a lot of money from them. The more interest he could generate in them, the more valuable they would come. He had finally decided to help Sveta's old boss in arranging for Olya to make the trip to research the Italian painter who had vanished.

***

As Danny drove to the old studio site in the old van, he hoped he would look like a simple delivery boy making a delivery, that is, if he ran into anyone. With any luck, he would soon have Olya with him and she would simply disappear just as the Panov family had earlier.

The place looked different as he approached the old house. New fences had been erected around the old studio location. Apparently the old house had been placed under a lot of security since the police discovered the farmhouse. "I see the house ahead," Danny smiled as he whispered to Sveta.

"Just go slow and as if this is a normal shipment." Her voice became a slight whisper.

Danny drove slowly and entered the main road leading to the house. "I see no guards anywhere. The place seems to be deserted."

"The stillness is a good sign. Now keep driving."

Danny soon drove in front of the house. "I see no one here and I'm not sure if Olya is around or not. I'll have to go to the door and knock."

"I'll be here waiting for you. If you feel anything is wrong at all, give me the signal and I'll let Papa and Amos know. They aren't far away. We need to get in and out of here as fast as we can."

"Trust me; I won't be here any longer than I have to." Danny walked to the front door where he looked around and banged on the door. No one answered.

He knocked again and much louder this time. A dull sound echoed from the center of the house. Something felt wrong. He moved to one side and listened intensely. After a long wait, he heard the same sound. He raised his hand and signaled to Sveta.

A voice addressed him from a side window in Russian. "Come inside and move slowly—I have a gun pointed at your head."

Danny had no choice but to obey. "Don't shoot."

As he entered the room, he saw a girl he assumed to be Olya tied to a chair in the center of the room. She looked like she had been brutally mistreated for a while. Olya cried out as best she could when she saw him, but her mouth was taped. Danny did his best to identify her from photos he had seen of her before he turned to the man pointing a gun at him. "What's going on?" he asked.

"You'll know soon enough. Have a seat. Who's in the van with you?"

Danny thought about lying, but stared back at him. He hoped Sveta had enough sense to make a run for it.

A loud noise came from outside the house. It sounded like a crash. He tried to move to a window, but the large gun was shoved in his face again. "Do not make me shoot you. Stay still."

Danny stared at him and waited for what he knew had happened. He heard a scream as Sveta came flying through the door. When Danny moved to help her, Denis hit him with the butt of his gun. He fell hard to the floor as the world went black.

***

Sveta tried to move toward him, but was stopped by a large hand reaching out and holding her tight. "Let me help him," She begged.

She heard a loud laugh as he shoved her to the floor beside him. "I don't think you can do anything for him now."

Sveta stared at Denis who had contortions registering on his face which made his normal Swedish looks disappear. "What are you doing here, you bastard?" Sveta violently yelled at him.

"What do you think I'm doing here? I'm looking for

you and your papa."

"Why are you doing this?" Her voice trembled as she attempted to get closer to Danny.

"I have a score to settle with your papa. He messed with the wrong people and he should have simply stayed dead. Since I suspect he's here somewhere it will only be a while until he dies for real this time."

When Sveta saw Olya trying to stand and fall, she tried to rush to her, but Denis immediately pushed her to the floor again. Danny also tried to stand, but Denis knocked him down, hitting him with the butt of the gun again.

Sveta suddenly recognized the guy who had grabbed her and dragged her inside. "I should have known you would be in on this, Andrew."

Andrew and Denis laughed in a devilish exchange. "Do you think we were taking you two dancing for the fun of it?" He removed the tape from Olya's mouth before shoving her next to the ground by Sveta. "She is nothing special to us, and can only be used as one of our whores."

Olya cried as she glanced up. "I'm so sorry. They gave me no choice. I had no way I could warn you."

"I understand. Are you okay?"

Her deep, sullen eyes gave Sveta the answer. Olya looked like she had been abused for a while. It made Sveta sick to look at her friend. She quickly raised her head to scream at Andrew. "What have you done to her?"

"Me . . . I'm getting her ready for her new occupation." Andrew sneered before following it with another evil laugh. "I think guys will pay good money to fuck her. Personally, I think she is better at giving a good blow job. Isn't that right, bitch?"

Danny stayed on the floor, groaning. While the blow to the back of his head looked serious, Denis kicked him again for good measure. "I think you picked a weak boyfriend. Such a shame."

"You're a bastard. I can't believe I had thoughts of making you a good wife at one time."

"I guess I am a bastard of sorts. What you don't know is the man your father set up to be murdered was my father."

"What?" Sveta asked.

"Boris Lisin was my real father. He had a Swedish mistress. While this was something he didn't advertise . . . it was something I had to live with it all my life. Yes . . . he was my papa and made my life comfortable as long as I remained quiet, but that's all been taken from me now. I have nothing now. Don't you understand that?"

"Do you think killing us will help anything? I had nothing to do with your papa being killed."

"Your papa planned all of this and he will pay for this. He will be found soon and then he'll wish he had died a long time ago."

"I think you'll be the one who'll wish you had never come looking for him. If you hurt us, he'll find you."

Laughing and smiling, Denis walked over to Sveta. "We're not planning on hurting you. I think you'll make a lot for money for us. Some men pay top dollar for a nice young Russian virgin, don't you think?"

Sveta saw red. She never knew she could despise someone so much as she charged at Denis with all her fingernails ready to dig into him. Denis, however, slapped her hard in the face to send her to the floor before she could inflict any damage. "Your actions aren't too smart." While looking beside her on the floor Denis saw where a mobile phone had popped out of her pocket. He retrieved it and laughed. "I assume you know how to reach your Papa on this."

After Sveta didn't say a word, Denis looked at the

menu and dialed the first one. A voice soon answered, "Hello."

Denis spoke in deep Russian, "I think you'll want to know I have your daughter." As the phone went dead, he looked at it and said, "I don't think he wanted to talk."

Within minutes, a loud voice yelled at the house. "This is Nickolay. I think it's me you want. I'm coming in unarmed."

Denis scrambled to the front door. "Hold your hands high where I can see them."

"I have some items we need to discuss."

"I think I have all the answers I need. Without you, much of the information about my family will never be acknowledged. You've caused hell for us and you're responsible for the death of my papa."

"Your papa?" Nickolay's surprise reflected on his face.

"Yes, Boris Lisin was my father. I thought you'd like to know."

"Perhaps, but it doesn't surprise me at all. He had several children by many women."

In a sudden rage, Denis punched Nickolay in the face, sending him backwards. "It's going to be nice to watch you die, but before you do, I think you should see the life your daughter will have for the rest of her life." He turned to Andrew. "I think we need to introduce Sveta to her new life properly. I know of nothing better than having a virgin in the romantic countryside of Italy."

Andrew's smile turned evil as he walked over to Sveta and lifted her from the floor. "This is going to be a real treat."

As he reached around to the front of her blouse and started to rip the material, a large voice from the back of the room startled him: "Let her go."

Andrew swirled and pointed his gun toward the back of

the house, but he had reacted too slow as Amos fired and hit him in the head. Sveta screamed as he pulled her down with him. Denis quickly fired back and hit Amos in the side. He would have fired another round, but Danny managed to rise slightly from the floor, remove a gun from his ankle holster, and fire at Denis first. The bullet found its mark and Denis went down, stumbling backwards with blood spraying everywhere.

Nickolay ran to Denis and removed his gun. He looked badly wounded, but still alive as Nicolay held his hand over it trying to stop the bleeding. "We need to drive him to a hospital."

Amos rushed over to Nickolay. "He looks bad."

"Yes. What about you? You're bleeding."

"It isn't too bad. I think I'll live." He held his side, but wasn't losing much blood.

Denis started coughing blood. His eyes flashed wildly, and he seemed to know he would die soon. "Why did you have to come back and cause all of this?"

Nickolay lowered his head as Denis died in his arms. Denis would never know that his own half brother had shot him. After glancing around, he moved over to Danny to examine his bloody head, knowing that he might also have a concussion. He yelled at Sveta, "We need to find Danny and Amos some help fast."

Sveta quickly pulled a dazed Olya to her feet as she worried about what all they had put her through. Knowing they had to move now, Sveta also helped Danny and Amos to the van as Olya slowly followed them.

After everyone entered the van, Danny moaned softly in Sveta's lap as she held his face in her hands. "Don't worry, Danny. We'll be at a hospital soon. I love you."

Nickolay reached over and held Danny's shoulder. "You saved all of us today and we'll never forget it. I'm so sorry you had to kill Denis. I didn't know he was a son of Boris. Please forgive me."

Sveta failed to understand what her papa said as Danny passed out again. Her father quickly looked over at Sveta, as his jaw quivered. "I've raised Danny as my own for all his life. His mother saved my life, and I owed her everything. She had become pregnant with Danny when all this first happened in New York."

"Are you saying Danny isn't your biological son?" Sveta asked as her heart raced.

"Danny's real biological father was Boris Lisin. He raped Danny's mother many times when she was brought to America. Yes . . . Denis would have been his half brother."

"Wow." Sveta could not move.

"Don't worry. I think Danny will be fine. We'll have him in the emergency room soon. He's the best son I could ever have."

Sveta continued to hold Danny in her lap as Amos and Olya made their way to the back of the van. "Then . . . this means we're not really brother and sister."

"Yes and no; I'll let you both decide your own future, but for right now we need to get him and Amos to the hospital."

"What about the dead bodies? They'll be found soon, won't they?"

"I think Ivan Lisin will be able to take care of this situation. This is the one last thing he'll want to handle in order to make a full break with the past. We'll send word to him soon. This will finally tie up all the loose ends for all of us."

"Well almost." She held Danny closer, knowing that they had a future together, not as brother and sister, but hopefully as husband and wife. She loved him, and she knew, even as he was unconscious, that he loved her too.

THE END